For Alexia — F.B.

For Fred — I.A.

Jane,
the fox
&me

First published in French in 2012 as *Jane, le renard & moi* by
Les Éditions de la Pastèque, Montreal, Quebec

First published in English in Canada and the USA in 2013 by
Groundwood Books

Groundwood Books / House of Anansi Press
110 Spadina Avenue, Suite 801, Toronto, Ontario M5V 2K4
or c/o Publishers Group West
1700 Fourth Street, Berkeley, CA 94710

We acknowledge for their financial support of our publishing program the Canada Council for the Arts, the Government of Canada through the Canada Book Fund (CBF) and the Ontario Arts Council.

Canada Council for the Arts | Conseil des Arts du Canada
ONTARIO ARTS COUNCIL
CONSEIL DES ARTS DE L'ONTARIO

Library and Archives Canada Cataloguing in Publication
Britt, Fanny
Jane, the fox and me / written by Fanny Britt ; illustrated by Isabelle Arsenault ; translated by Christelle Morelli and Susan Ouriou.
Translation of: Jane, le renard et moi.
Issued also in electronic format.
ISBN 978-1-55498-360-5
1. Graphic novels. I. Arsenault, Isabelle
II. Morelli, Christelle III. Ouriou, Susan IV. Title.
PN6733.B75J3513 2013 j741.5'971 C2013-900392-4

The illustrations were done in mixed media (pencil, color crayon, gouache, ink and watercolor), and some were assembled or touched up digitally.
Printed and bound in Singapore

FSC www.fsc.org
MIX
Paper from responsible sources
FSC® C019704

FANNY BRITT
ISABELLE ARSENAULT

Jane,
the fox
& me

TRANSLATED BY
CHRISTELLE MORELLI AND SUSAN OURIOU

GROUNDWOOD BOOKS / HOUSE OF ANANSI PRESS
TORONTO BERKELEY

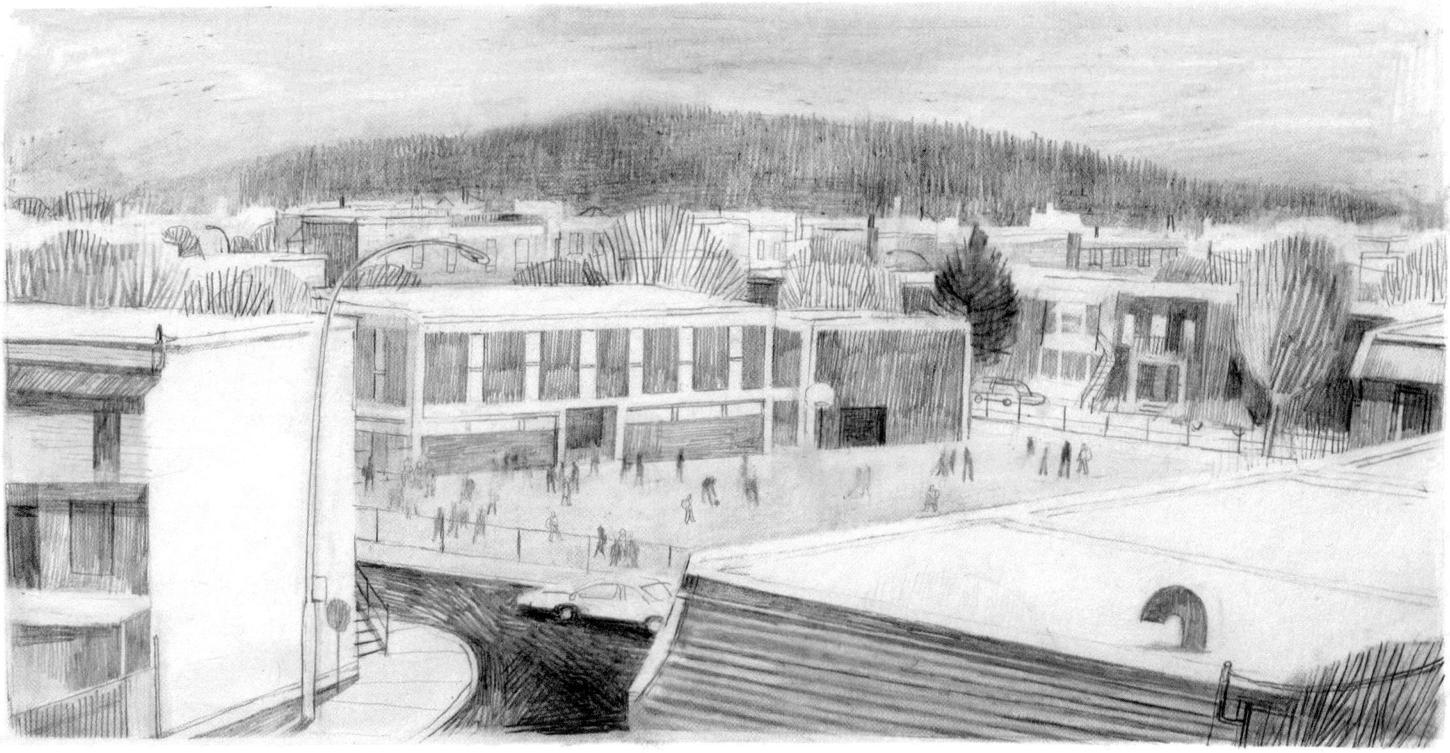

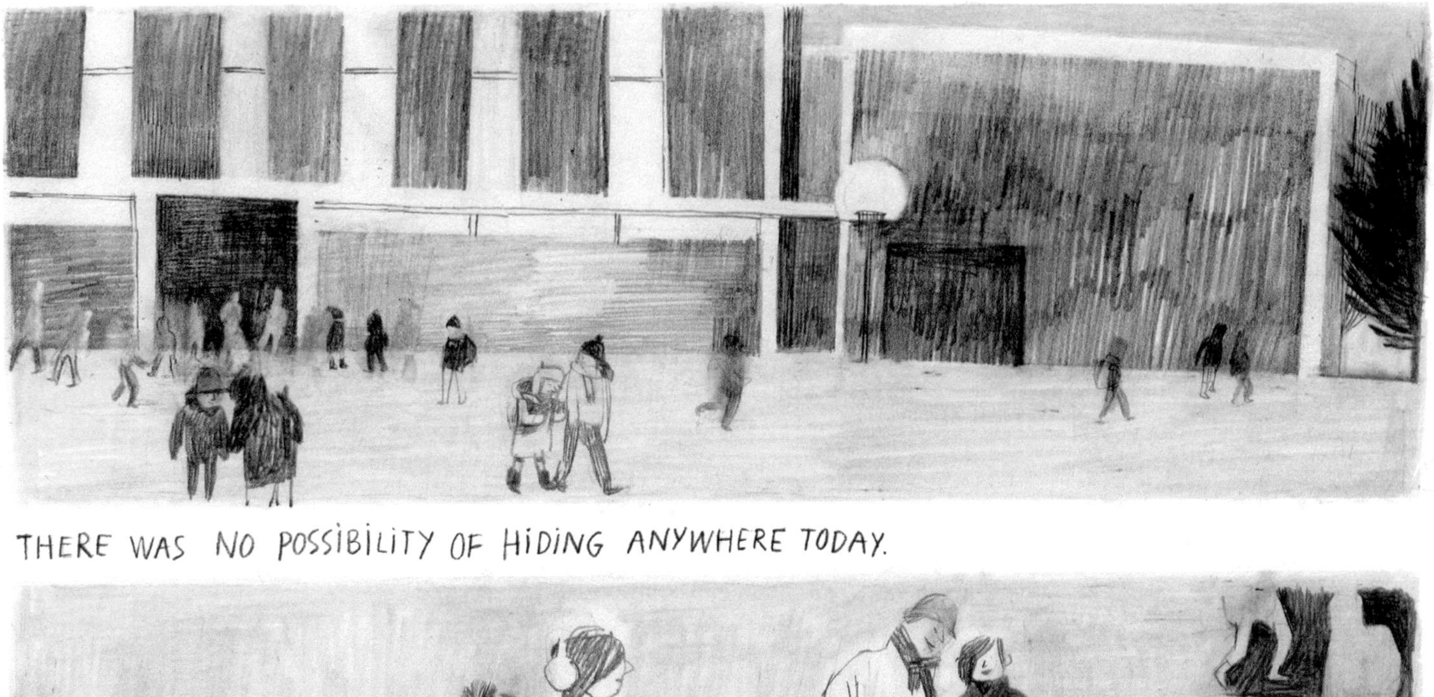

THERE WAS NO POSSIBILITY OF HIDING ANYWHERE TODAY.

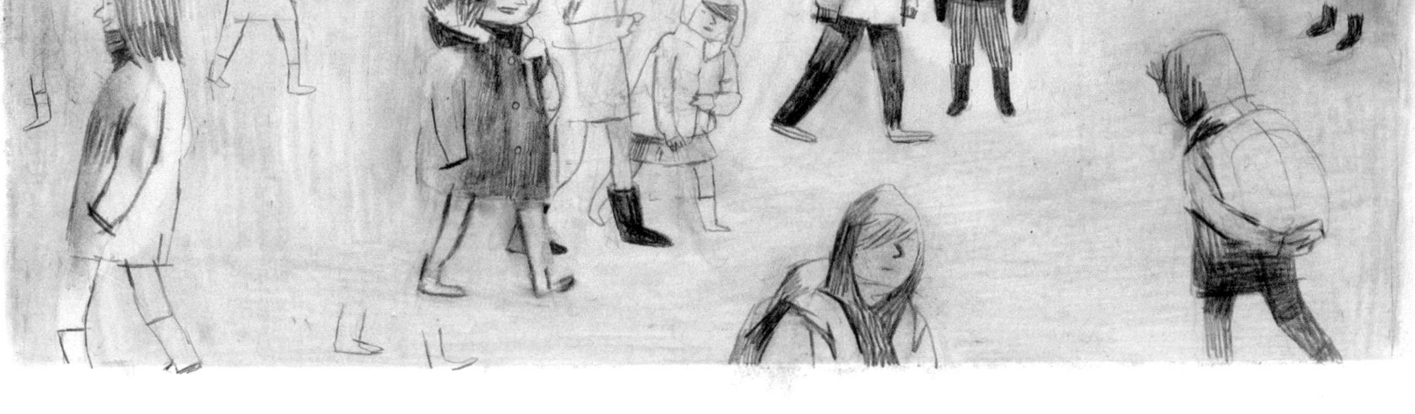

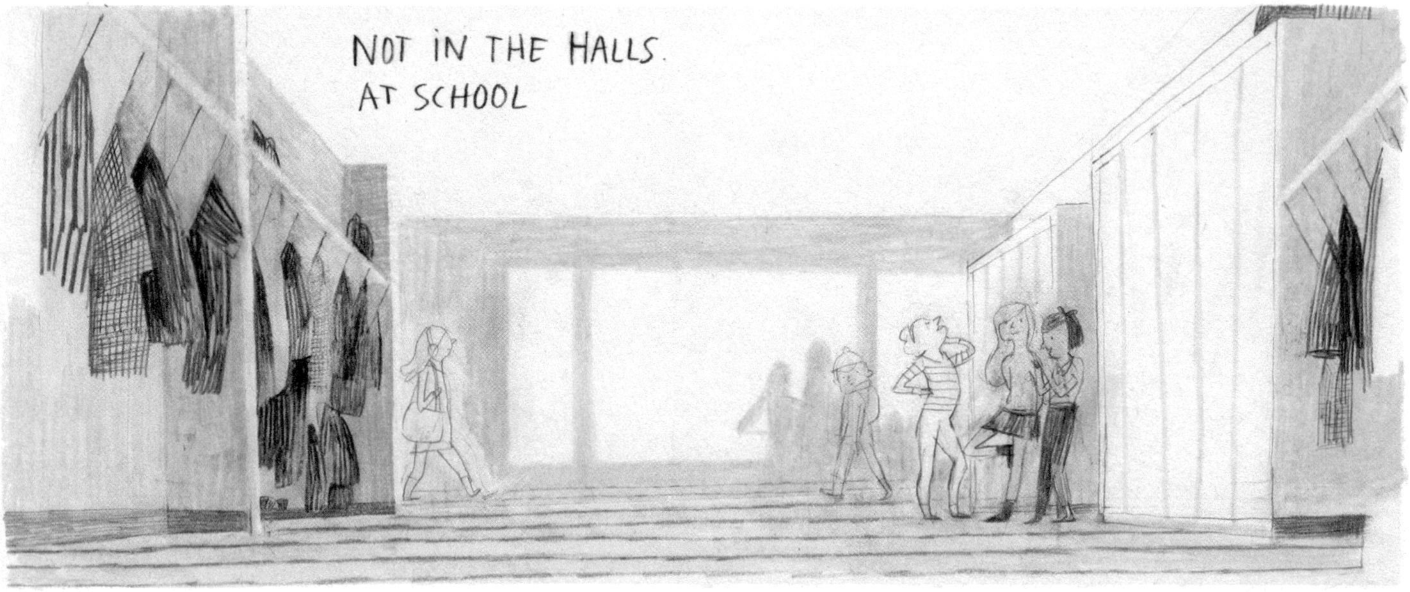
NOT IN THE HALLS
AT SCHOOL

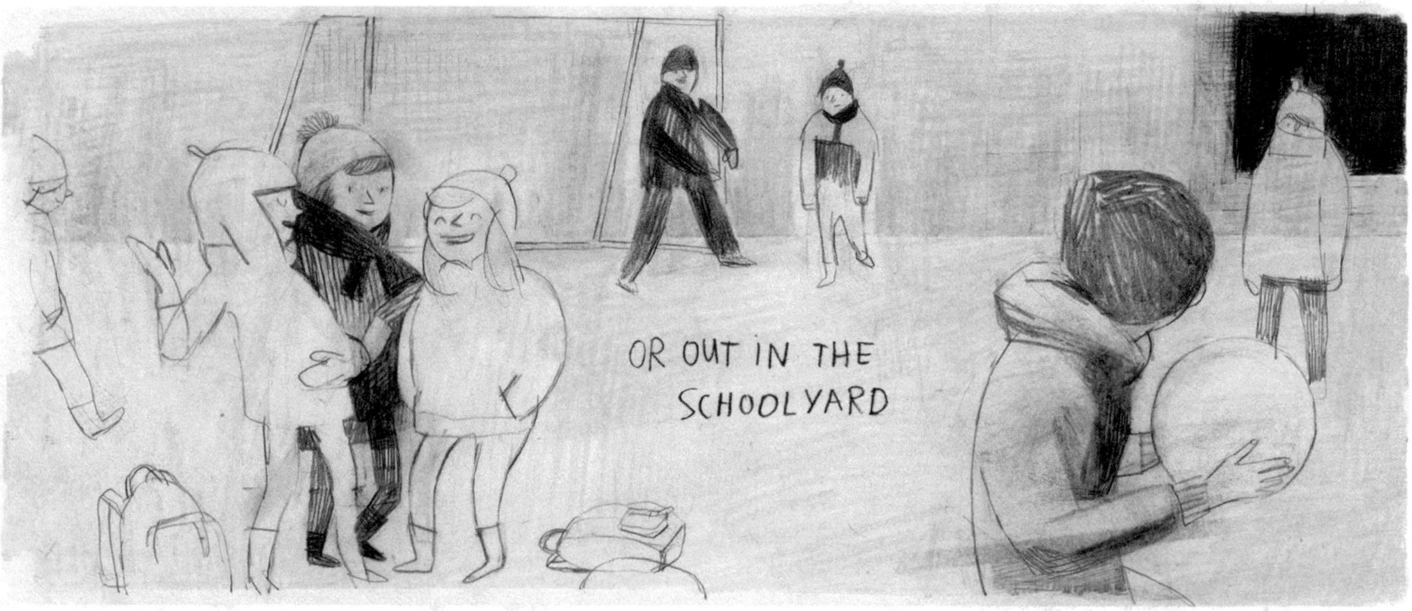
OR OUT IN THE
SCHOOLYARD

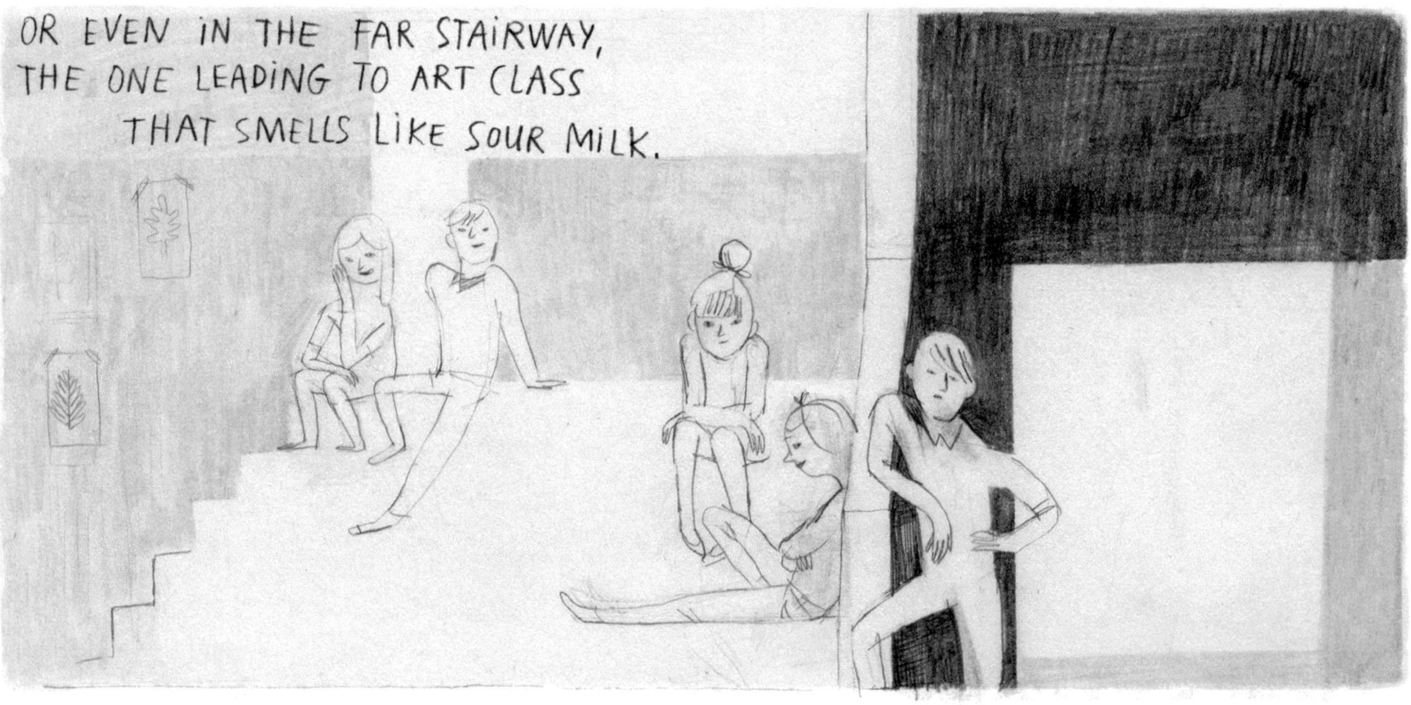
OR EVEN IN THE FAR STAIRWAY,
THE ONE LEADING TO ART CLASS
THAT SMELLS LIKE SOUR MILK.

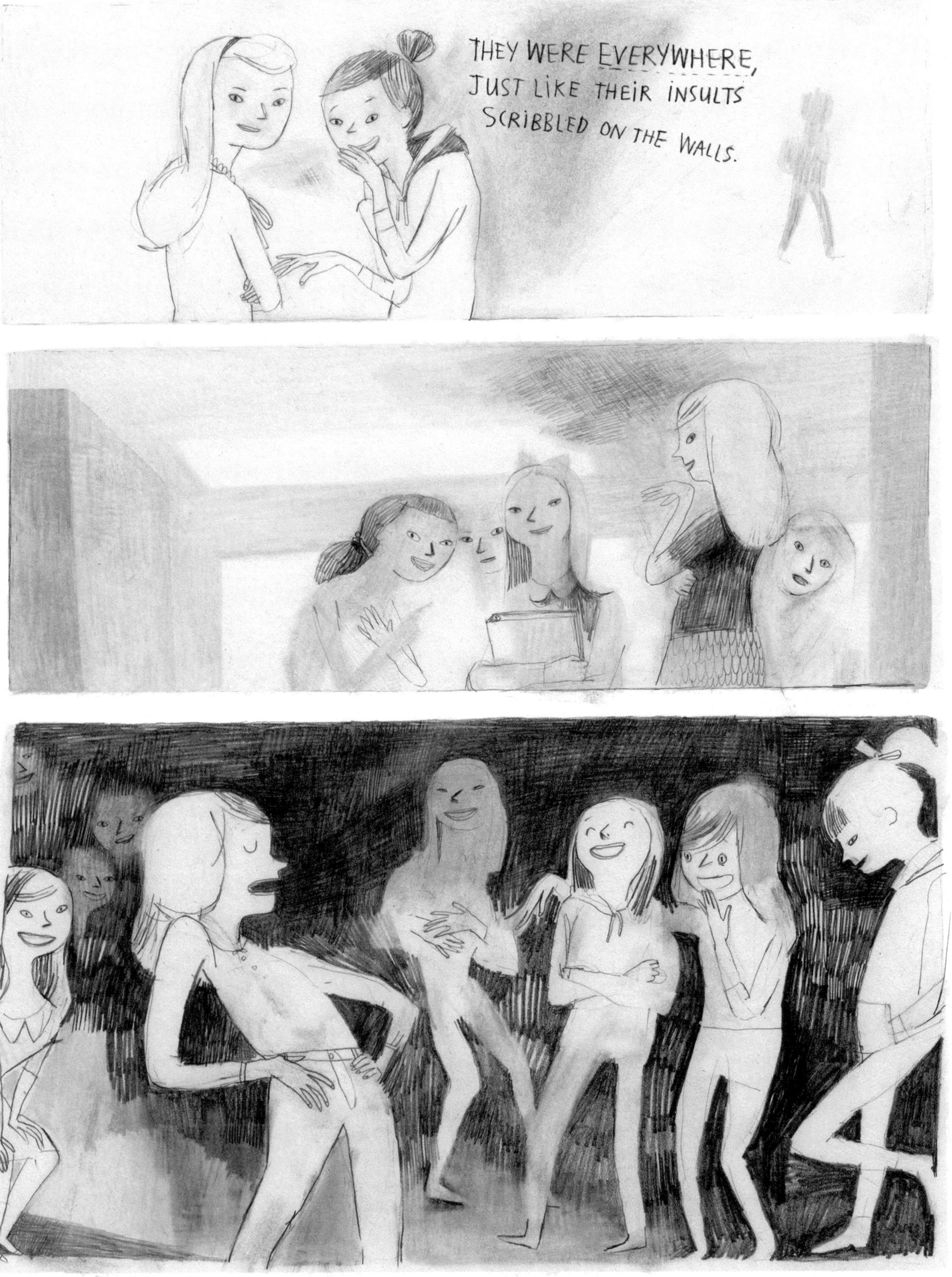
THEY WERE EVERYWHERE,
JUST LIKE THEIR INSULTS
SCRIBBLED ON THE WALLS.

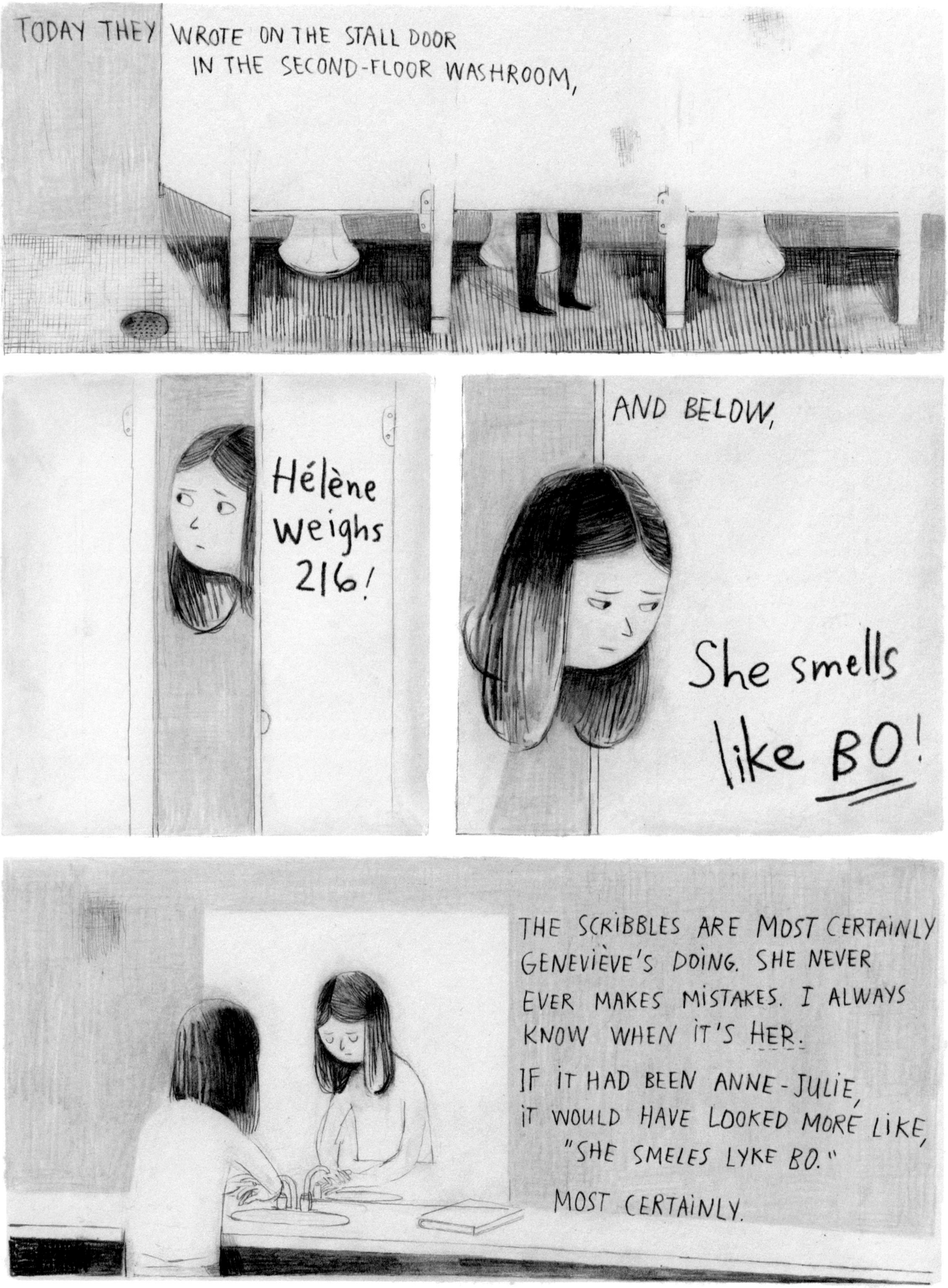
TODAY THEY WROTE ON THE STALL DOOR IN THE SECOND-FLOOR WASHROOM,
Hélène weighs 216!
AND BELOW,
She smells like BO!
THE SCRIBBLES ARE MOST CERTAINLY GENEVIÈVE'S DOING. SHE NEVER EVER MAKES MISTAKES. I ALWAYS KNOW WHEN IT'S HER.
IF IT HAD BEEN ANNE-JULIE, IT WOULD HAVE LOOKED MORE LIKE, "SHE SMELES LYKE BO."
MOST CERTAINLY.

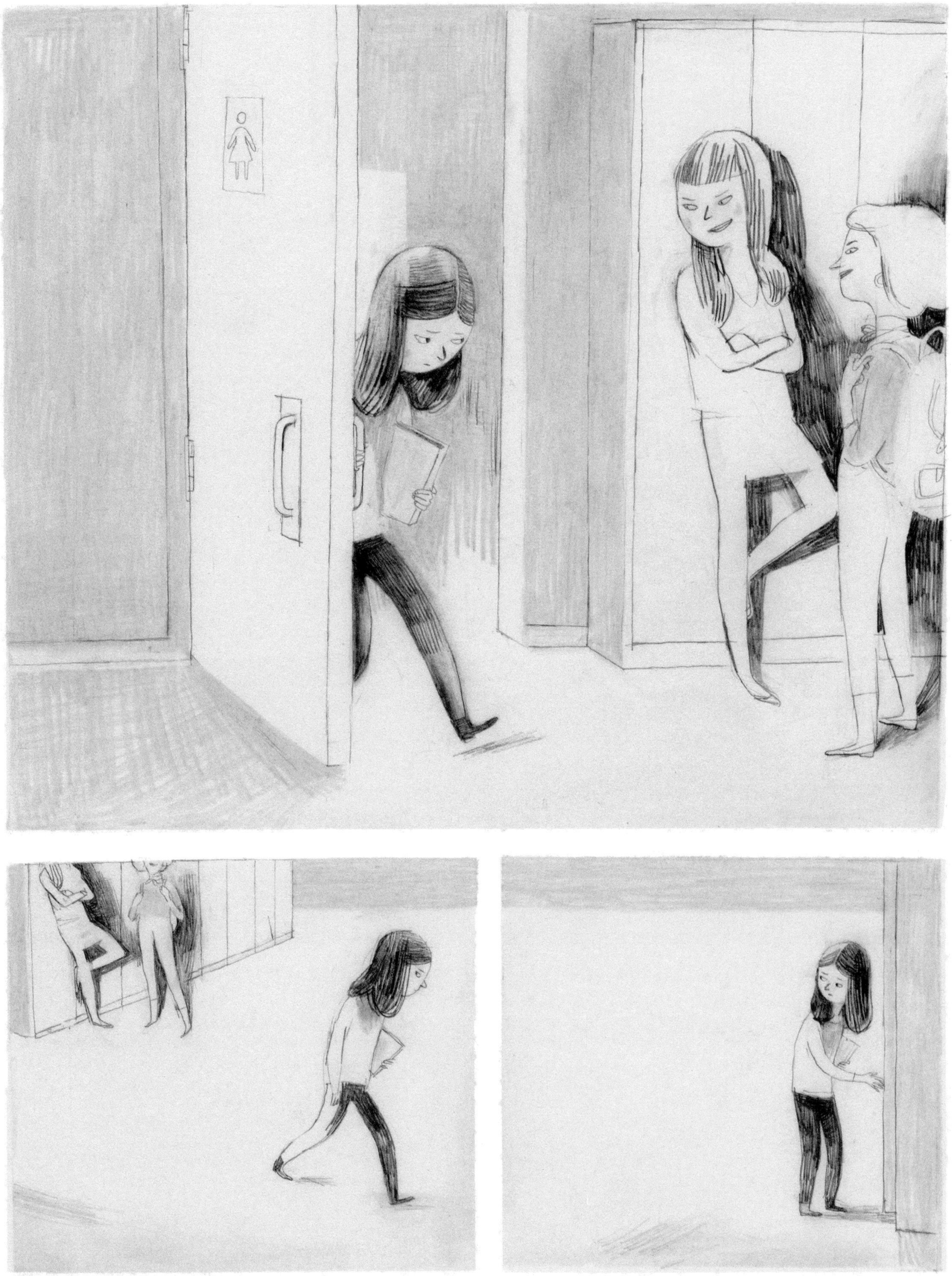

IT USED TO BE THAT WITH GENEVIÈVE AND ANNE-JULIE, SARAH AND CHLOÉ, WHAT WE LOVED MOST WERE CRINOLINE DRESSES.

JUST LIKE THE ONES IN THE INFOMERCIALS FOR TIME LIFE'S OLDIES COLLECTIONS WITH THE SONG TITLES SCROLLING DOWN.

OR LIKE DONNA, RITCHIE VALENS' GIRLFRIEND IN LA BAMBA.

GETTING A DRESS MEANT HEADING TO THE VINTAGE STORE, PICKING OUT THE PRETTIEST ONE, THE REAL THING SMELLING SLIGHTLY OF MOTHBALLS.

IT TOOK MONEY, LOTS OF IT.

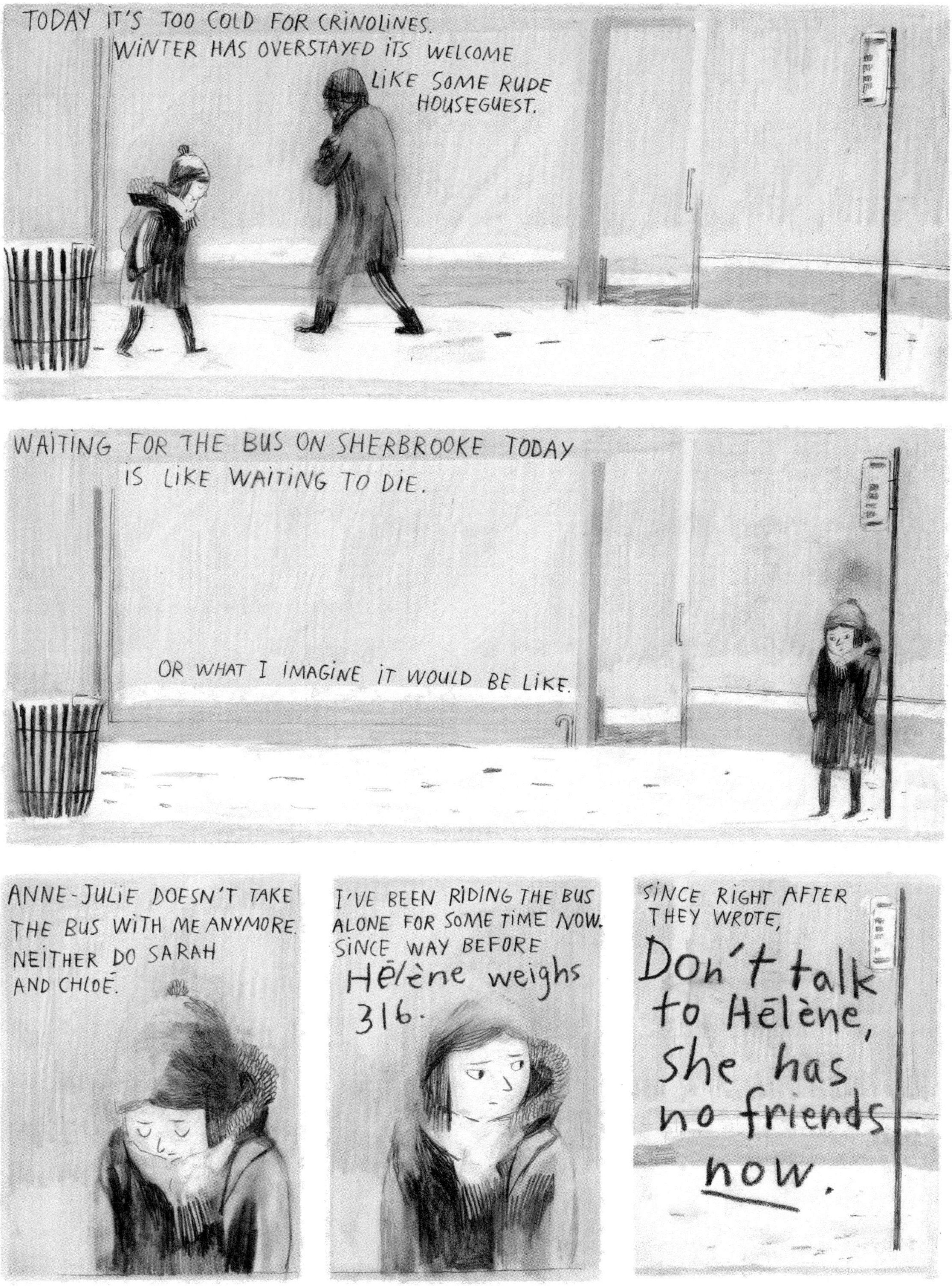
TODAY IT'S TOO COLD FOR CRINOLINES.
WINTER HAS OVERSTAYED ITS WELCOME
LIKE SOME RUDE HOUSEGUEST.
WAITING FOR THE BUS ON SHERBROOKE TODAY IS LIKE WAITING TO DIE.
OR WHAT I IMAGINE IT WOULD BE LIKE.
ANNE-JULIE DOESN'T TAKE THE BUS WITH ME ANYMORE. NEITHER DO SARAH AND CHLOÉ.
I'VE BEEN RIDING THE BUS ALONE FOR SOME TIME NOW. SINCE WAY BEFORE
Hélène weighs 316.
SINCE RIGHT AFTER THEY WROTE,
Don't talk to Hélène, She has no friends now.

On the bus, I pull out my book.

It's the best book I've ever read, even if I'm only halfway through.
It's called *Jane Eyre* by Charlotte Brontë,
with two dots over the e.

Jane Eyre lives in England in Queen Victoria's time.
She's an orphan who's taken in by a horrid rich aunt
who locks her in a haunted room to punish her for lying,
even though she didn't lie.

Then Jane is sent to a charity school, where all she gets to eat
is burnt porridge and brown stew for many years.
But she grows up to be clever, slender and wise anyway.

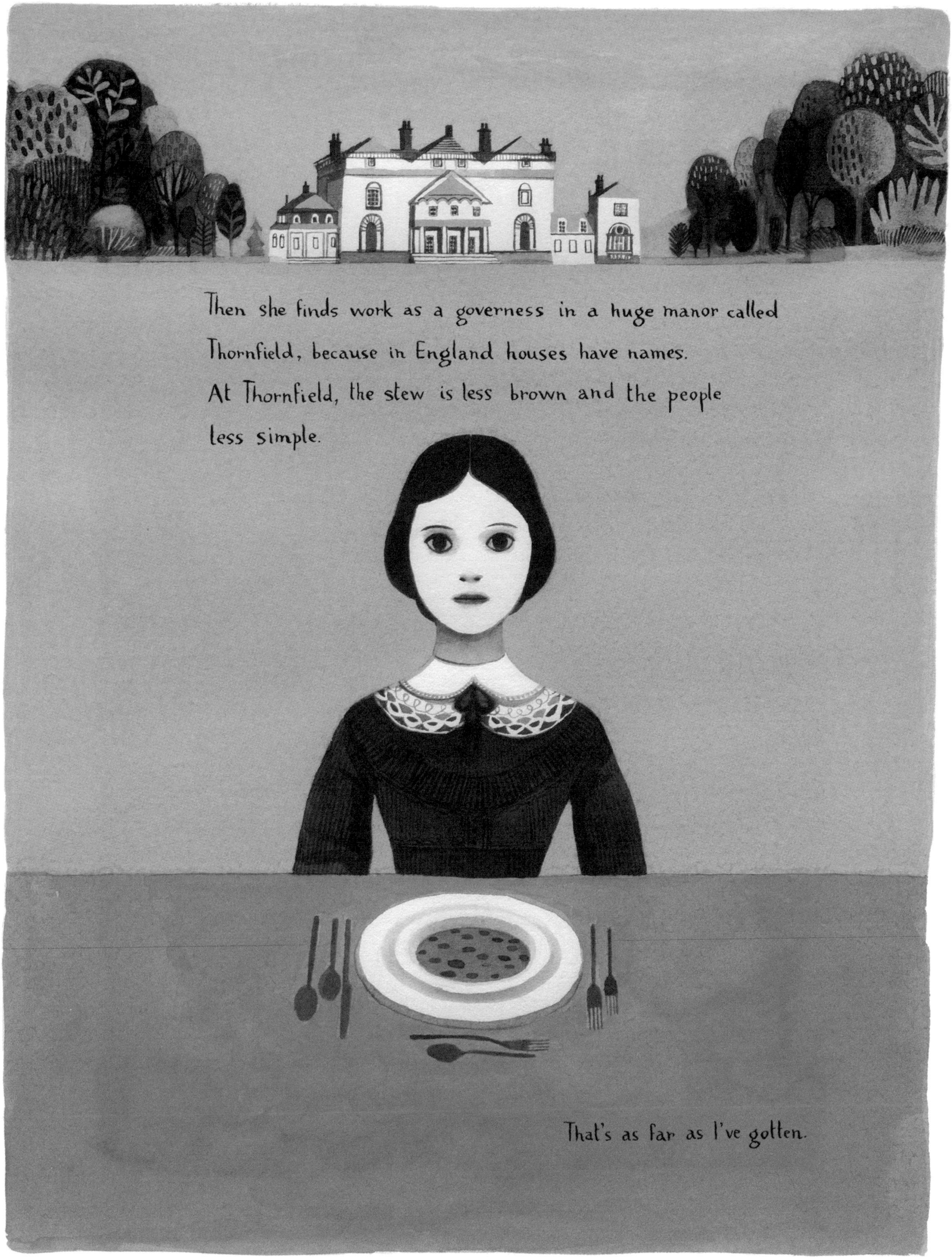
Then she finds work as a governess in a huge manor called Thornfield, because in England houses have names.
At Thornfield, the stew is less brown and the people less simple.
That's as far as I've gotten.

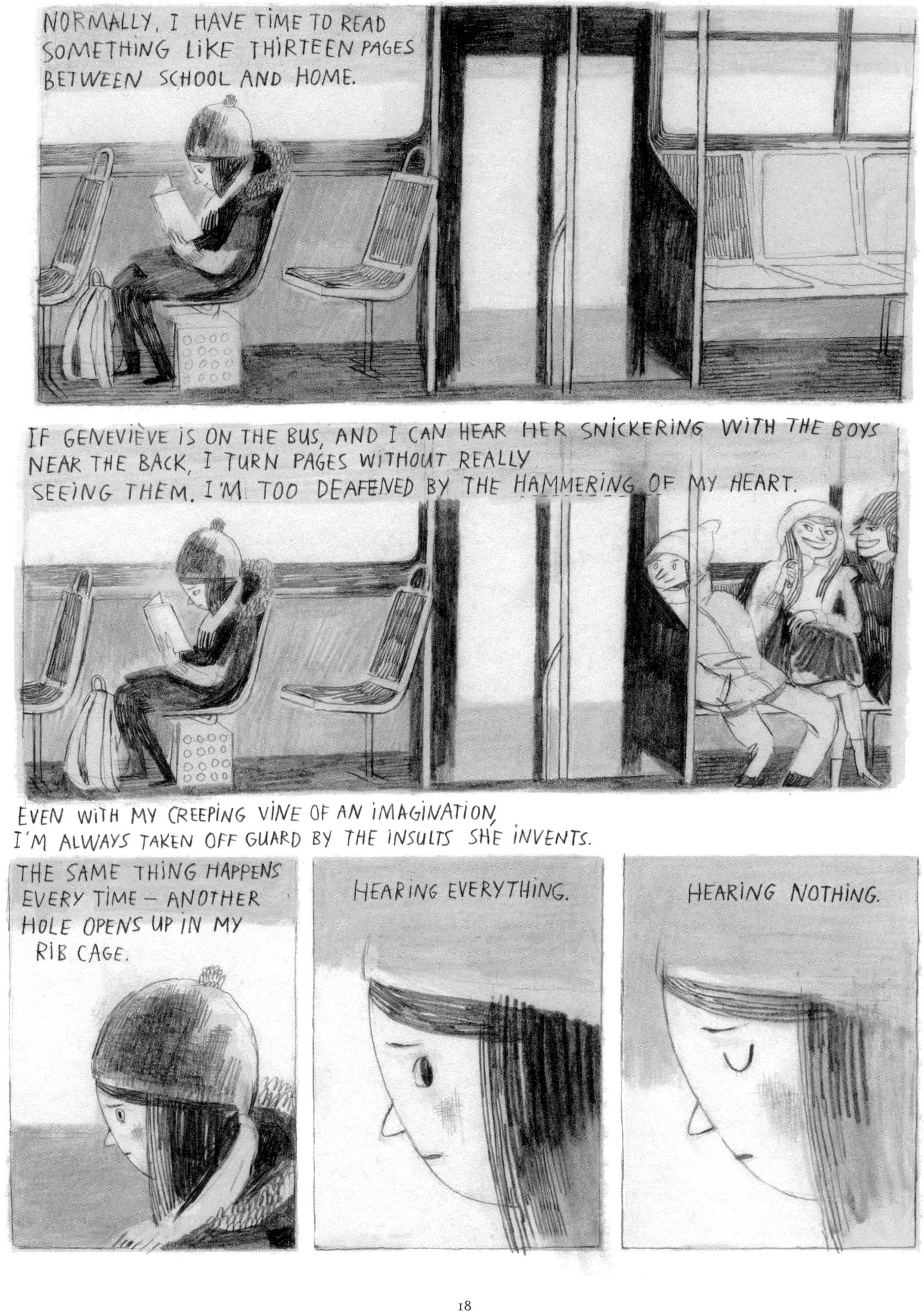
NORMALLY, I HAVE TIME TO READ SOMETHING LIKE THIRTEEN PAGES BETWEEN SCHOOL AND HOME.
IF GENEVIÈVE IS ON THE BUS, AND I CAN HEAR HER SNICKERING WITH THE BOYS NEAR THE BACK, I TURN PAGES WITHOUT REALLY SEEING THEM. I'M TOO DEAFENED BY THE HAMMERING OF MY HEART.
EVEN WITH MY CREEPING VINE OF AN IMAGINATION, I'M ALWAYS TAKEN OFF GUARD BY THE INSULTS SHE INVENTS.
THE SAME THING HAPPENS EVERY TIME — ANOTHER HOLE OPENS UP IN MY RIB CAGE.
HEARING EVERYTHING.
HEARING NOTHING.

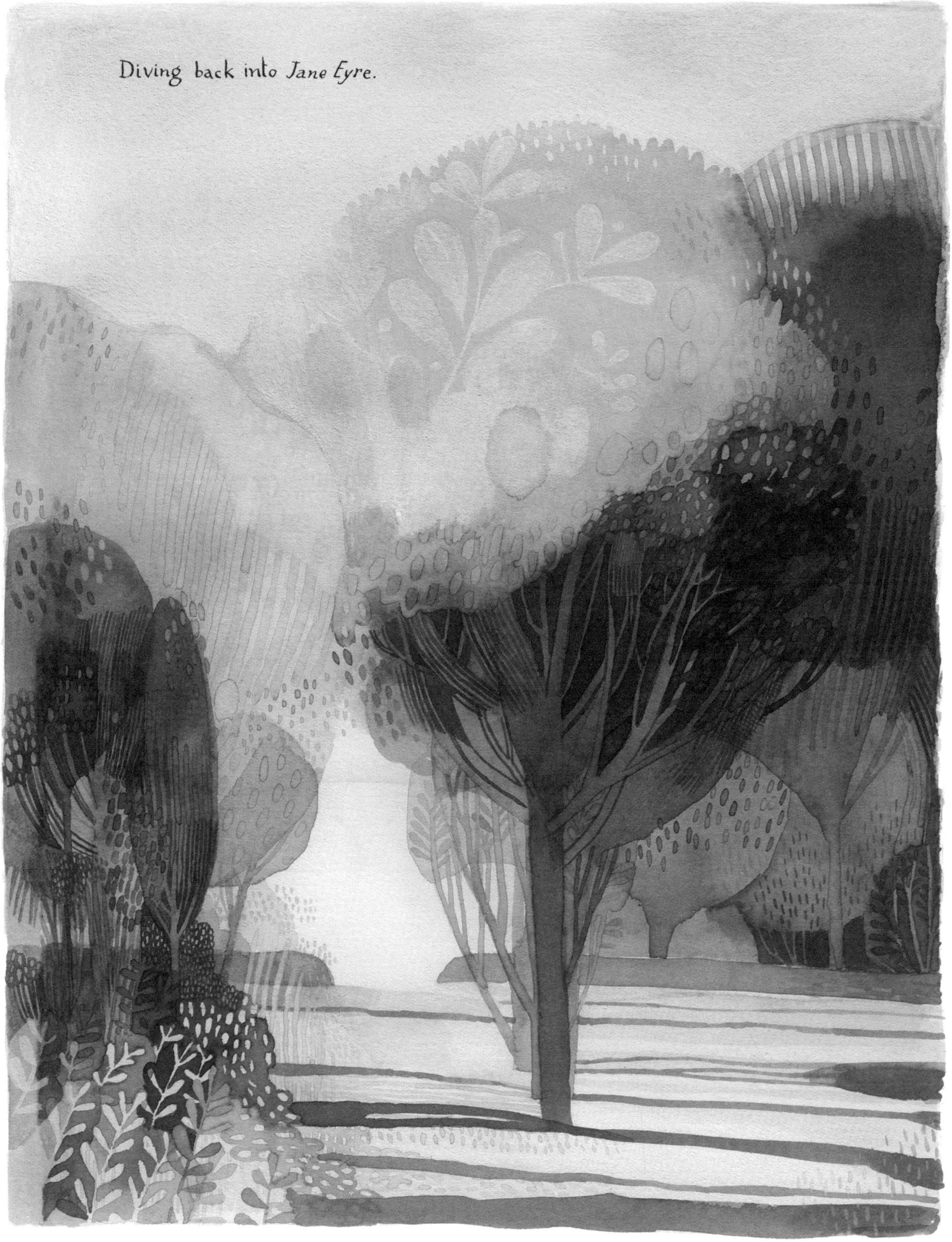
Diving back into Jane Eyre.

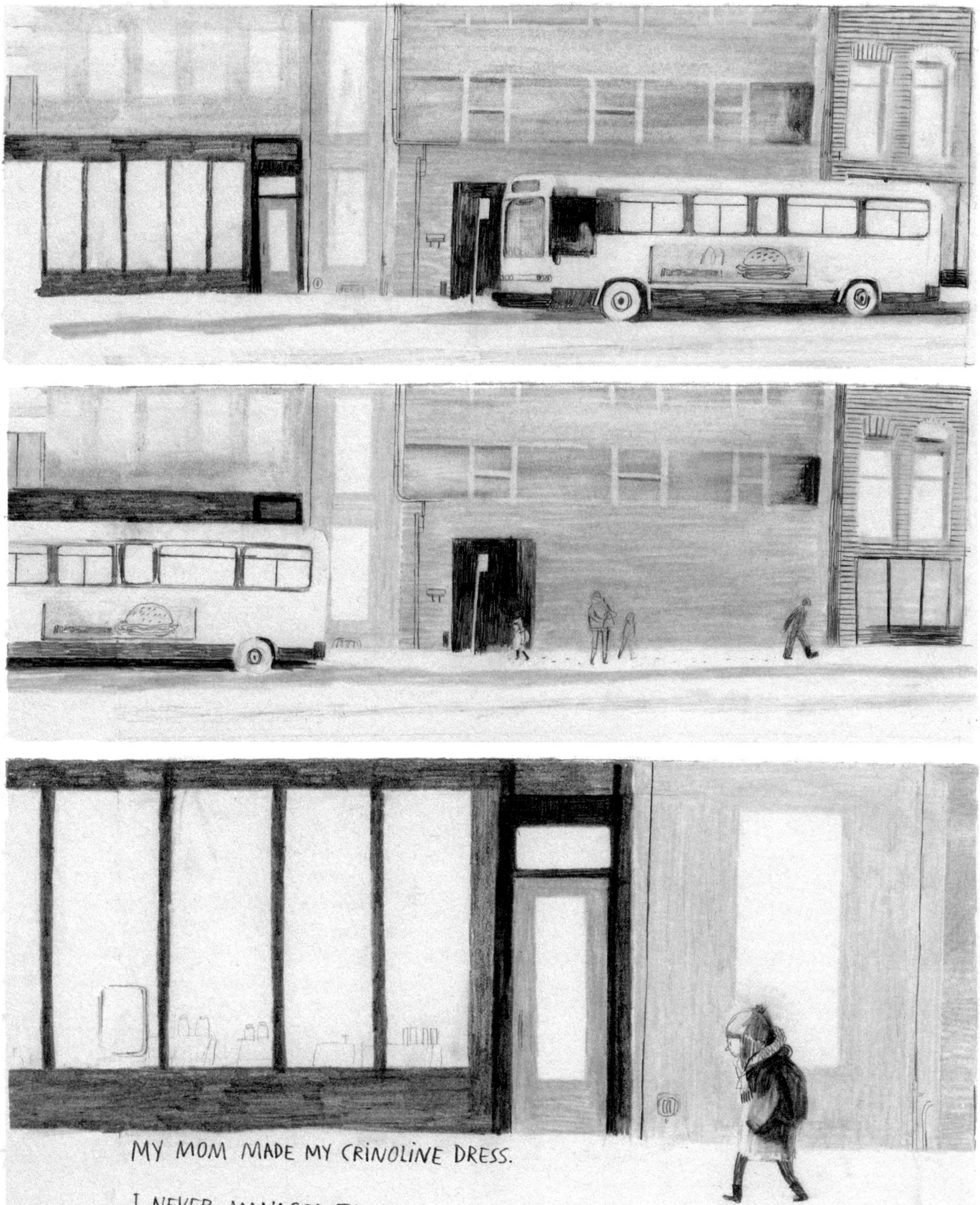

MY MOM MADE MY CRINOLINE DRESS.
I NEVER MANAGED TO SAVE ENOUGH MONEY.
I SPEND IT AS I GO.
IT'S BECAUSE OF THE RASPBERRY GUMMIES AT THE CORNER STORE.

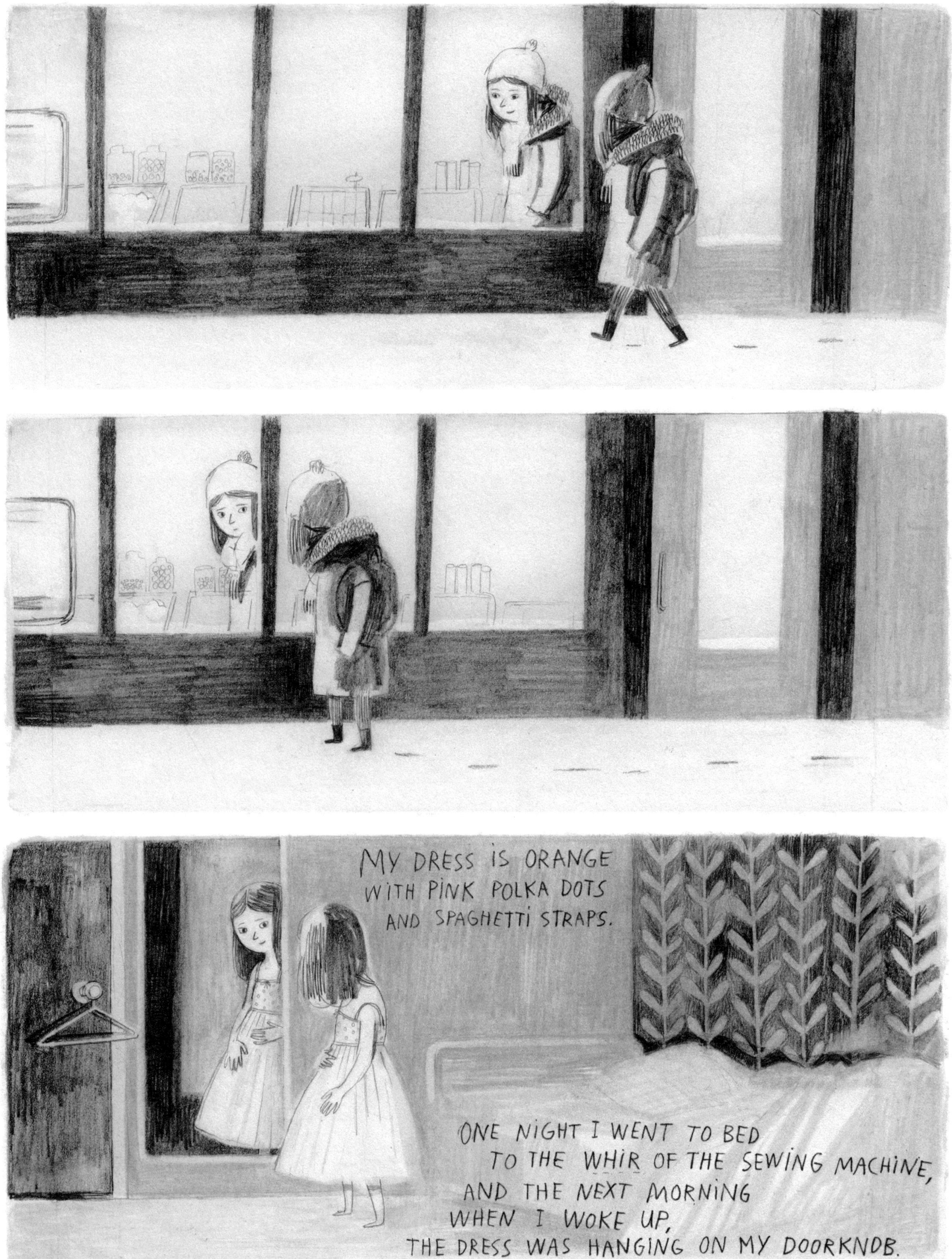
MY DRESS IS ORANGE
WITH PINK POLKA DOTS
AND SPAGHETTI STRAPS.
ONE NIGHT I WENT TO BED
TO THE WHIR OF THE SEWING MACHINE,
AND THE NEXT MORNING
WHEN I WOKE UP,
THE DRESS WAS HANGING ON MY DOORKNOB.

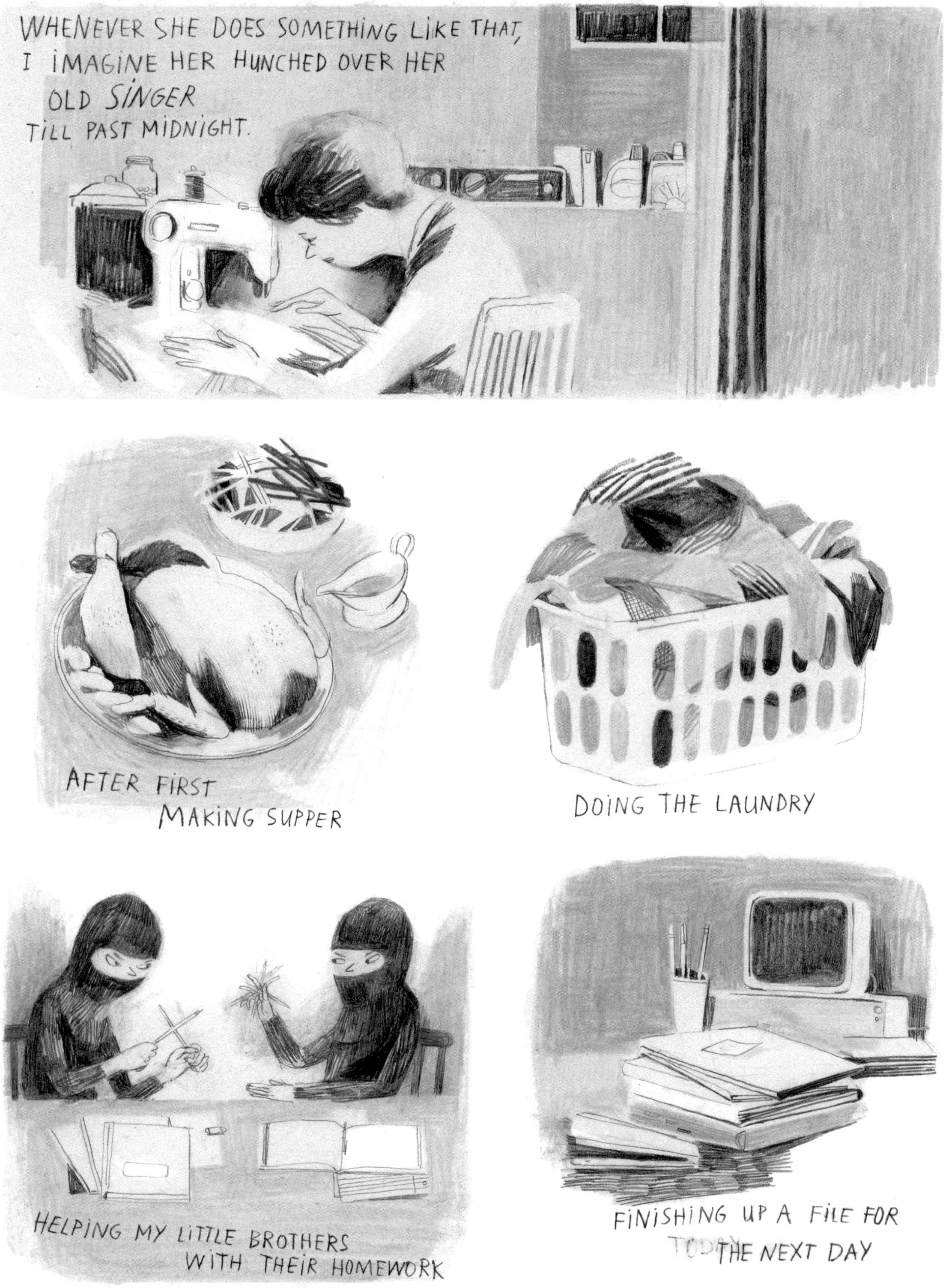
WHENEVER SHE DOES SOMETHING LIKE THAT, I IMAGINE HER HUNCHED OVER HER OLD SINGER TILL PAST MIDNIGHT.
AFTER FIRST MAKING SUPPER
DOING THE LAUNDRY
HELPING MY LITTLE BROTHERS WITH THEIR HOMEWORK
FINISHING UP A FILE FOR THE NEXT DAY

HANGING THE CLOTHES UP TO DRY

MAKING LUNCHES FOR TOMORROW

SENDING THE LOT OF US TO BED

CHANGING THE NEEDLE ON THE RECORD PLAYER

FOLDING THE LAUNDRY

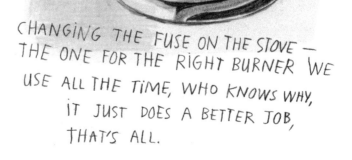

CHANGING THE FUSE ON THE STOVE — THE ONE FOR THE RIGHT BURNER WE USE ALL THE TIME, WHO KNOWS WHY, IT JUST DOES A BETTER JOB, THAT'S ALL.

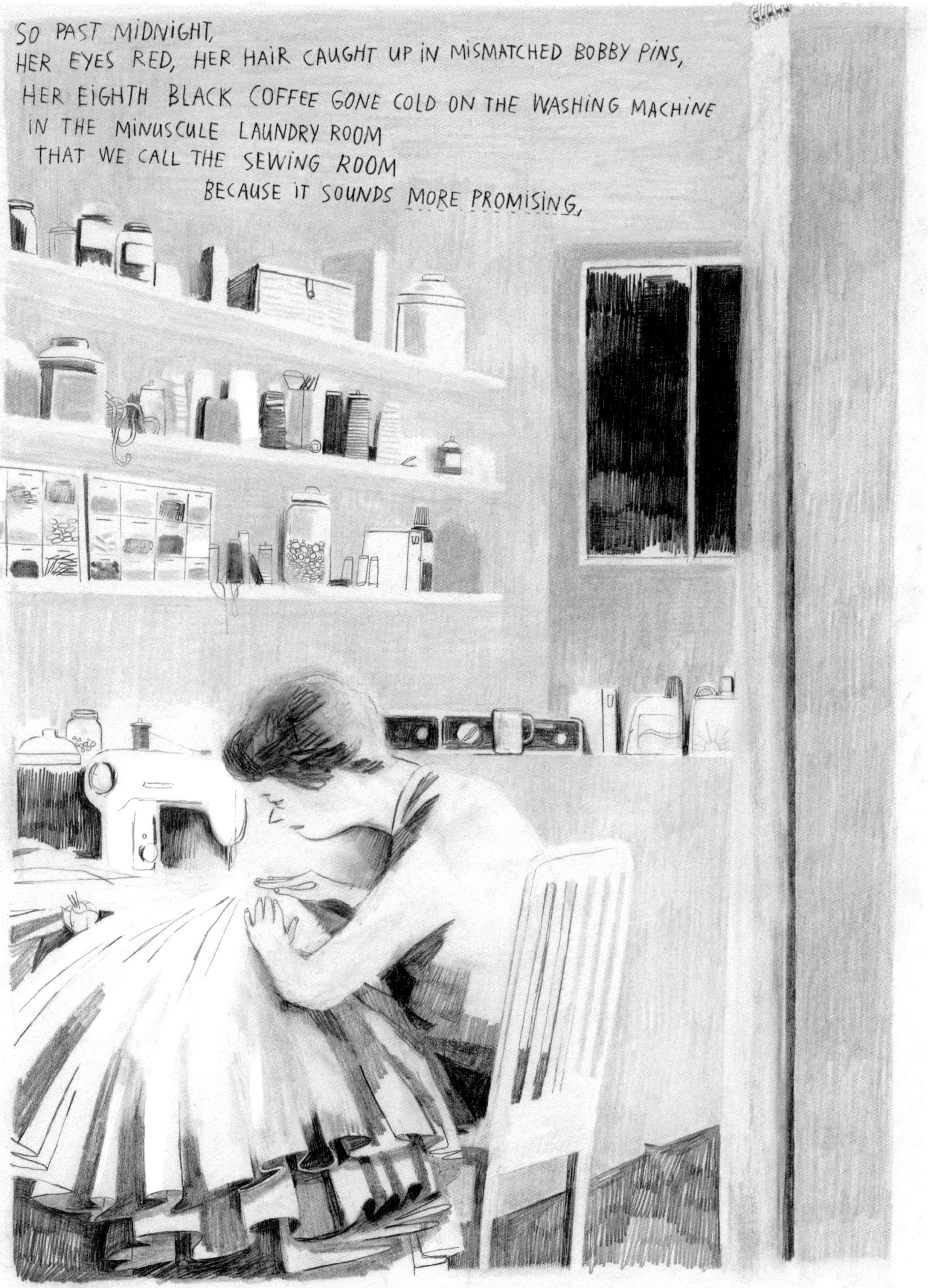
SO PAST MIDNIGHT,
HER EYES RED, HER HAIR CAUGHT UP IN MISMATCHED BOBBY PINS,
HER EIGHTH BLACK COFFEE GONE COLD ON THE WASHING MACHINE
IN THE MINUSCULE LAUNDRY ROOM
THAT WE CALL THE SEWING ROOM
BECAUSE IT SOUNDS MORE PROMISING,

I IMAGINE HER RUNNING OUT OF THREAD JUST BEFORE SHE'S DONE.

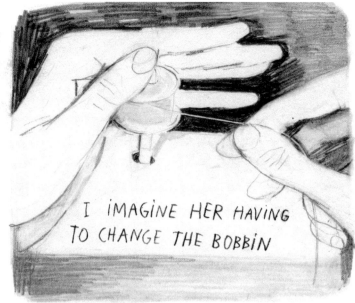

I IMAGINE HER HAVING TO CHANGE THE BOBBIN

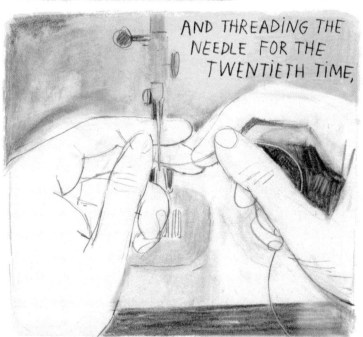

AND THREADING THE NEEDLE FOR THE TWENTIETH TIME,

SAYING TO HERSELF OUT LOUD SO JUST MAYBE SOMEONE WILL HEAR HER, EVEN THOUGH BY NOW EVERYONE'S IN BED,

I'm so tired I could die.

SO I STARE AT THE BEAUTIFUL BRAND-NEW CRINOLINE DRESS THAT'S MINE ALONE WITH NO WHIFF OF MOTHBALLS.

EVEN SO, IT DROOPS EVER SO SLIGHTLY.

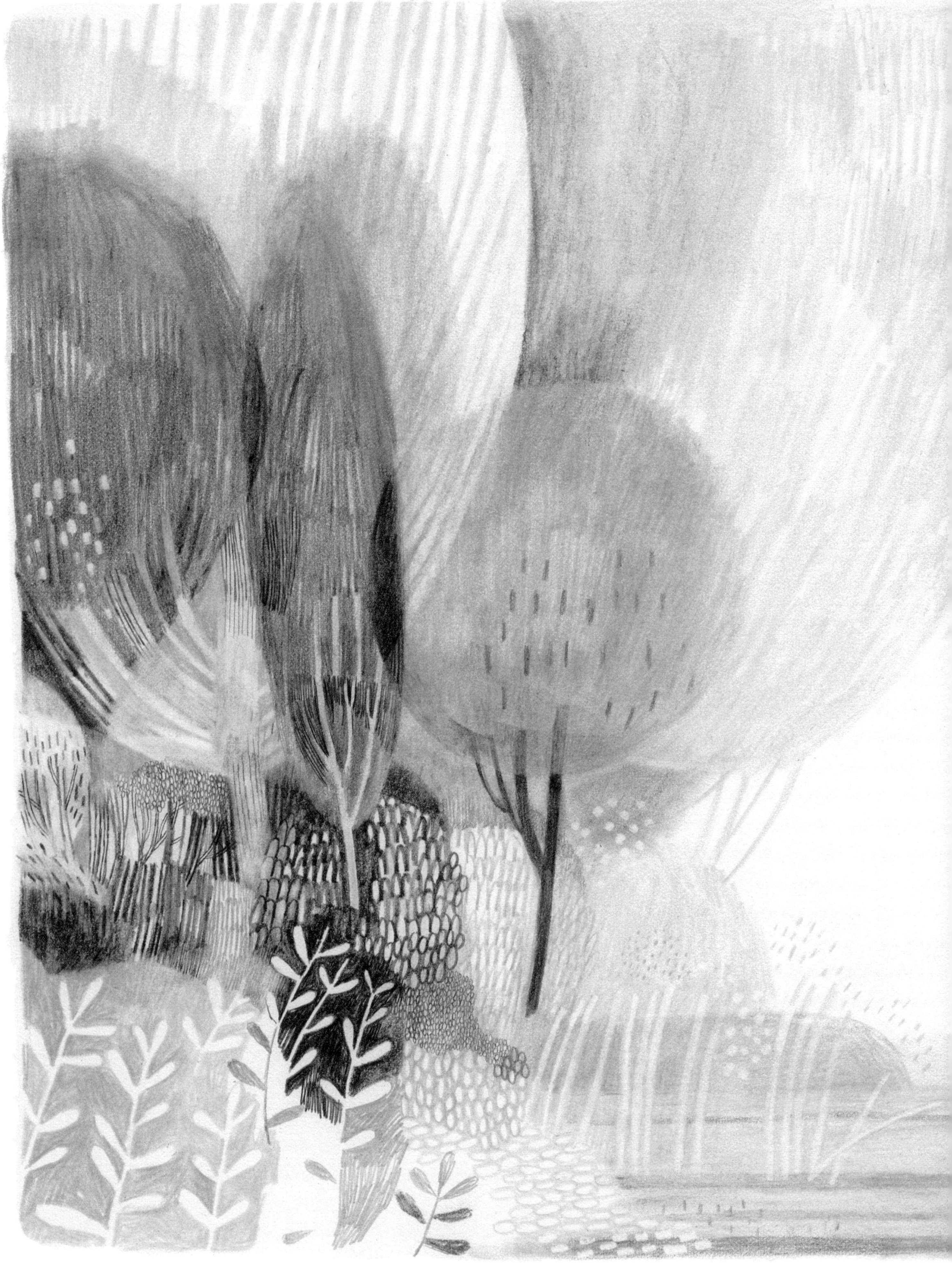

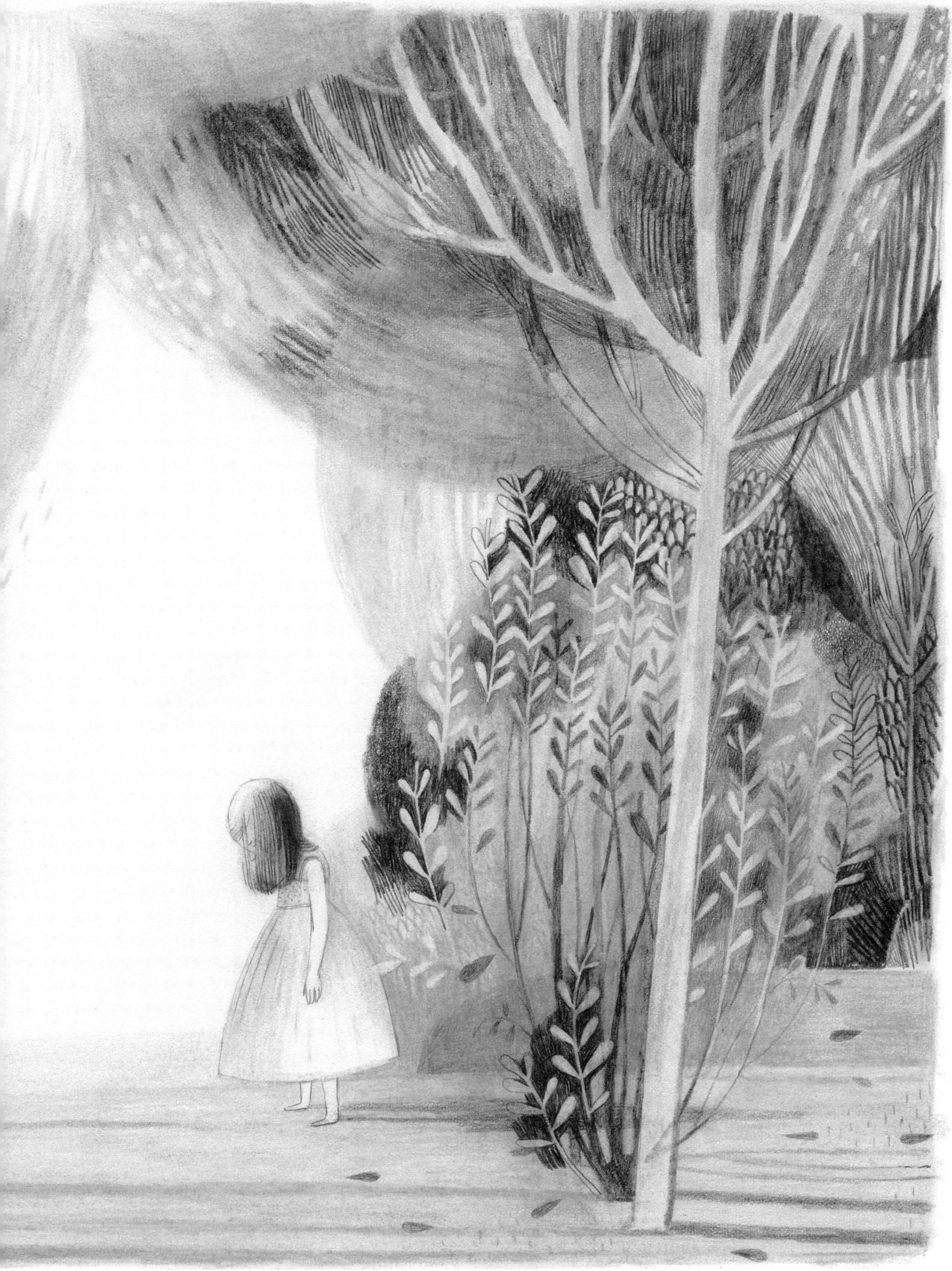

Because she grew up to be clever, slender and wise, no one calls
Jane Eyre a liar, a thief or an ugly duckling again. She tutors a young girl,
Adèle, who loves her, even though all she has to her name are three
plain dresses. Adèle thinks Jane Eyre's smart and always tells her so.

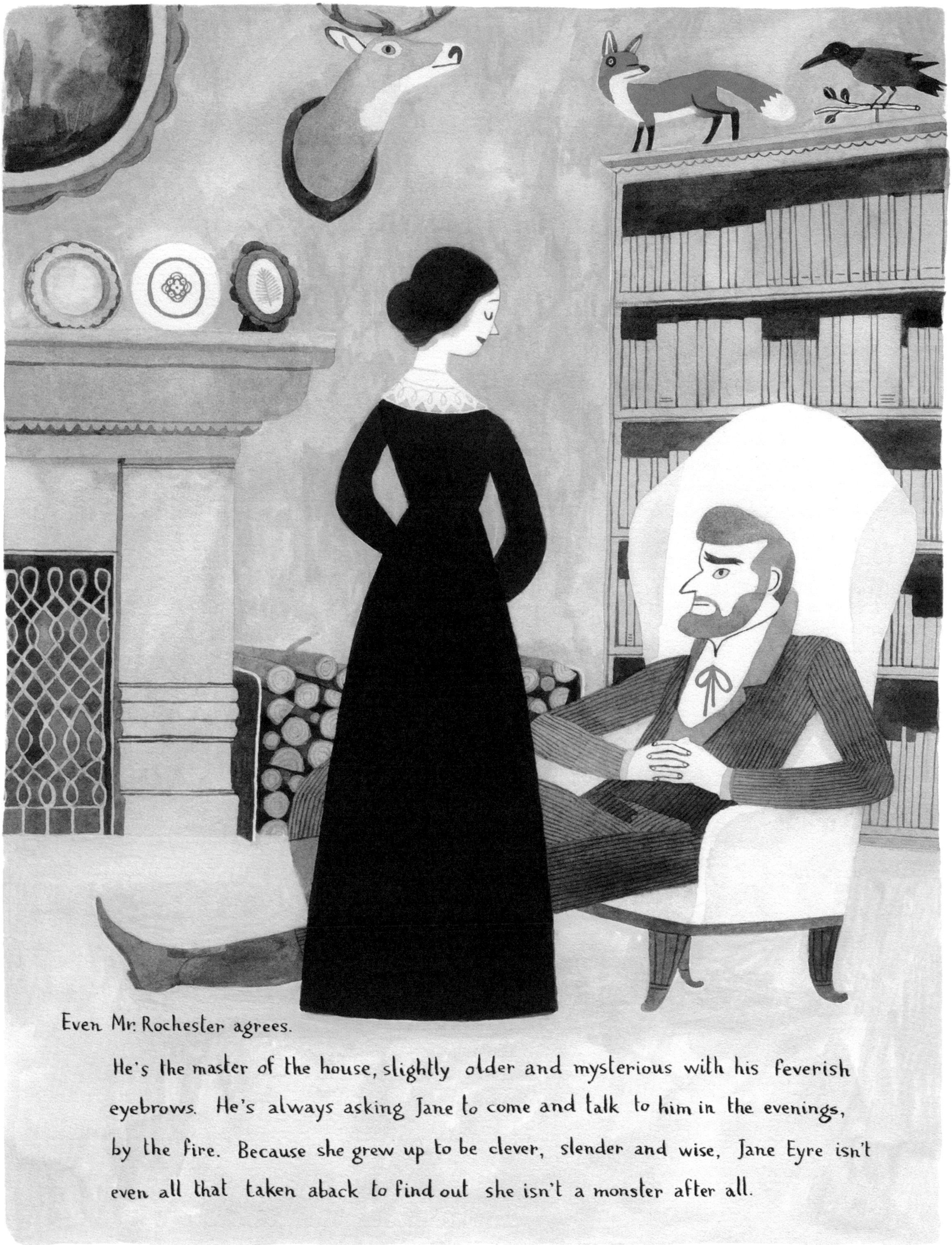

Even Mr. Rochester agrees.

He's the master of the house, slightly older and mysterious with his feverish eyebrows. He's always asking Jane to come and talk to him in the evenings, by the fire. Because she grew up to be clever, slender and wise, Jane Eyre isn't even all that taken aback to find out she isn't a monster after all.

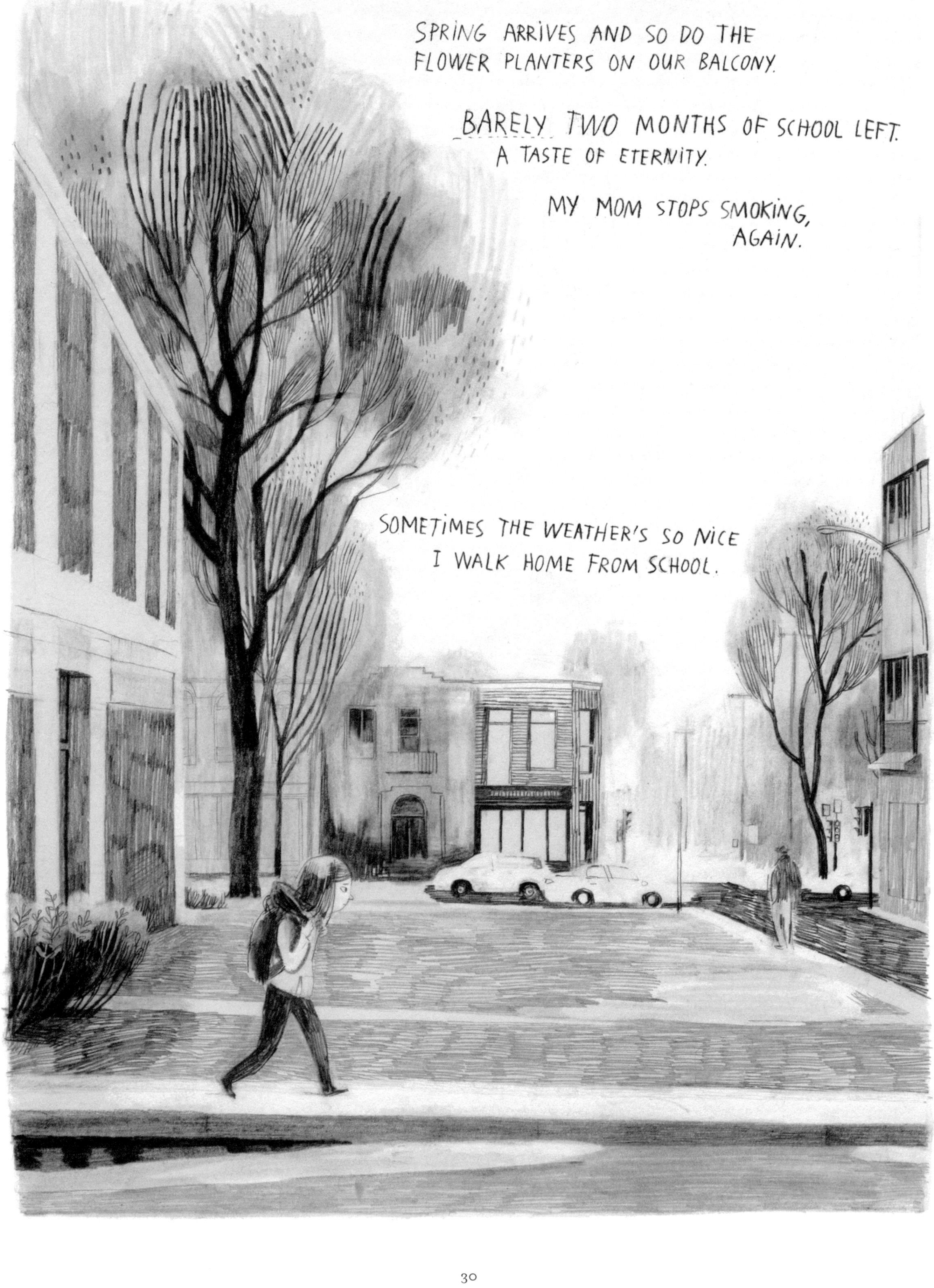
SPRING ARRIVES AND SO DO THE FLOWER PLANTERS ON OUR BALCONY.
BARELY TWO MONTHS OF SCHOOL LEFT. A TASTE OF ETERNITY.
MY MOM STOPS SMOKING, AGAIN.
SOMETIMES THE WEATHER'S SO NICE I WALK HOME FROM SCHOOL.

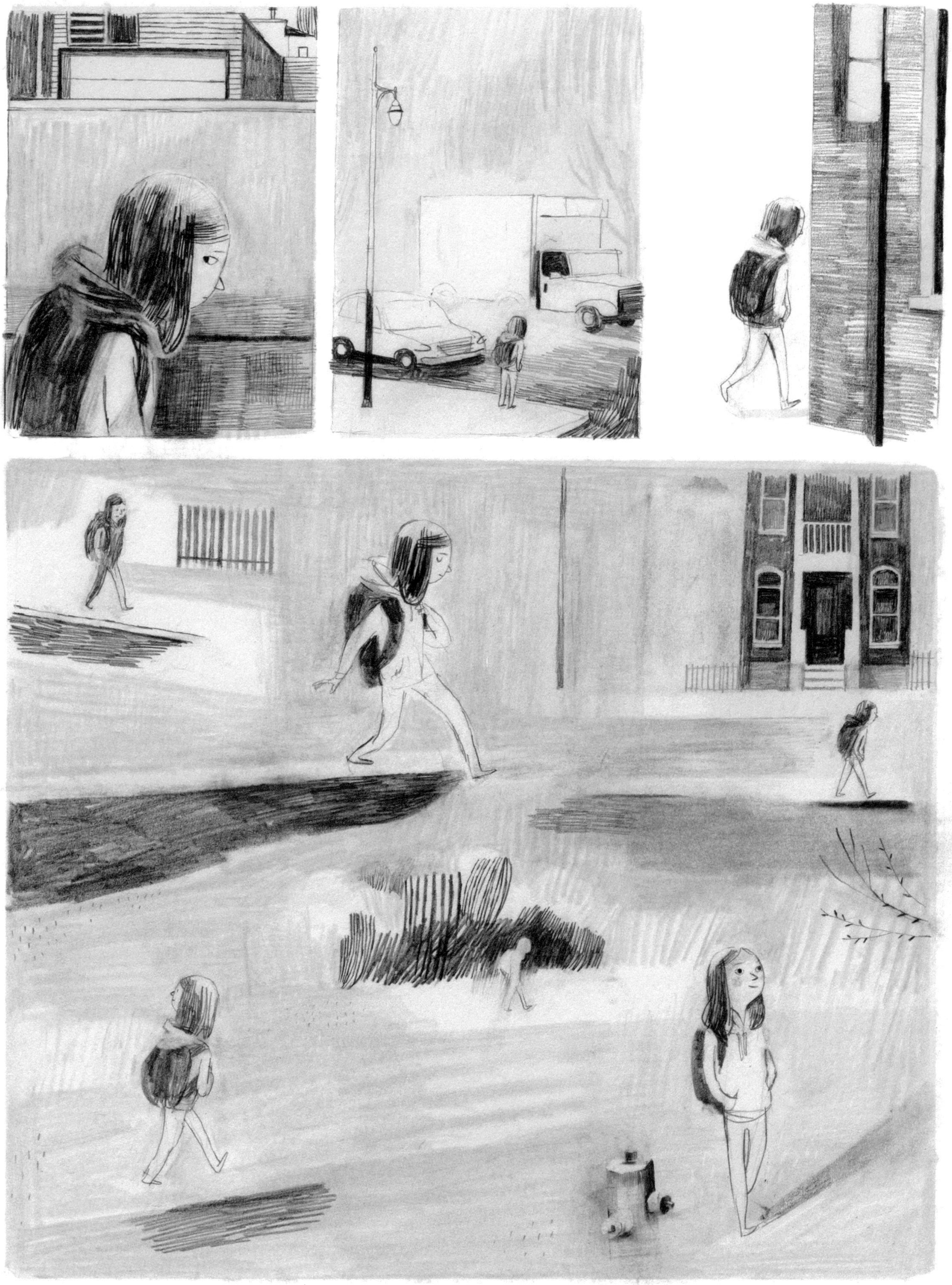

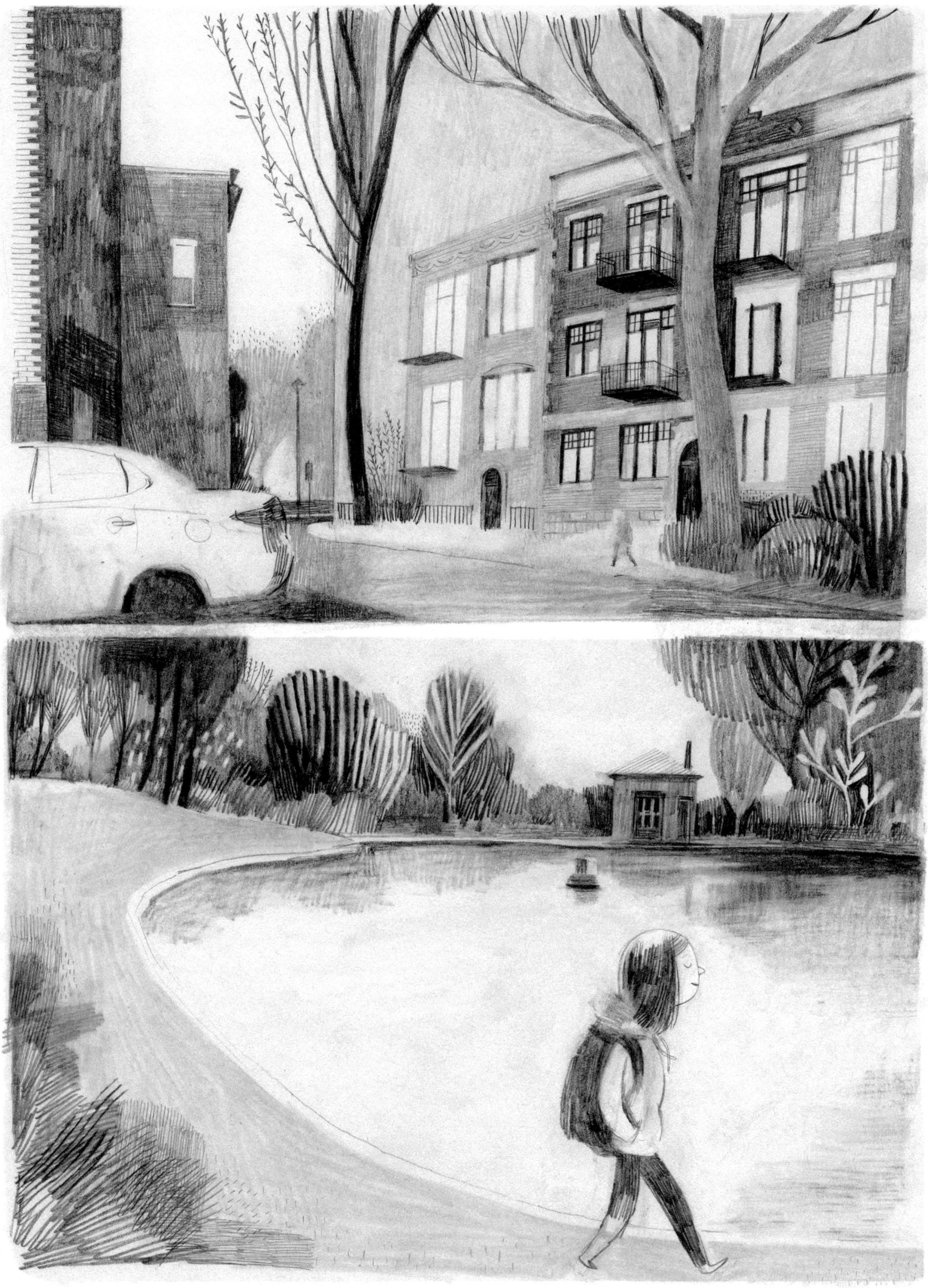

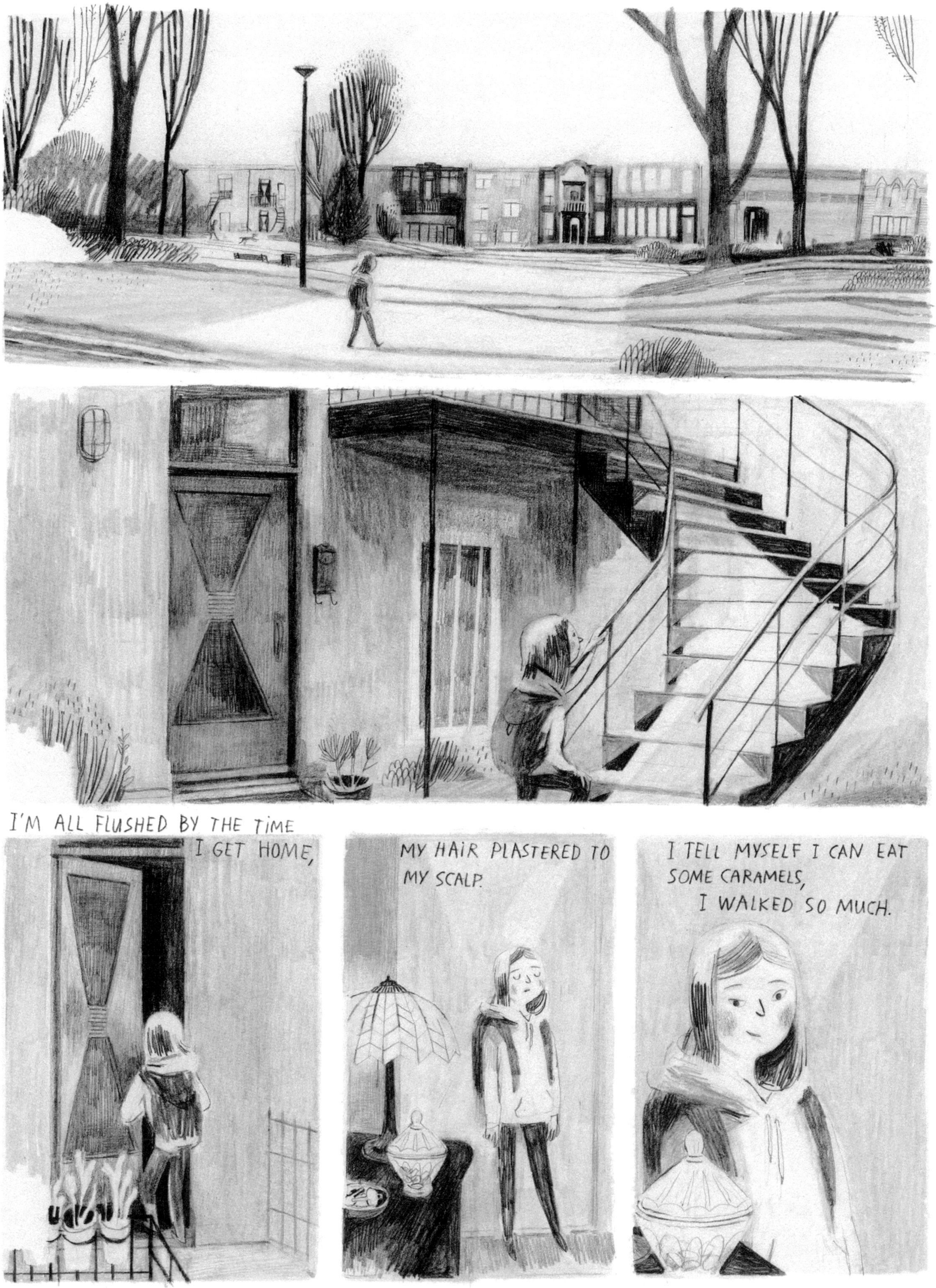
I'M ALL FLUSHED BY THE TIME
I GET HOME,
MY HAIR PLASTERED TO MY SCALP.
I TELL MYSELF I CAN EAT SOME CARAMELS,
I WALKED SO MUCH.

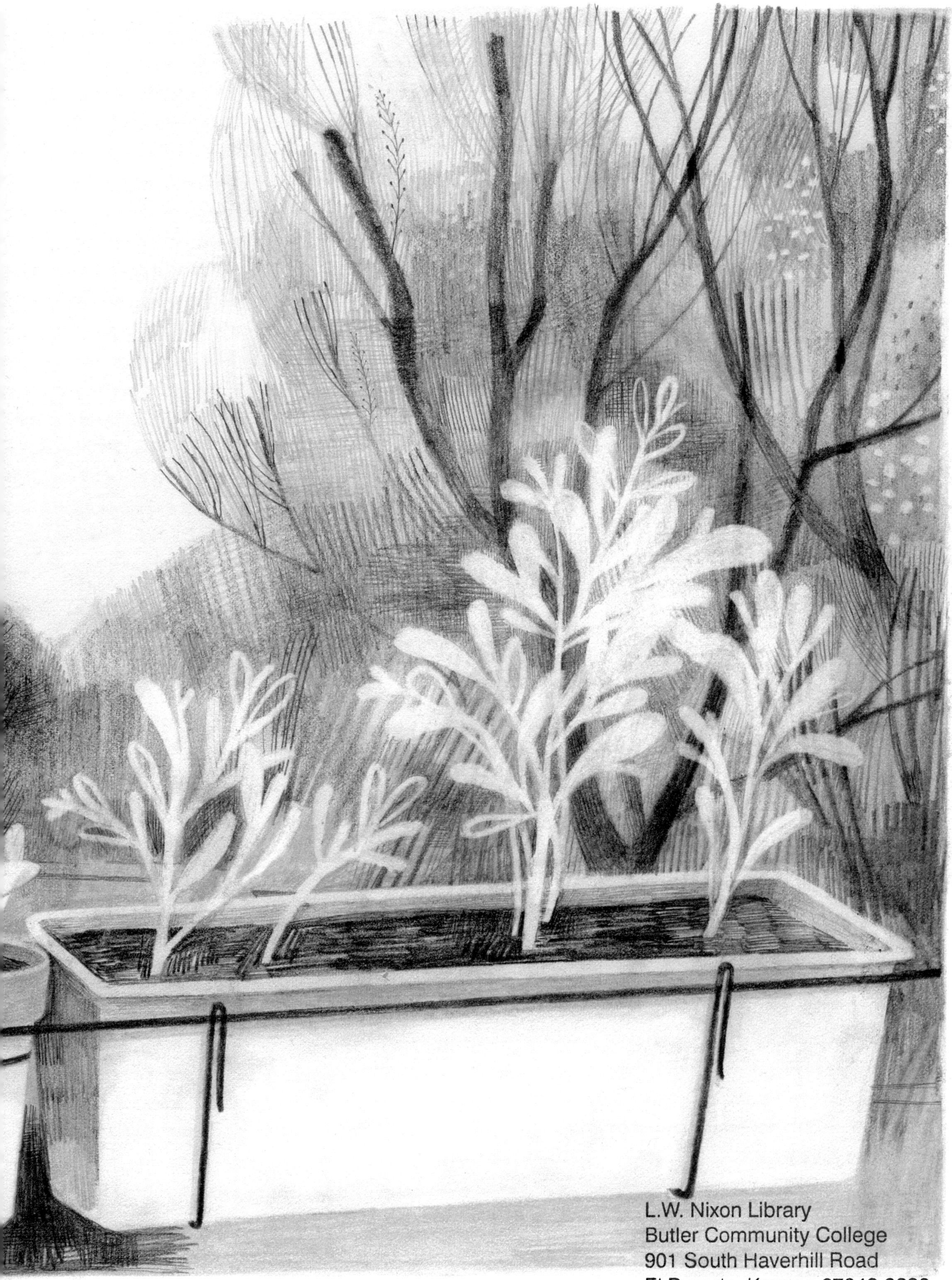

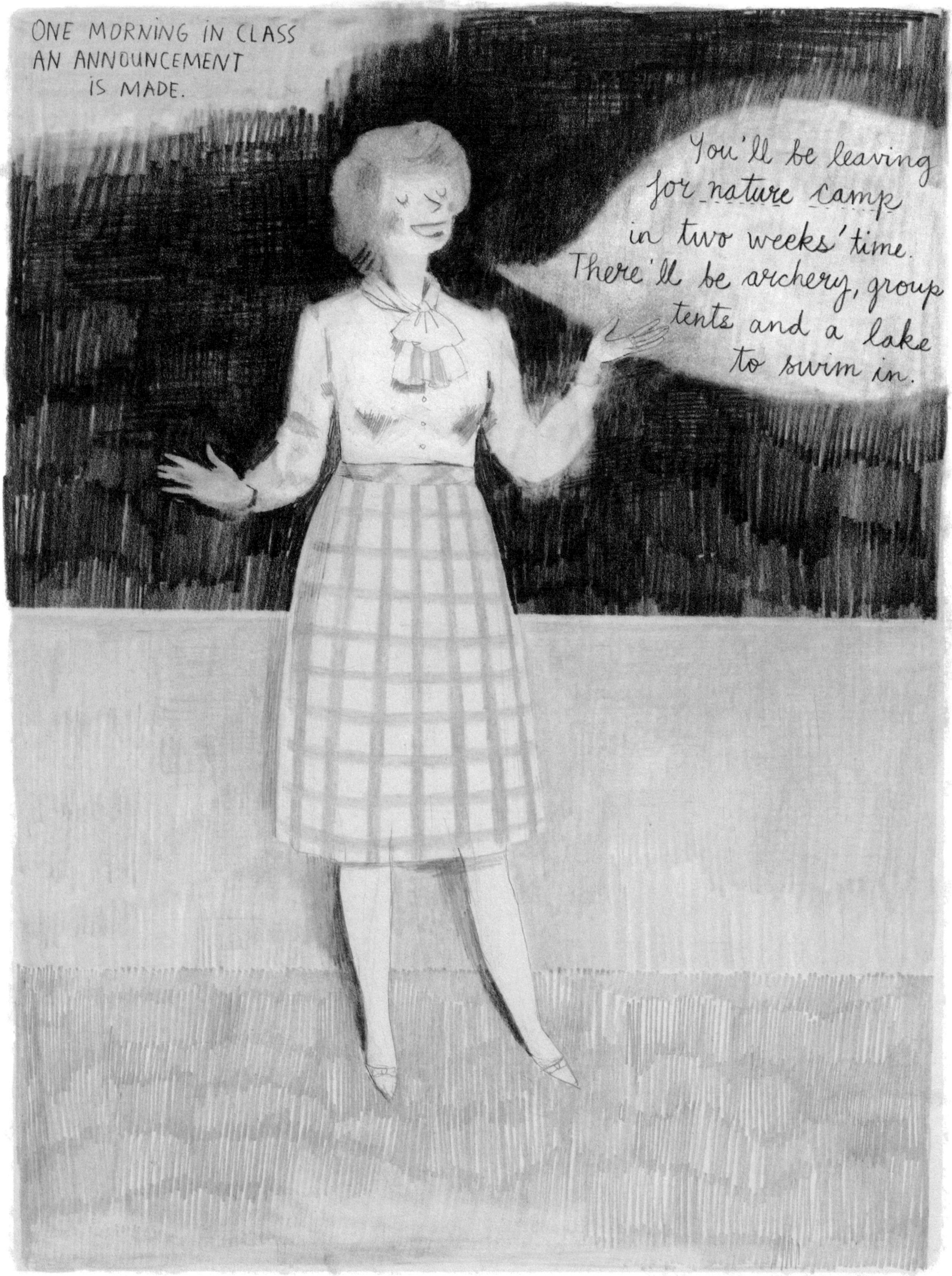
ONE MORNING IN CLASS AN ANNOUNCEMENT IS MADE.
You'll be leaving for nature camp in two weeks' time. There'll be archery, group tents and a lake to swim in.

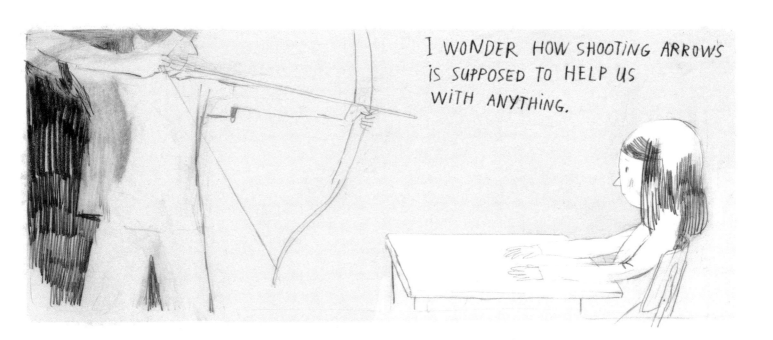

I WONDER HOW SHOOTING ARROWS IS SUPPOSED TO HELP US WITH ANYTHING.

BUT THERE'S NO GETTING AROUND IT.
EVERYTHING'S BEEN ORGANIZED.
FOUR NIGHTS,
FORTY STUDENTS.
OUR WHOLE CLASS.

Geneviève
Sarah
Anne-Julie
Chloé

EVERYONE'S GOING.

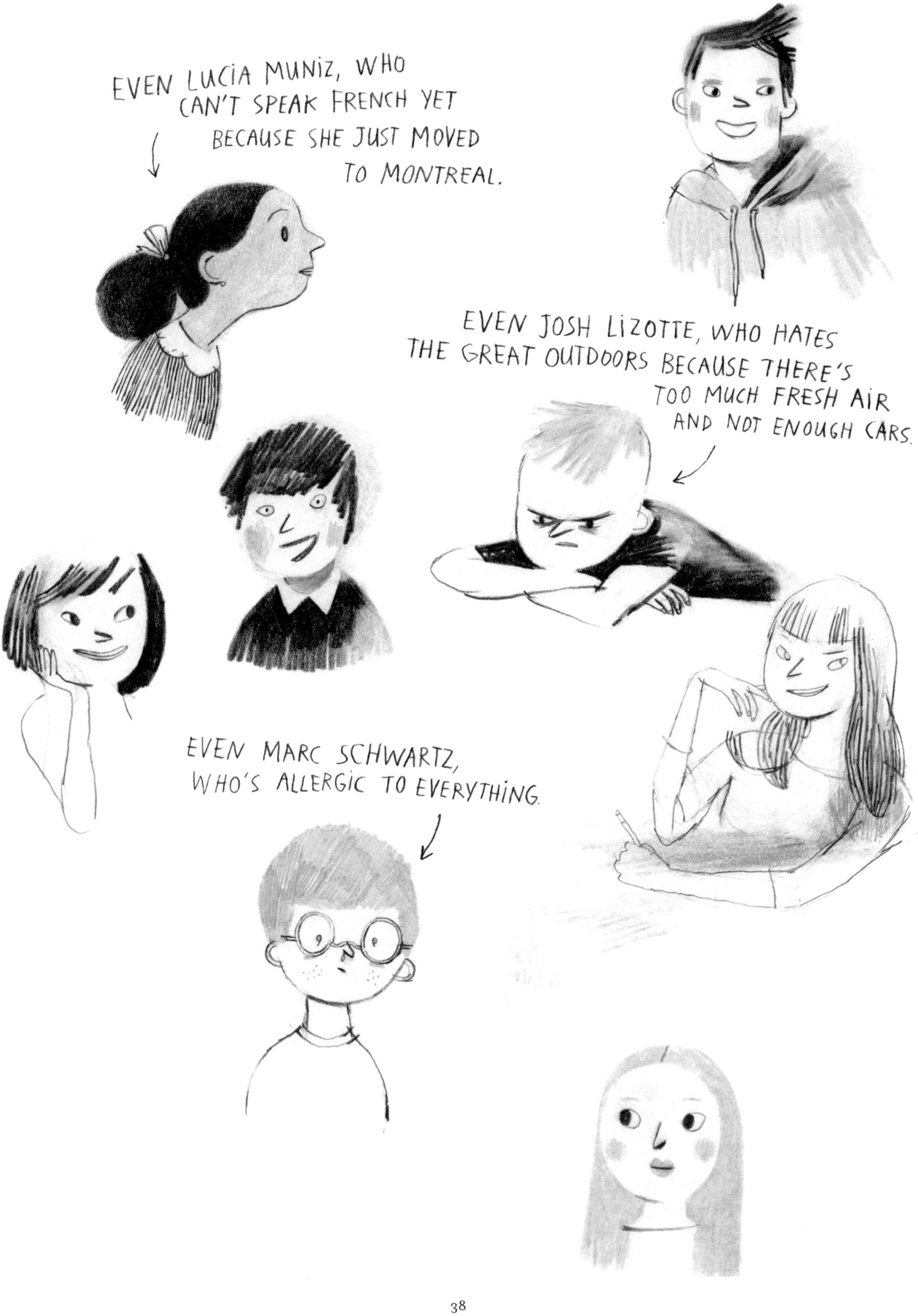
EVEN LUCIA MUNIZ, WHO CAN'T SPEAK FRENCH YET BECAUSE SHE JUST MOVED TO MONTREAL.
EVEN JOSH LIZOTTE, WHO HATES THE GREAT OUTDOORS BECAUSE THERE'S TOO MUCH FRESH AIR AND NOT ENOUGH CARS.
EVEN MARC SCHWARTZ, WHO'S ALLERGIC TO EVERYTHING.

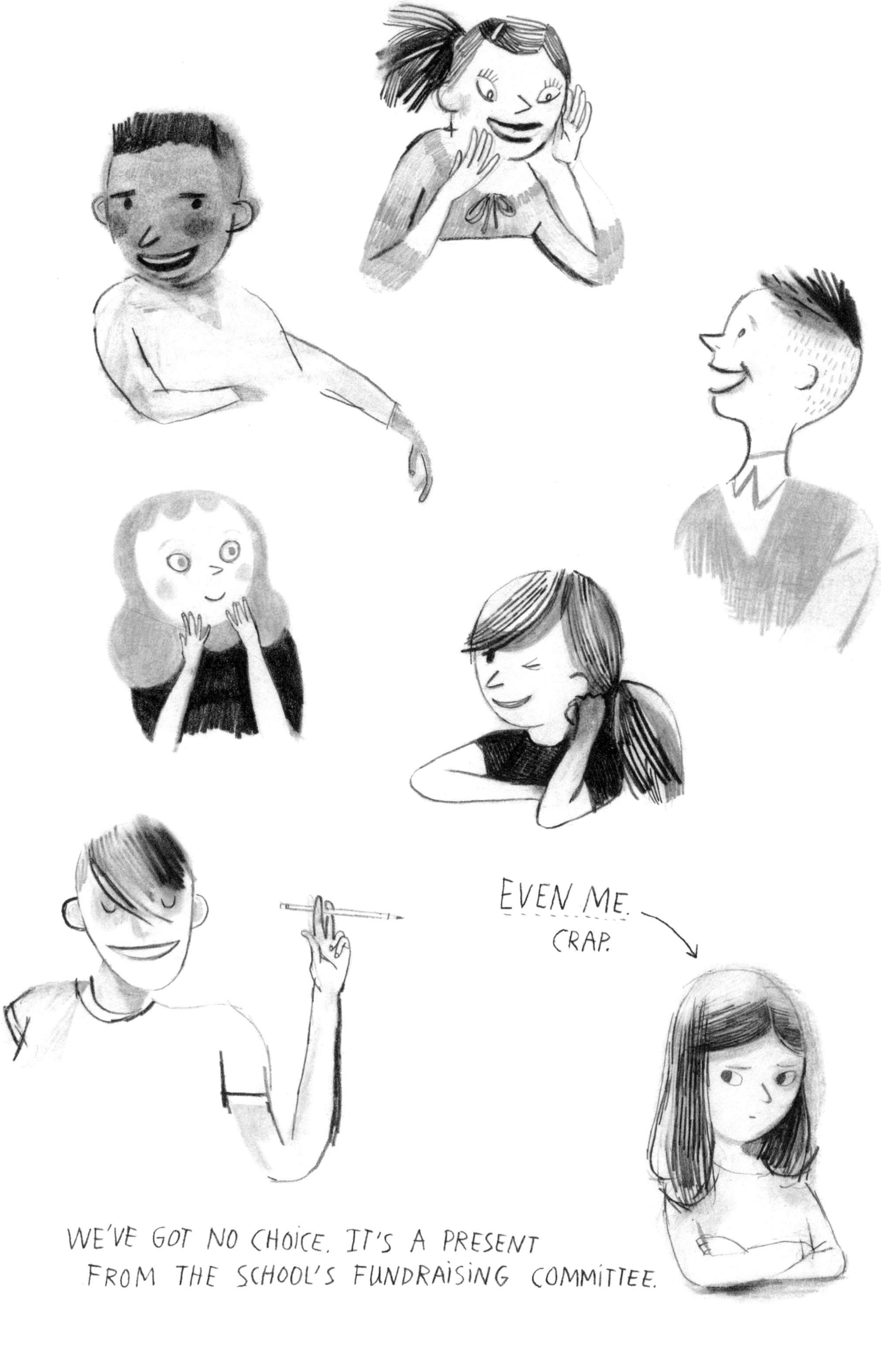
EVEN ME.
CRAP.
WE'VE GOT NO CHOICE. IT'S A PRESENT FROM THE SCHOOL'S FUNDRAISING COMMITTEE.

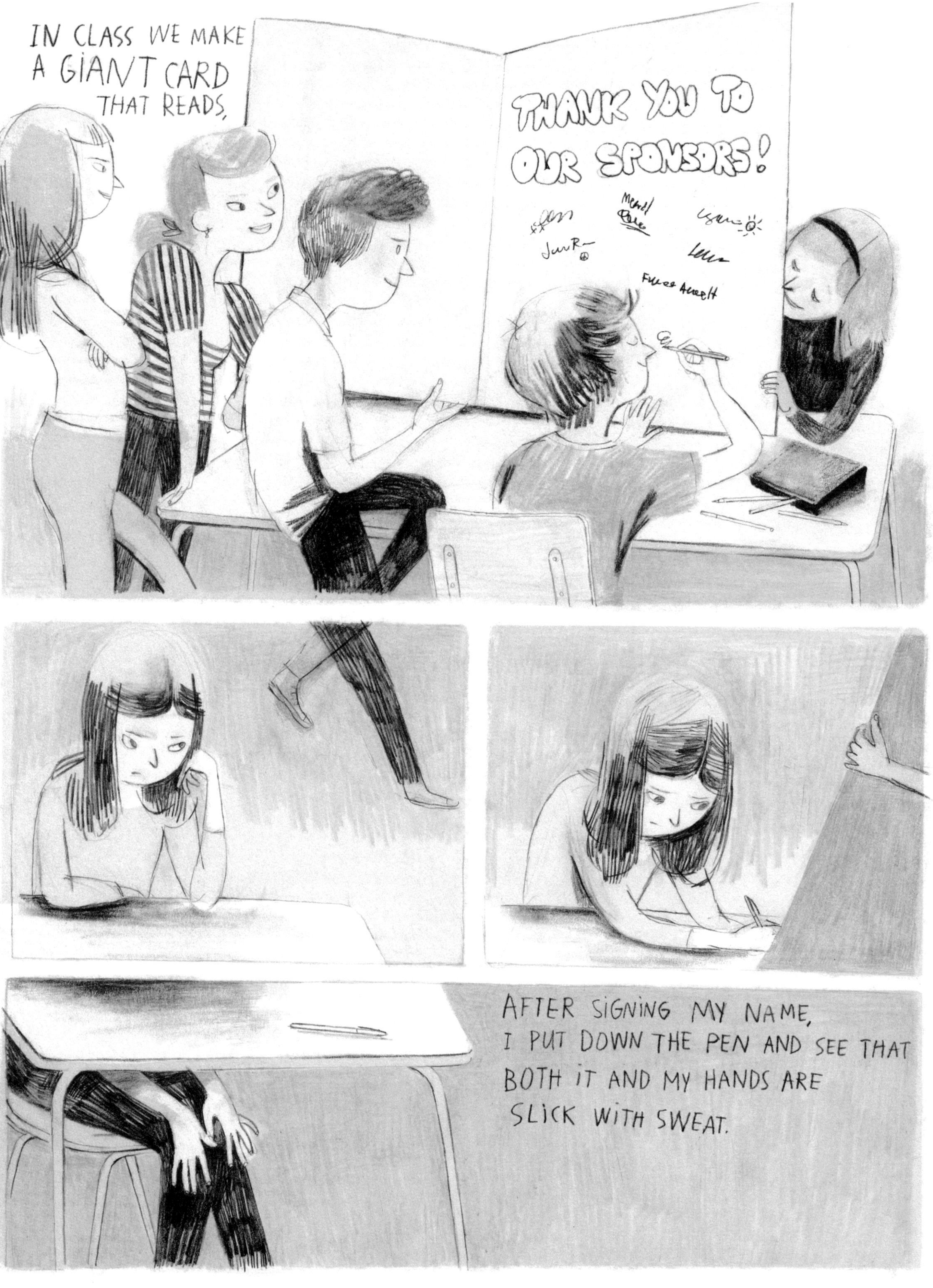
IN CLASS WE MAKE A GIANT CARD THAT READS,
THANK YOU TO OUR SPONSORS!
AFTER SIGNING MY NAME, I PUT DOWN THE PEN AND SEE THAT BOTH IT AND MY HANDS ARE SLICK WITH SWEAT.

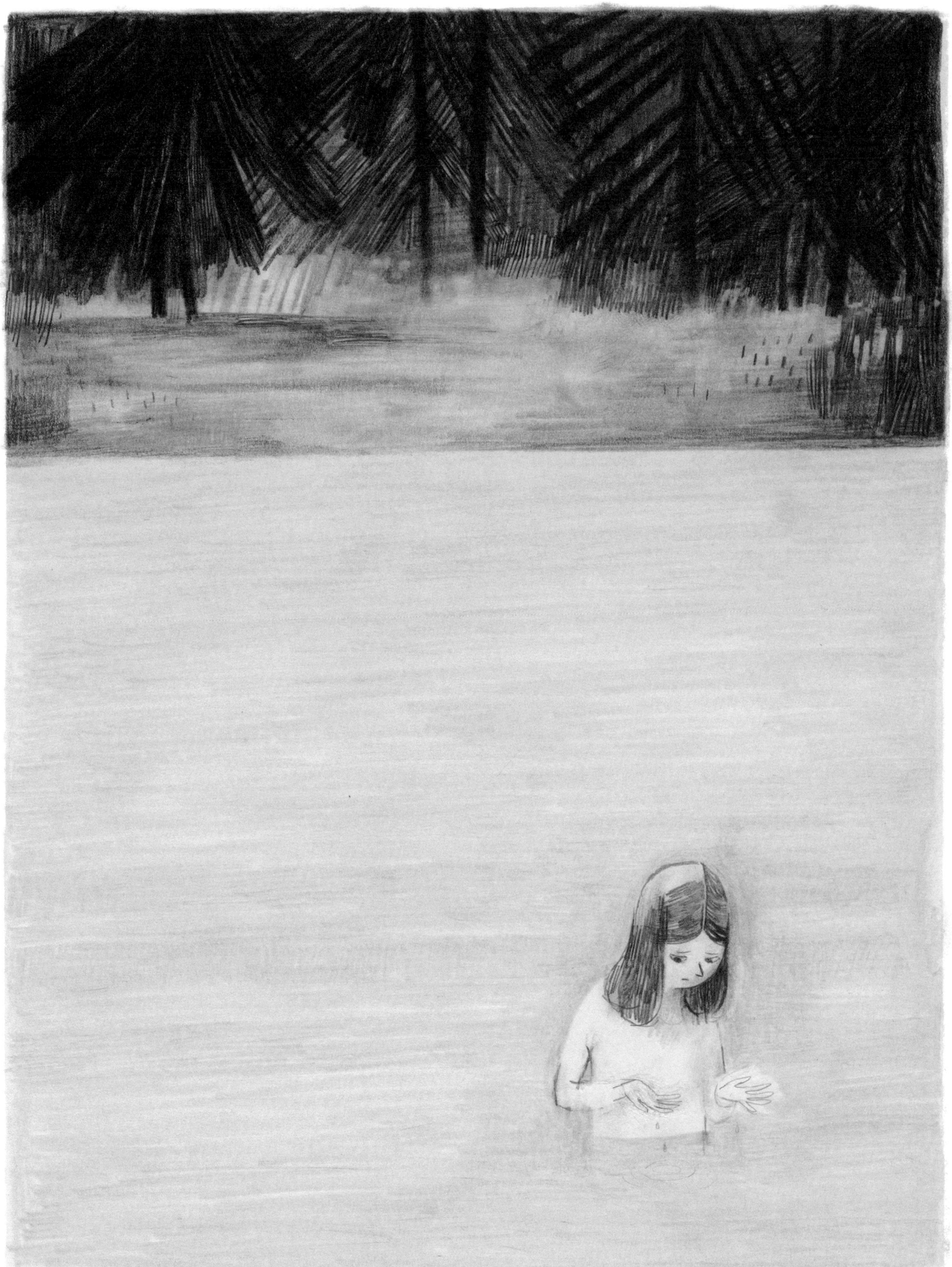

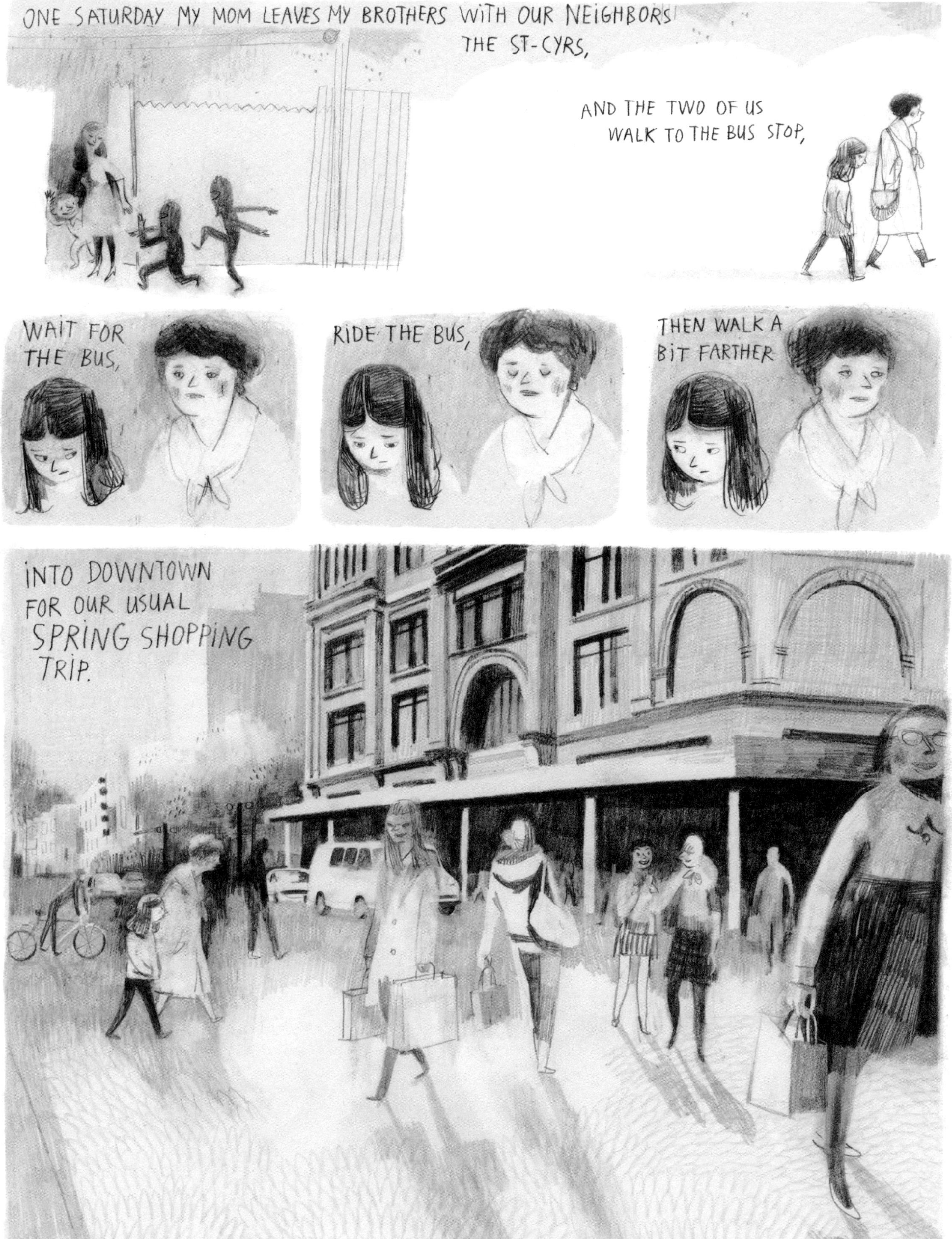
ONE SATURDAY MY MOM LEAVES MY BROTHERS WITH OUR NEIGHBORS THE ST-CYRS,
AND THE TWO OF US WALK TO THE BUS STOP,
WAIT FOR THE BUS,
RIDE THE BUS,
THEN WALK A BIT FARTHER
INTO DOWNTOWN FOR OUR USUAL SPRING SHOPPING TRIP.

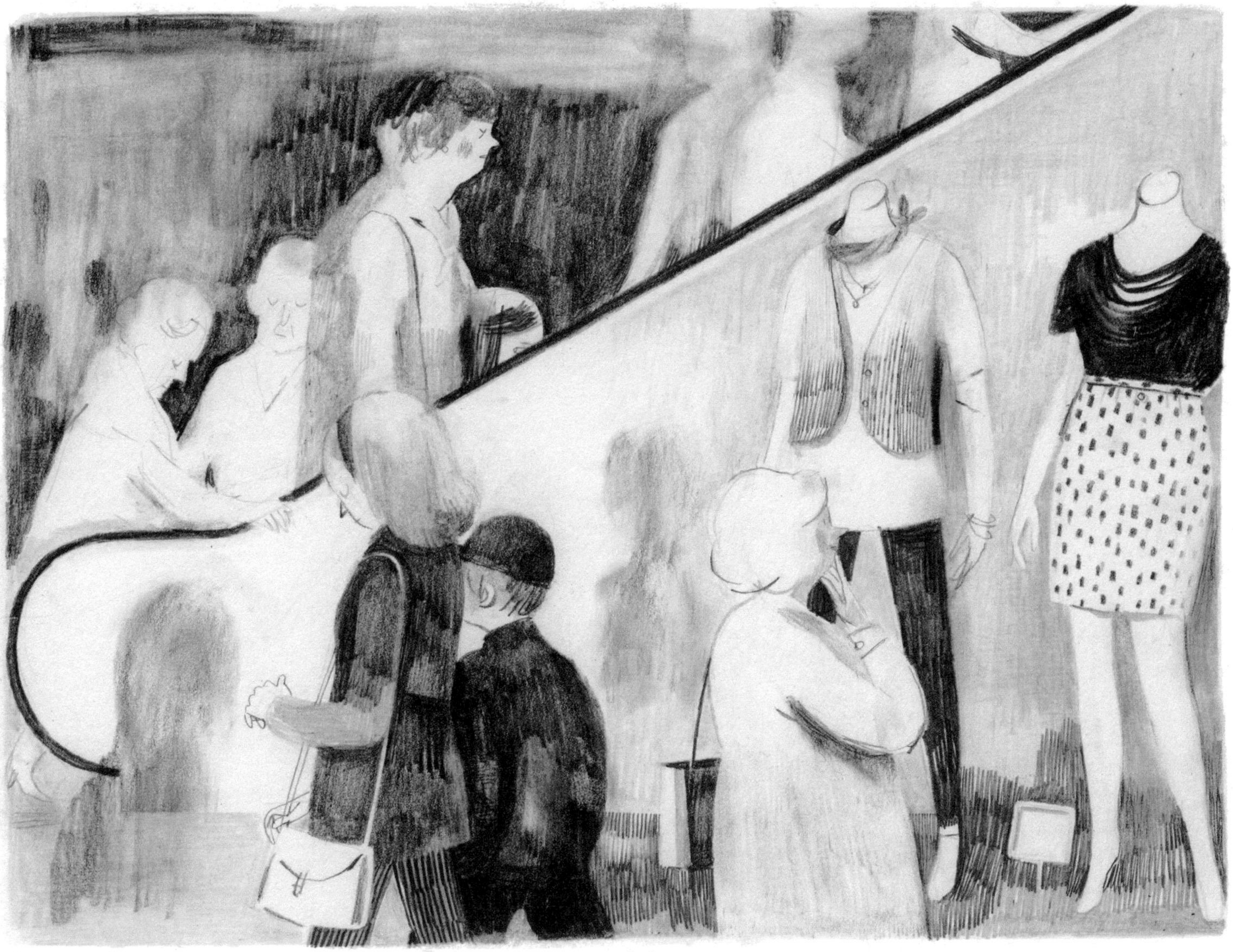

ESCALATORS TAKE US TO THE THIRD FLOOR OF THE BAY AND THE SWIMSUIT DEPARTMENT.

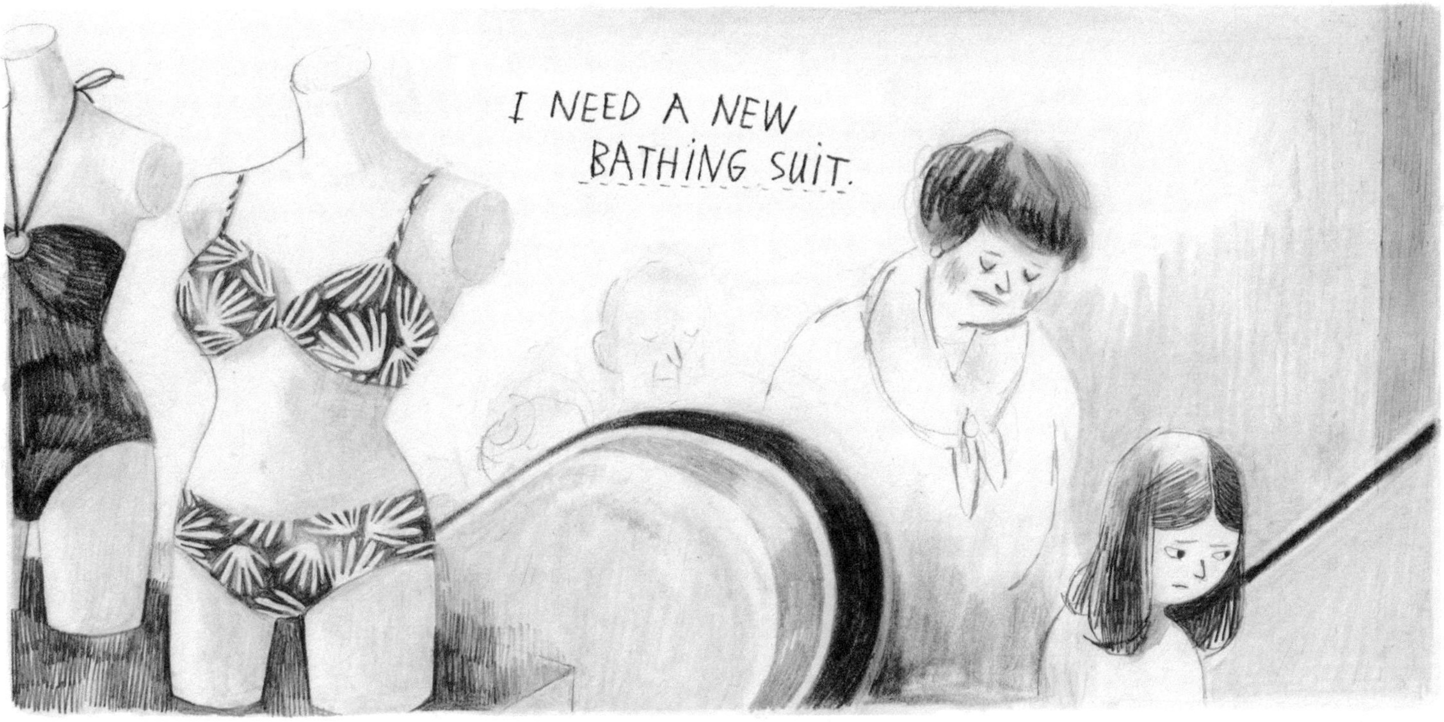
I NEED A NEW BATHING SUIT.

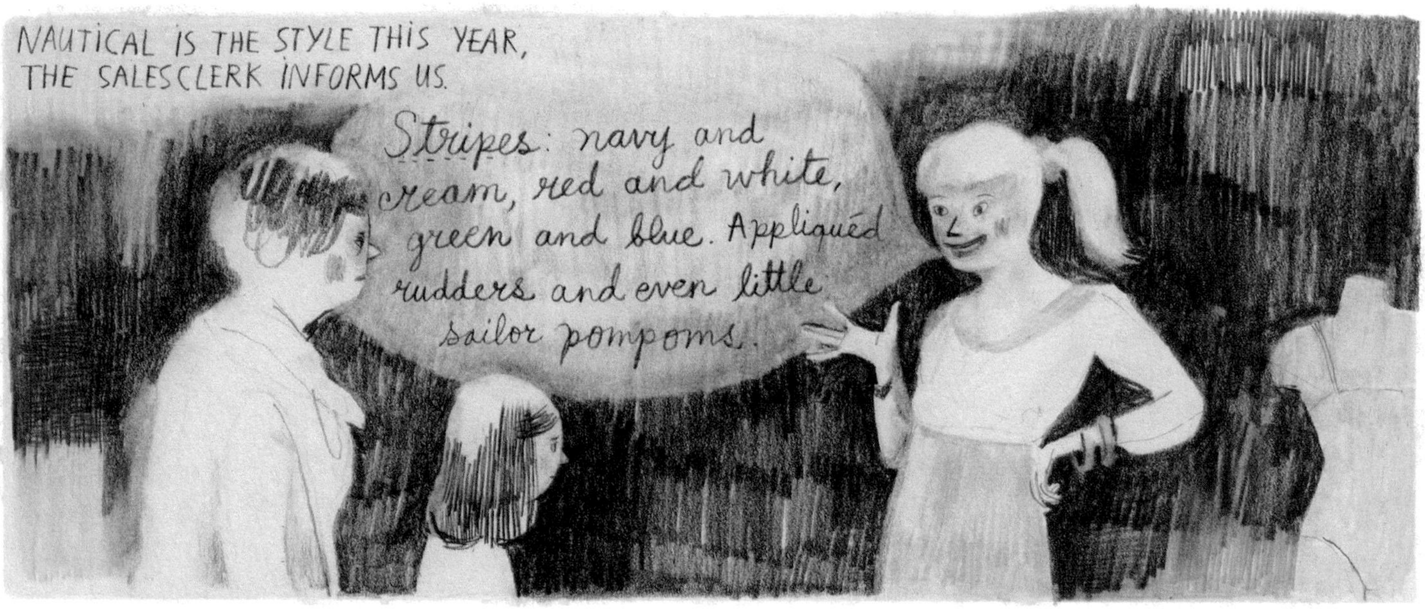
NAUTICAL IS THE STYLE THIS YEAR, THE SALESCLERK INFORMS US.
Stripes: navy and cream, red and white, green and blue. Appliquéd rudders and even little sailor pompoms.

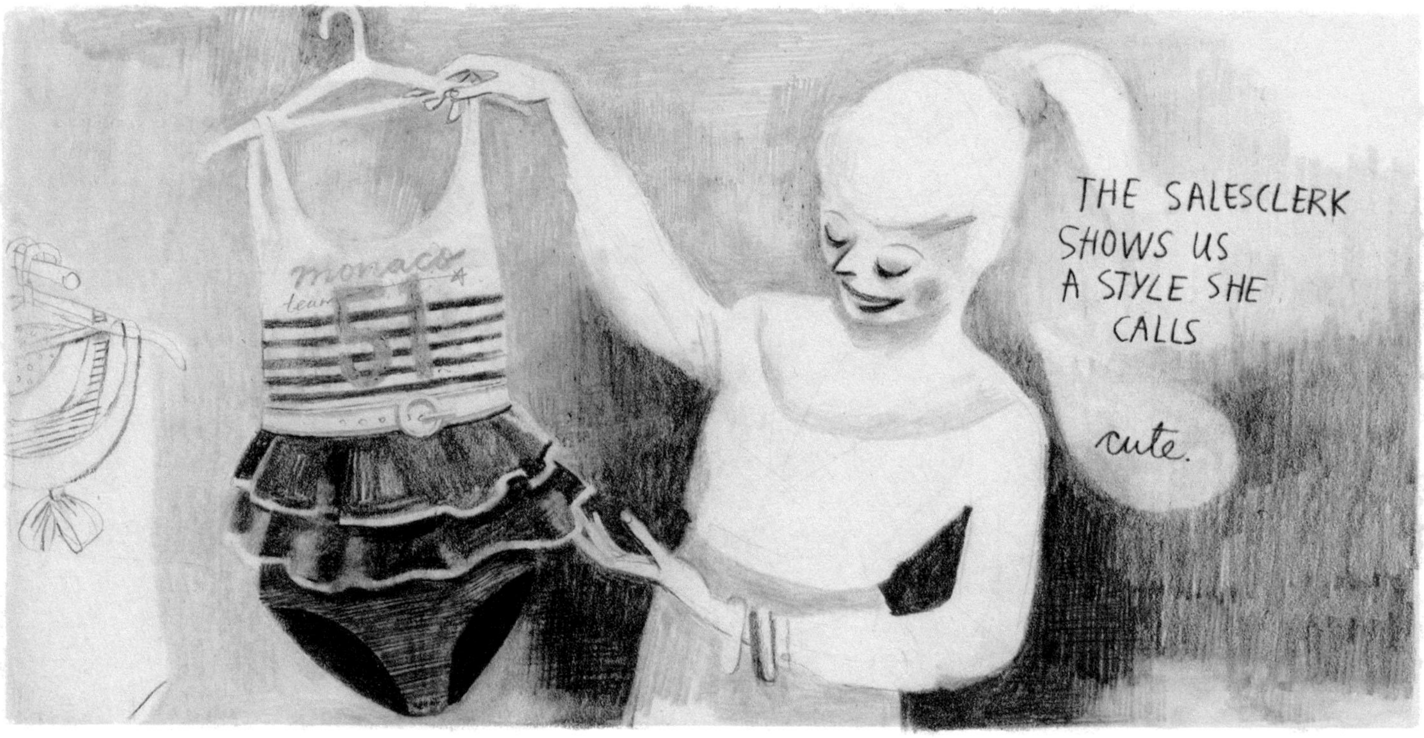
THE SALESCLERK SHOWS US A STYLE SHE CALLS
cute.

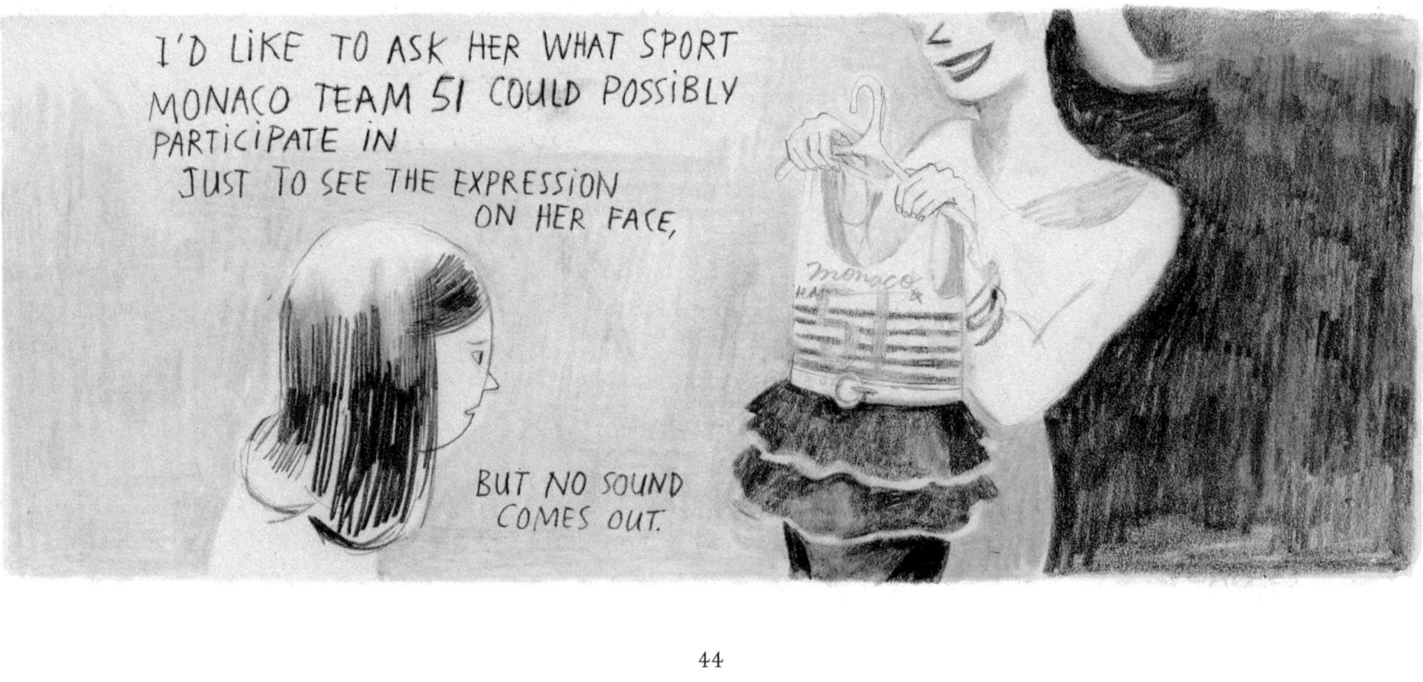
I'D LIKE TO ASK HER WHAT SPORT MONACO TEAM 51 COULD POSSIBLY PARTICIPATE IN
JUST TO SEE THE EXPRESSION ON HER FACE,
BUT NO SOUND COMES OUT.

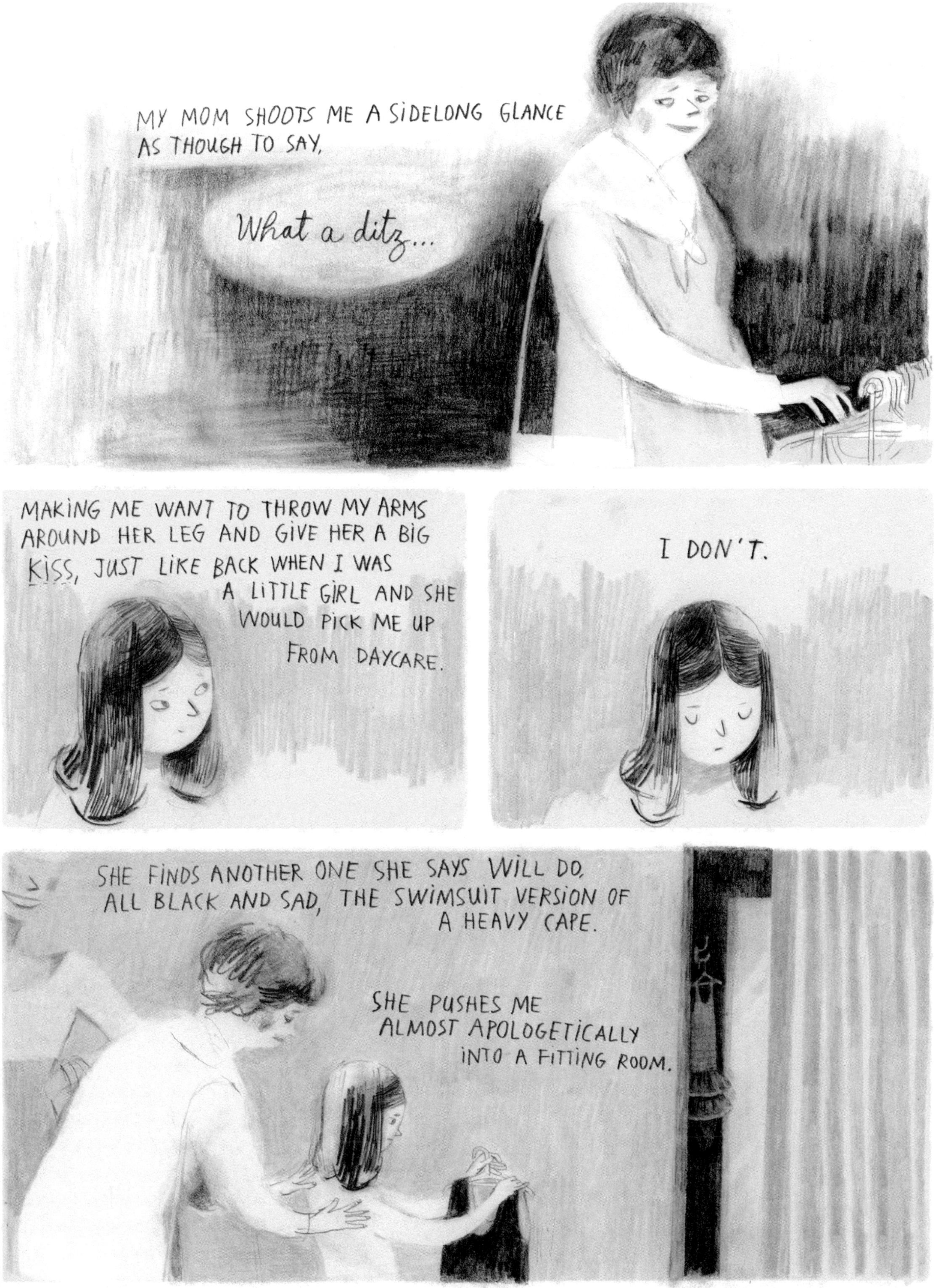
MY MOM SHOOTS ME A SIDELONG GLANCE AS THOUGH TO SAY,
What a ditz...
MAKING ME WANT TO THROW MY ARMS AROUND HER LEG AND GIVE HER A BIG KISS, JUST LIKE BACK WHEN I WAS A LITTLE GIRL AND SHE WOULD PICK ME UP FROM DAYCARE.
I DON'T.
SHE FINDS ANOTHER ONE SHE SAYS WILL DO, ALL BLACK AND SAD, THE SWIMSUIT VERSION OF A HEAVY CAPE.
SHE PUSHES ME ALMOST APOLOGETICALLY INTO A FITTING ROOM.

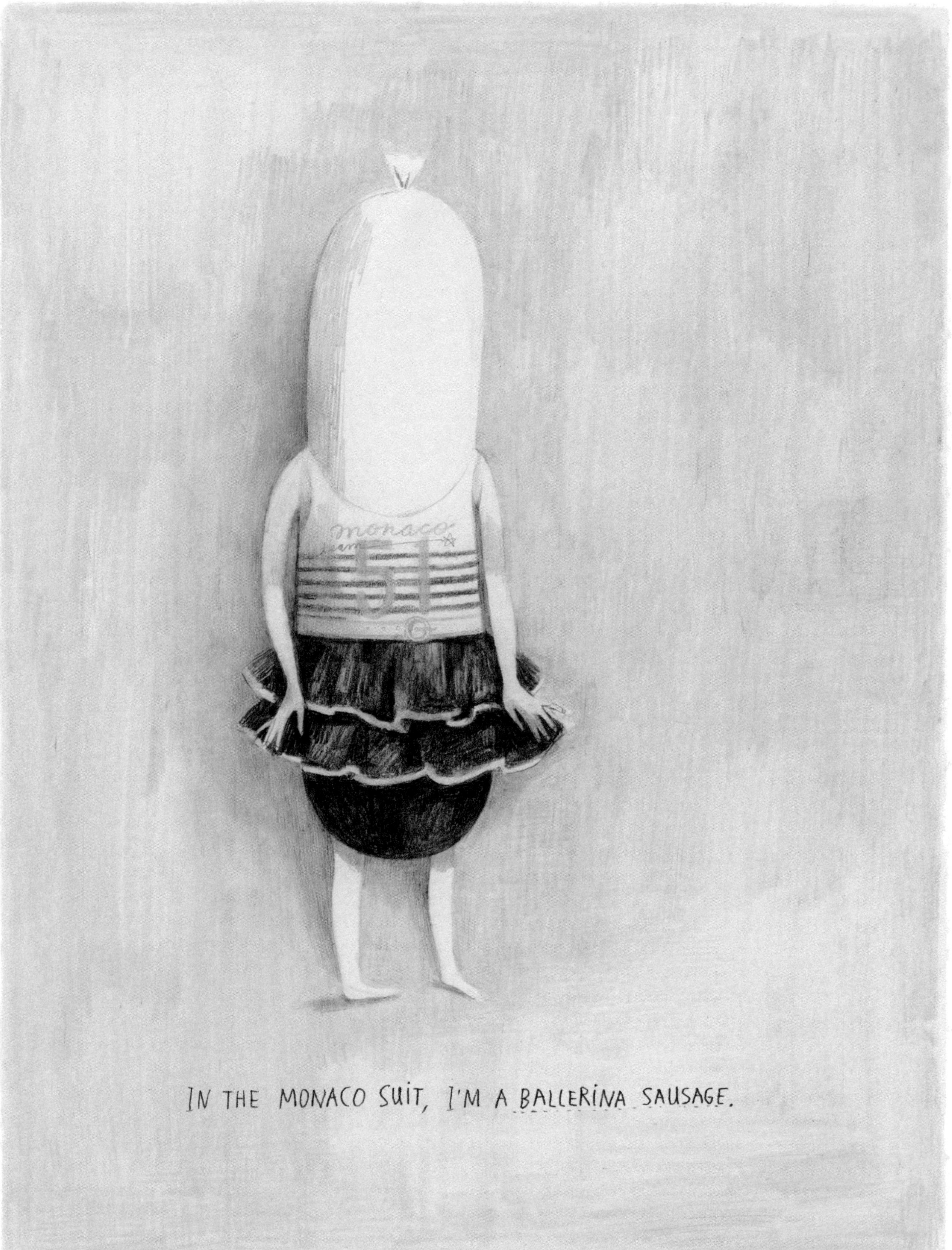
monaco
51
IN THE MONACO SUIT, I'M A BALLERINA SAUSAGE.

IN THE BLACK SUIT, I'M AN UNDERTAKER SAUSAGE.
I'M A SAUSAGE.
JANE EYRE MAY BE AN ORPHAN, HOMELY, BATTERED, ALONE AND
ABANDONED, BUT SHE IS NOT, NEVER HAS BEEN AND NEVER WILL BE
A BIG FAT SAUSAGE.

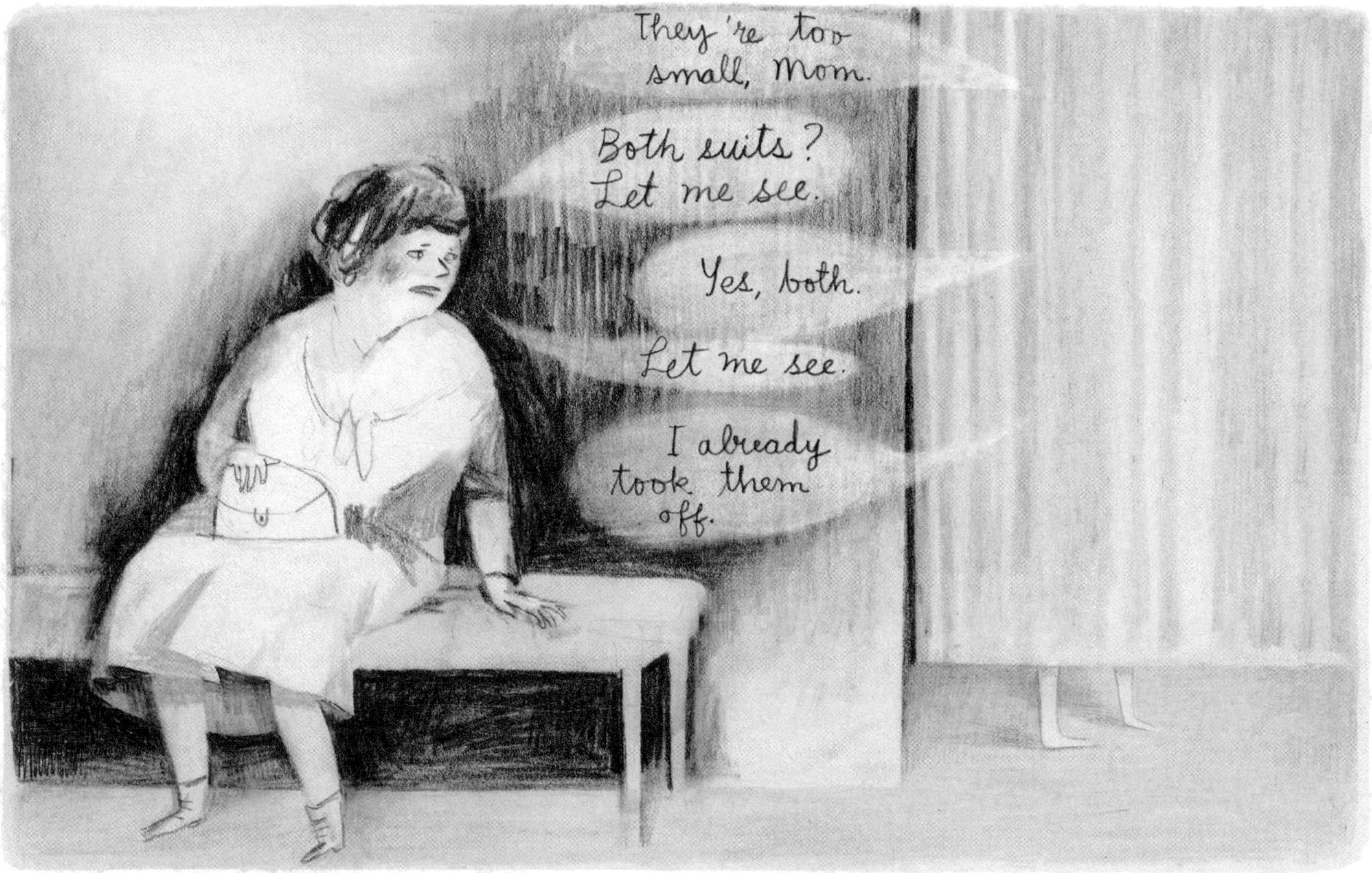
They're too small, Mom.
Both suits? Let me see.
Yes, both.
Let me see.
I already took them off.

THAT'S A LIE. I'M FROZEN IN FRONT OF THE MIRROR.

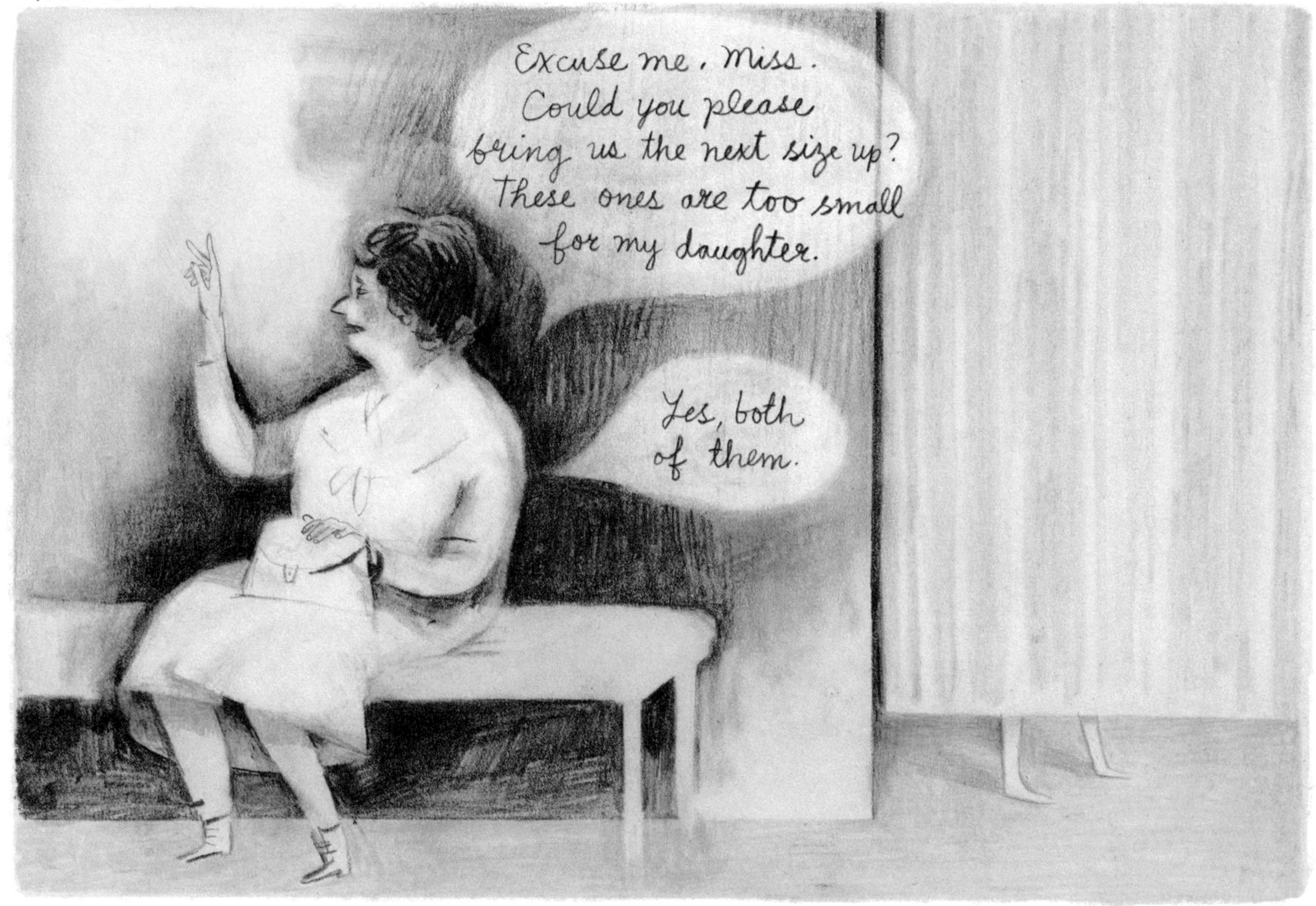
Excuse me, miss. Could you please bring us the next size up? These ones are too small for my daughter.
Yes, both of them.

I CAN'T TELL IF MY MOM'S ASHAMED OF ME

OR IF SHE'S JUST SICK AND TIRED OF THE BAY.

I CAN'T TELL IF MY MOM'S ASHAMED OF ME

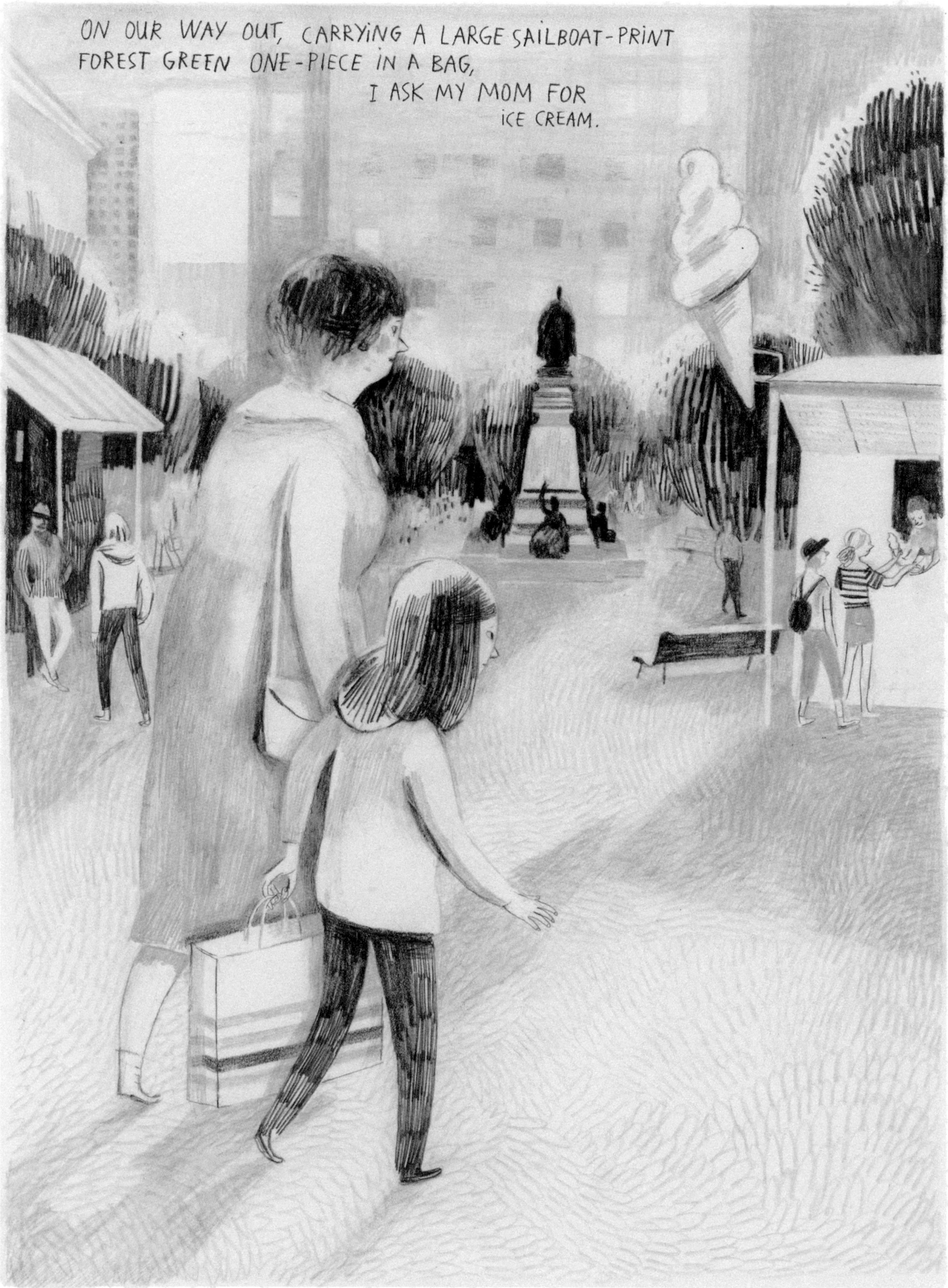
ON OUR WAY OUT, CARRYING A LARGE SAILBOAT-PRINT FOREST GREEN ONE-PIECE IN A BAG,
I ASK MY MOM FOR
ICE CREAM.

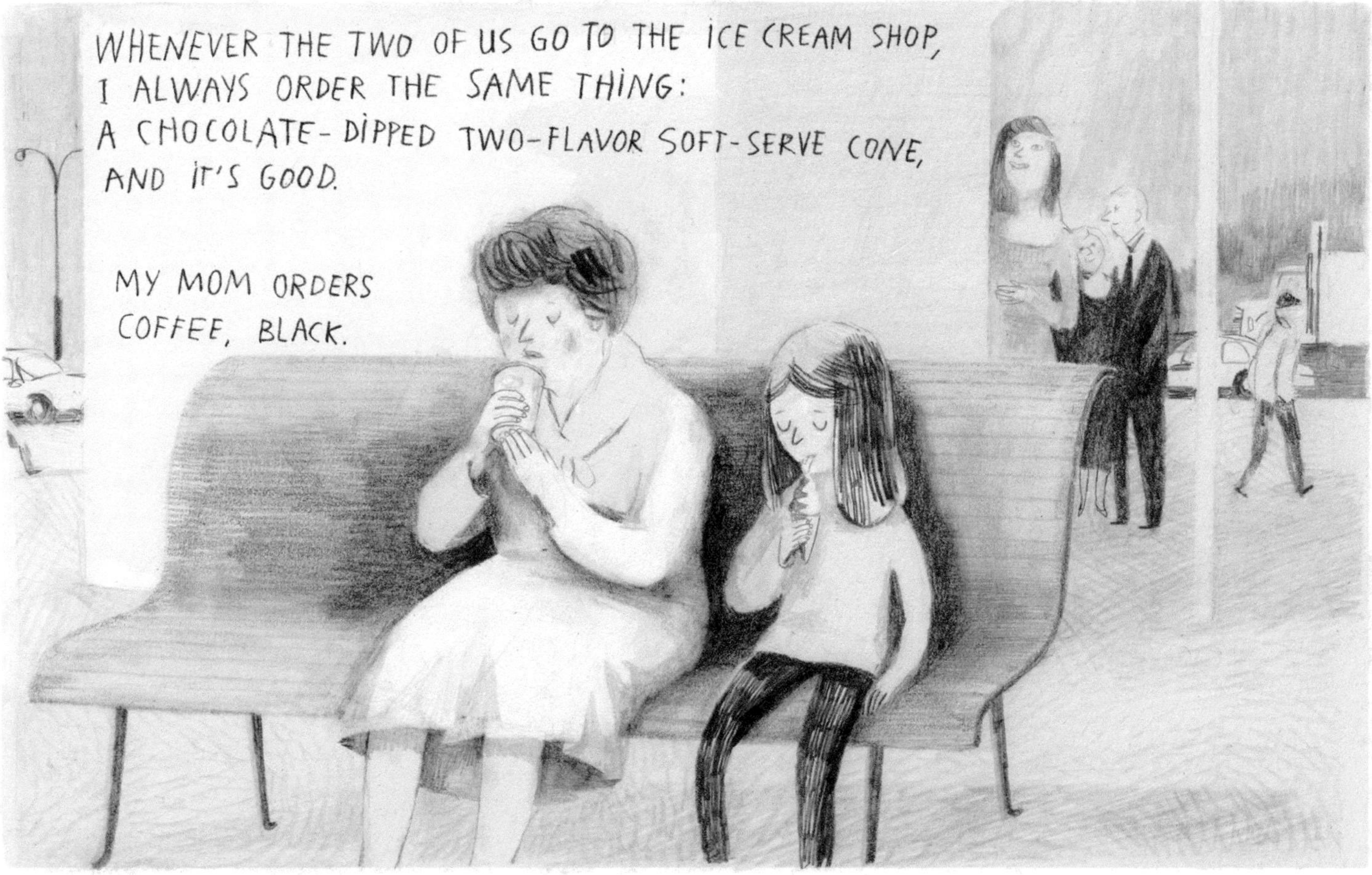
WHENEVER THE TWO OF US GO TO THE ICE CREAM SHOP, I ALWAYS ORDER THE SAME THING: A CHOCOLATE-DIPPED TWO-FLAVOR SOFT-SERVE CONE, AND IT'S GOOD.
MY MOM ORDERS COFFEE, BLACK.

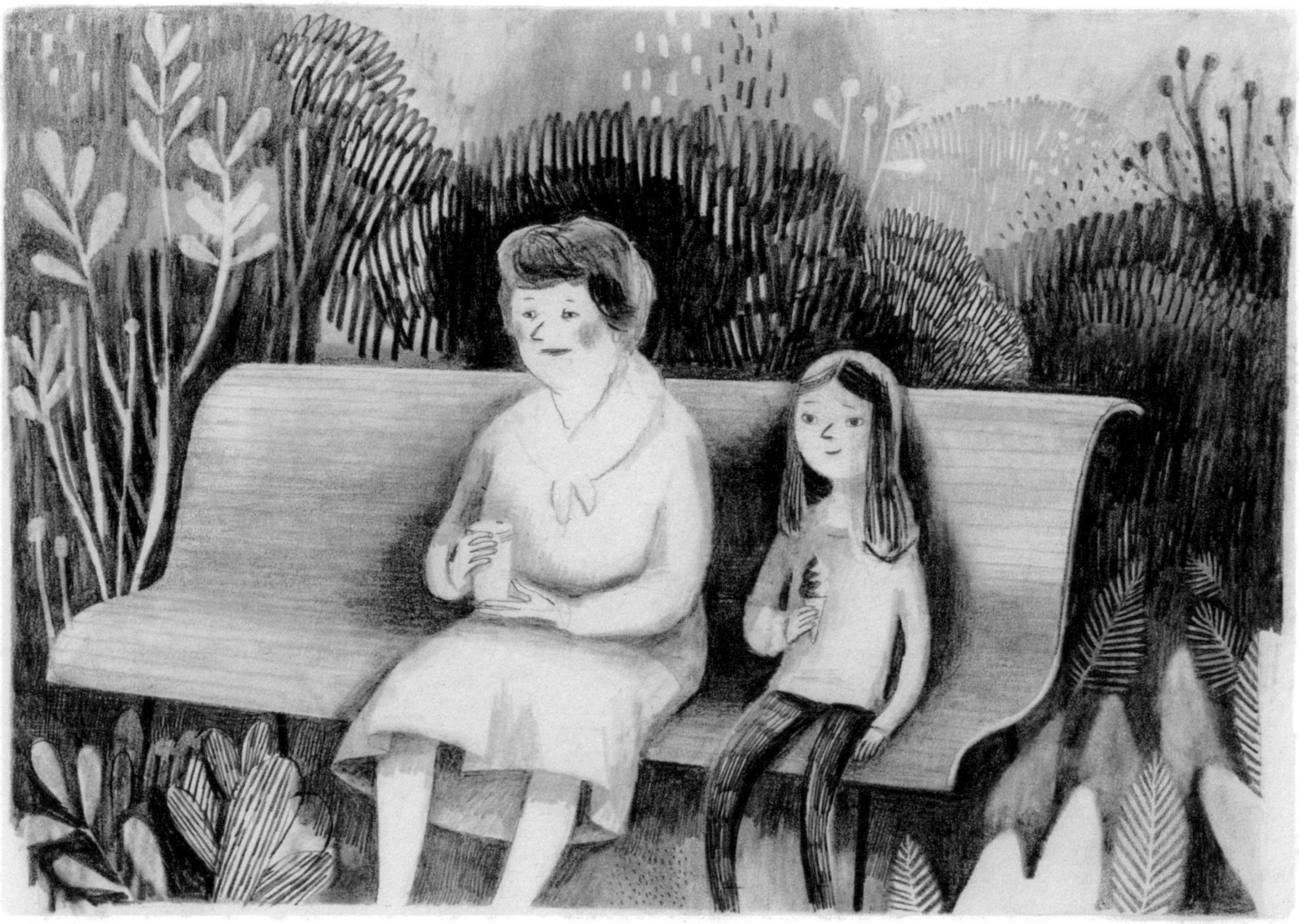

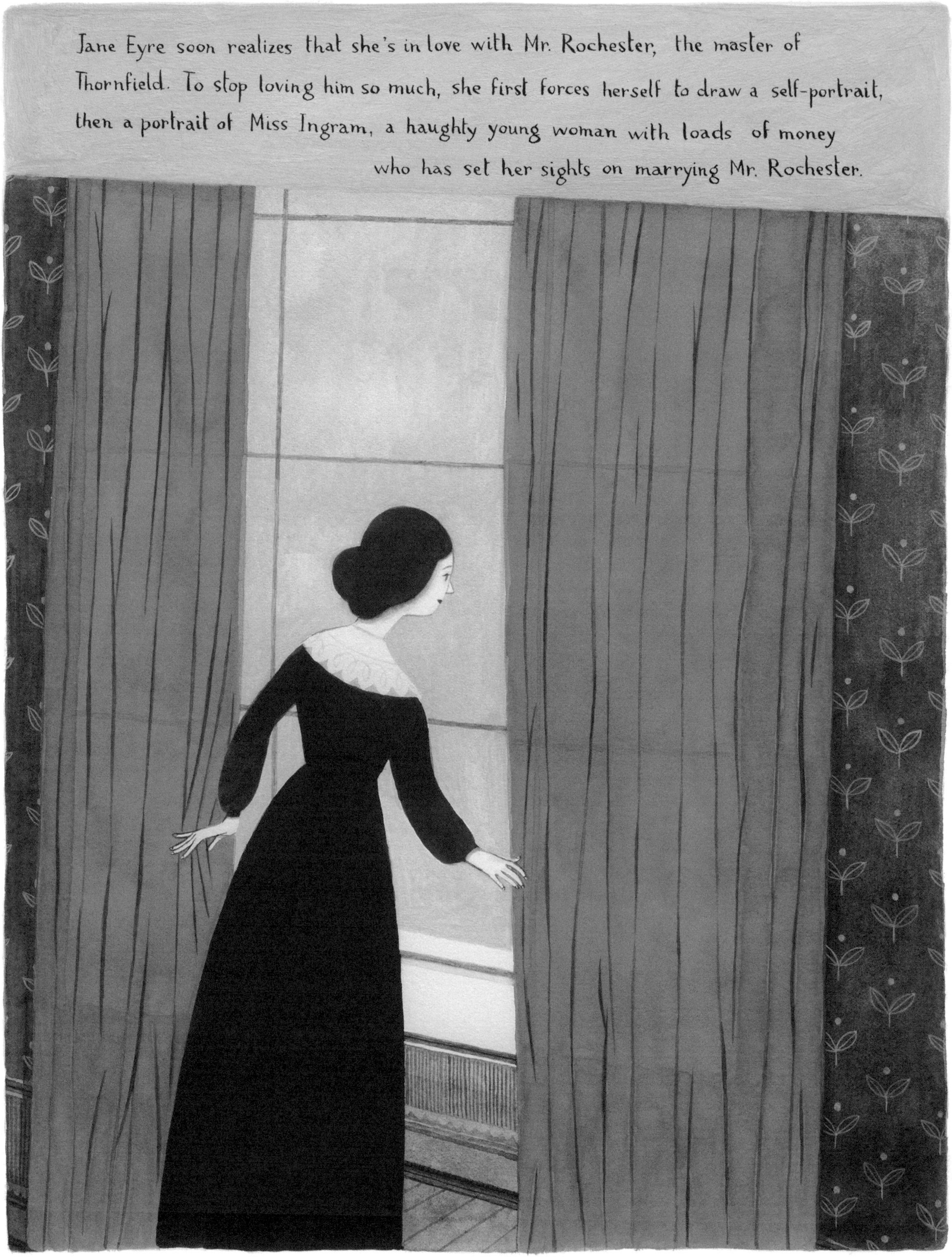
Jane Eyre soon realizes that she's in love with Mr. Rochester, the master of Thornfield. To stop loving him so much, she first forces herself to draw a self-portrait, then a portrait of Miss Ingram, a haughty young woman with loads of money who has set her sights on marrying Mr. Rochester.

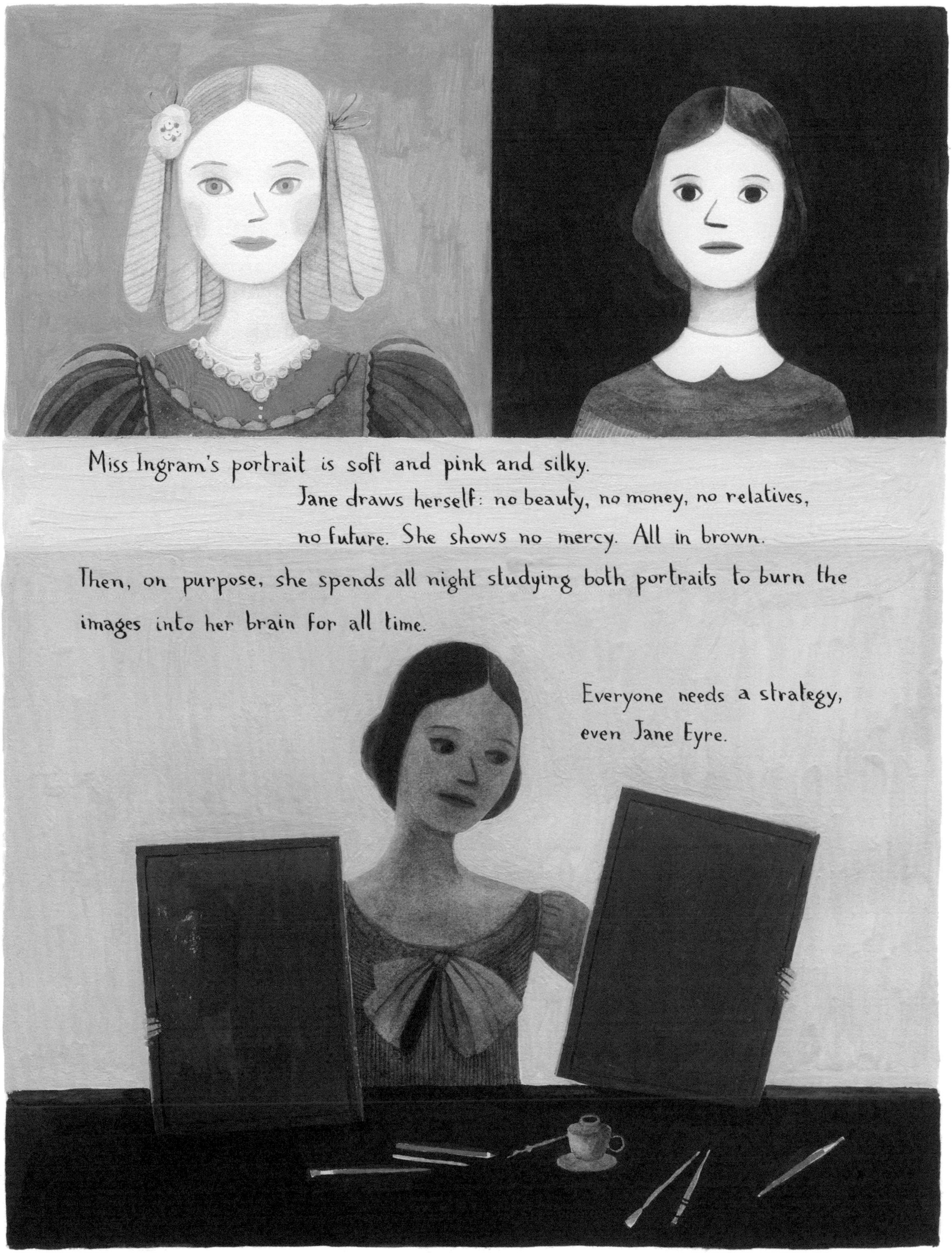
Miss Ingram's portrait is soft and pink and silky.
Jane draws herself: no beauty, no money, no relatives, no future. She shows no mercy. All in brown.
Then, on purpose, she spends all night studying both portraits to burn the images into her brain for all time.
Everyone needs a strategy, even Jane Eyre.

SOMETIMES MY MOM INVITES HER FRIENDS OVER FOR SUPPER. RUTH

LENNY   MARTHE   ANITA   GÉRARD

I LIE ON THE LIVING-ROOM FLOOR DOING MY HOMEWORK.
WITH ONE EAR, I HEAR THEIR VOICES IN THE KITCHEN,
WITH THE OTHER, I HEAR MY MOM'S MUSIC COMING FROM THE STEREO.

THESE DAYS IT'S KATE AND ANNA McGARRIGLE
OVER AND OVER AGAIN.

like a wheel...

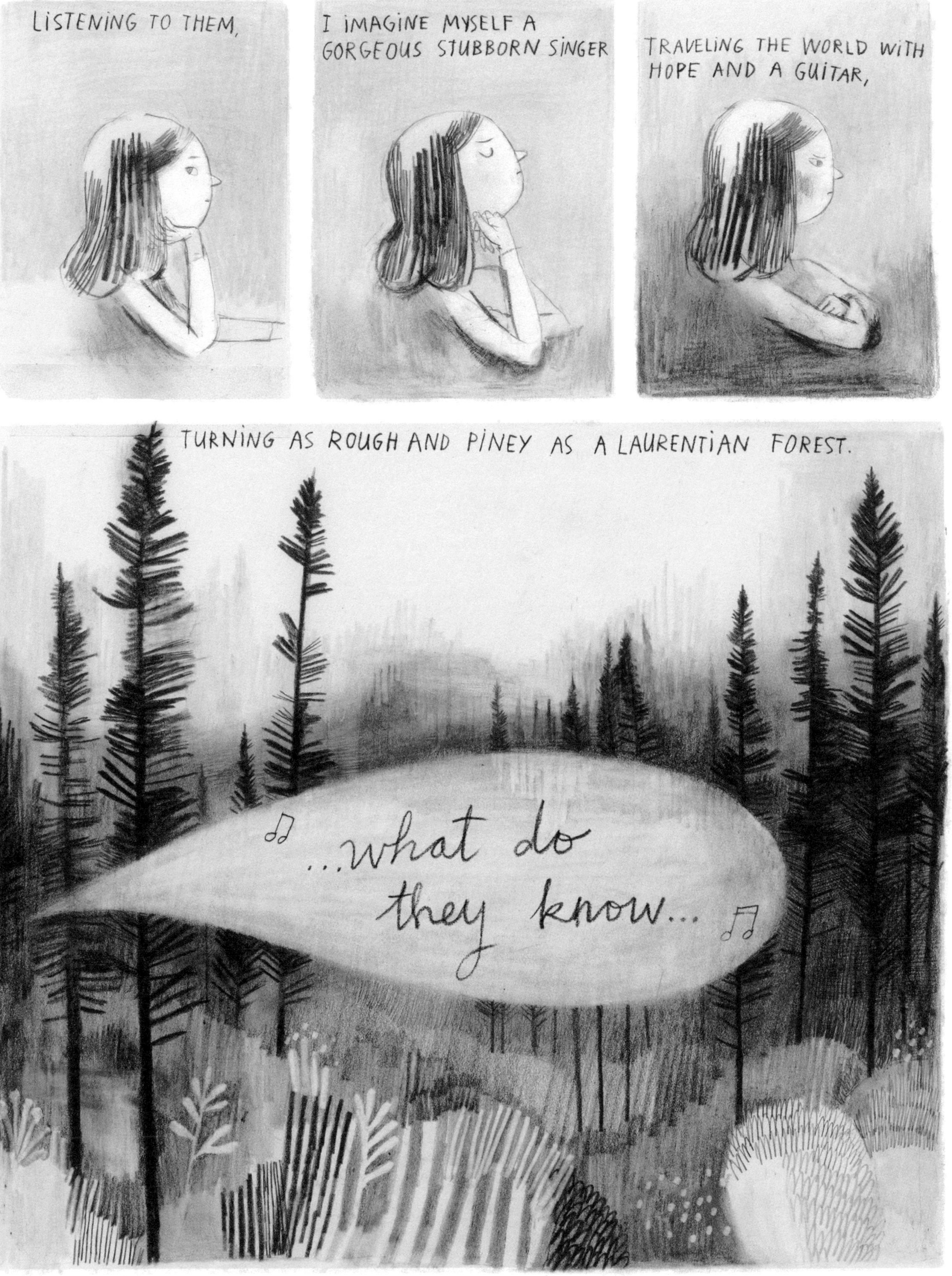
LISTENING TO THEM,
I IMAGINE MYSELF A GORGEOUS STUBBORN SINGER
TRAVELING THE WORLD WITH HOPE AND A GUITAR,
TURNING AS ROUGH AND PINEY AS A LAURENTIAN FOREST.
...what do they know...

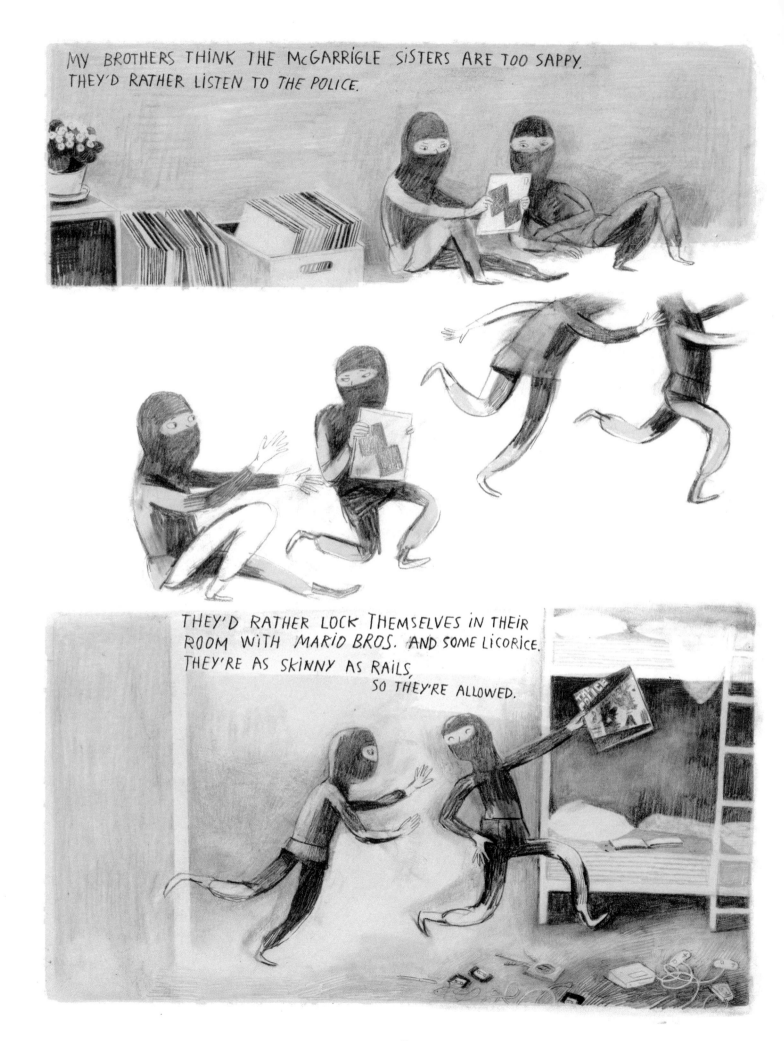

MY BROTHERS THINK THE McGARRIGLE SISTERS ARE TOO SAPPY.
THEY'D RATHER LISTEN TO THE POLICE.

THEY'D RATHER LOCK THEMSELVES IN THEIR
ROOM WITH MARIO BROS. AND SOME LICORICE.
THEY'RE AS SKINNY AS RAILS,
                    SO THEY'RE ALLOWED.

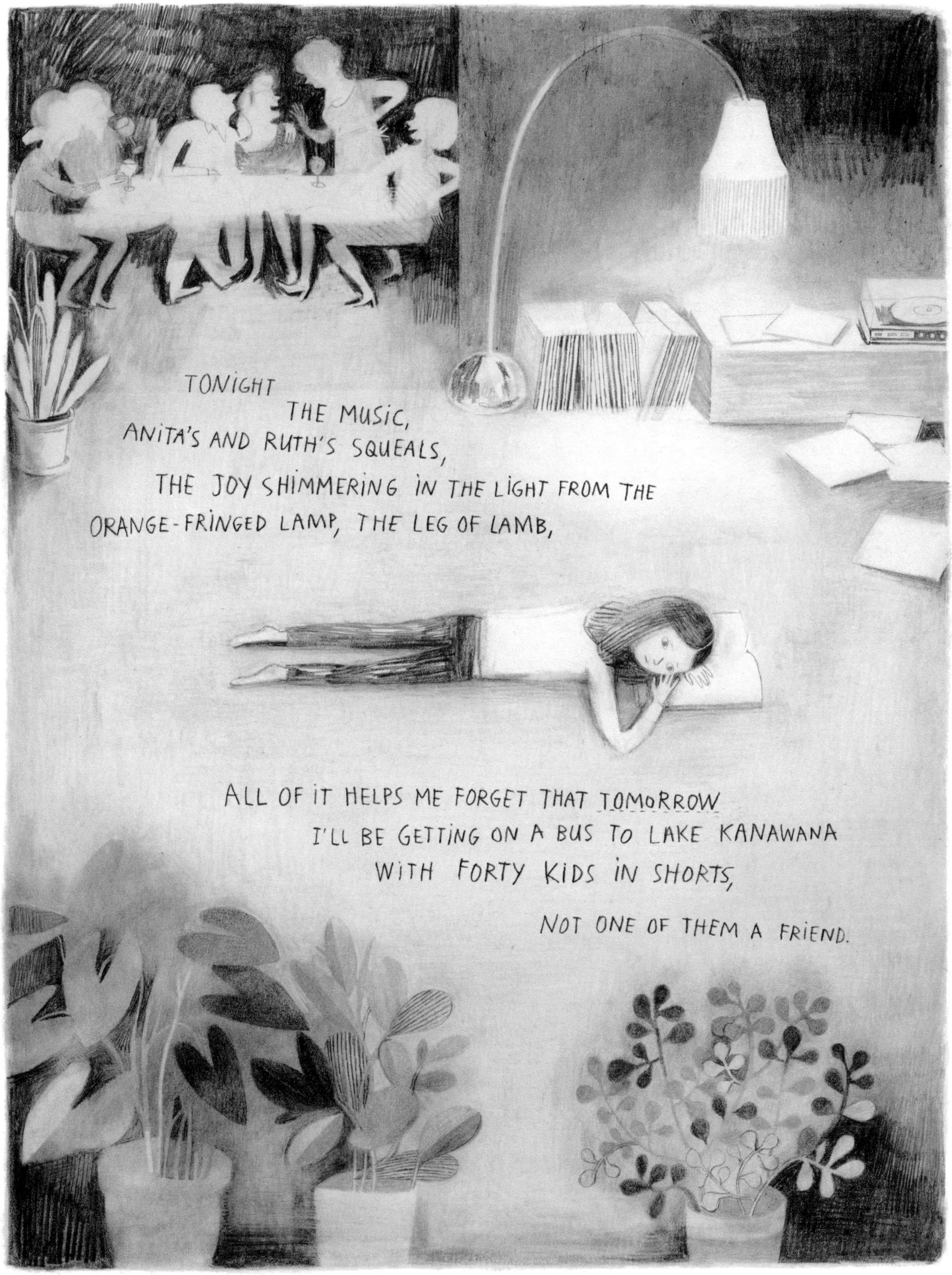
TONIGHT
THE MUSIC,
ANITA'S AND RUTH'S SQUEALS,
THE JOY SHIMMERING IN THE LIGHT FROM THE
ORANGE-FRINGED LAMP, THE LEG OF LAMB,
ALL OF IT HELPS ME FORGET THAT TOMORROW
I'LL BE GETTING ON A BUS TO LAKE KANAWANA
WITH FORTY KIDS IN SHORTS,
NOT ONE OF THEM A FRIEND.

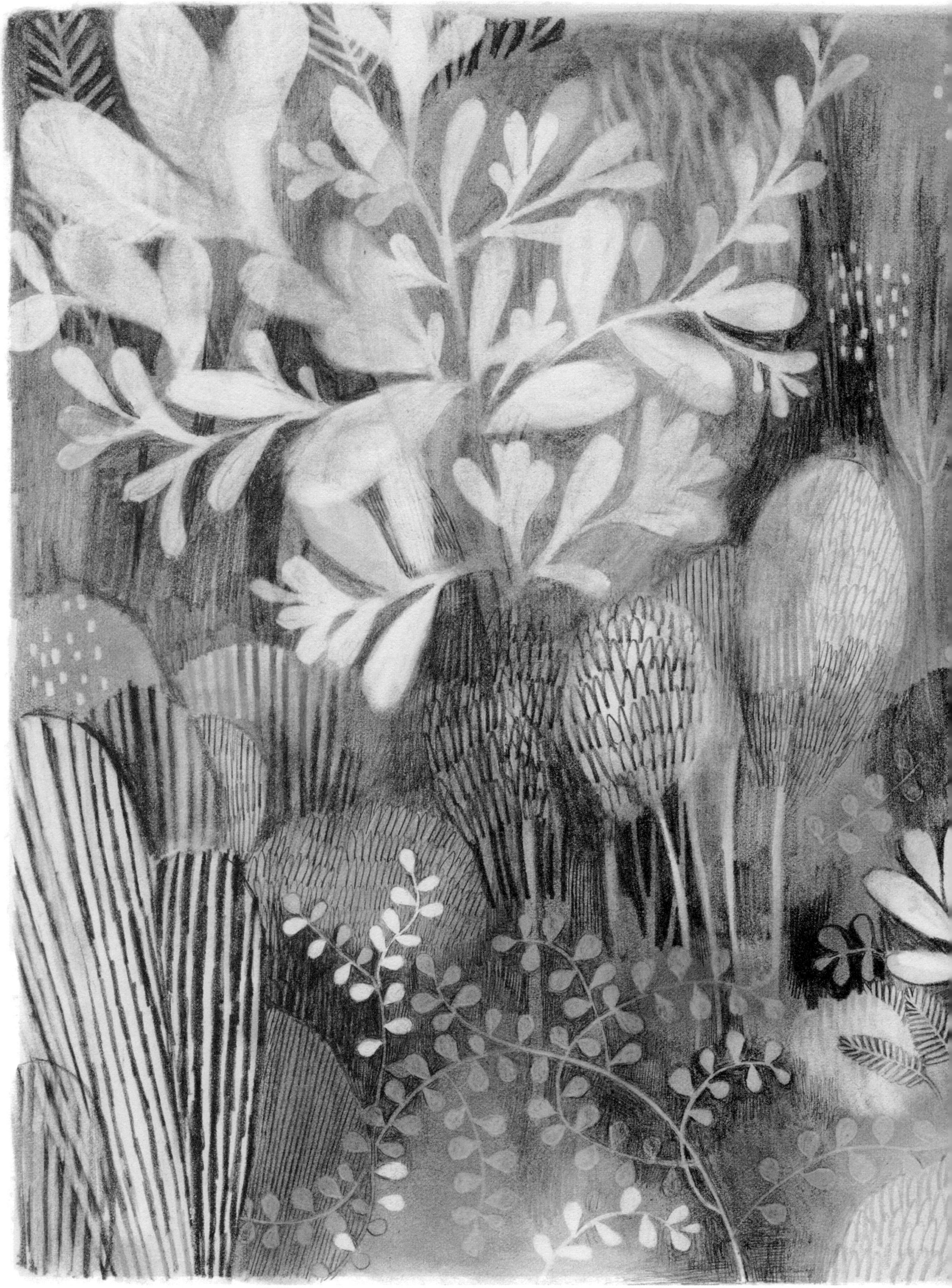

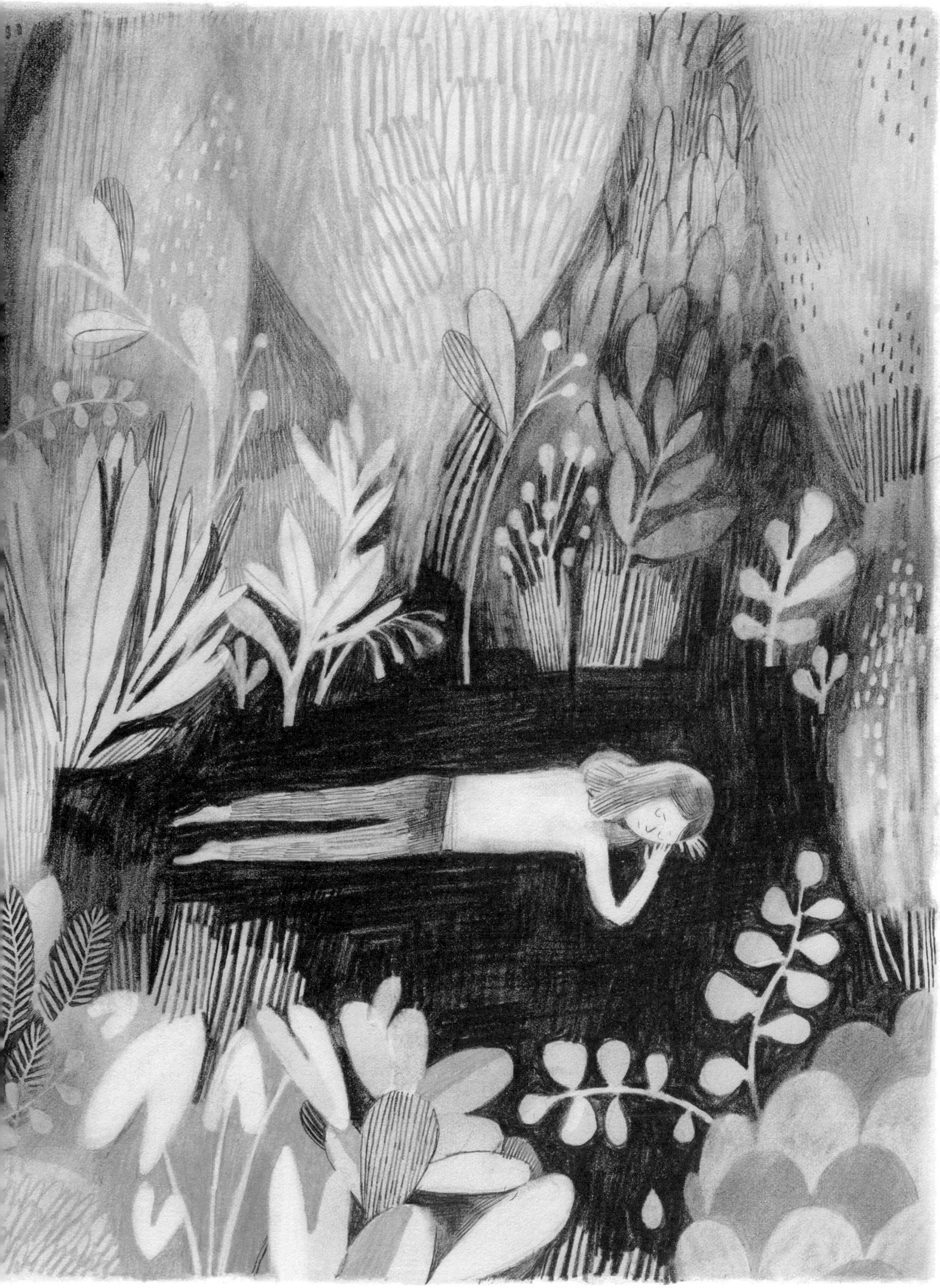

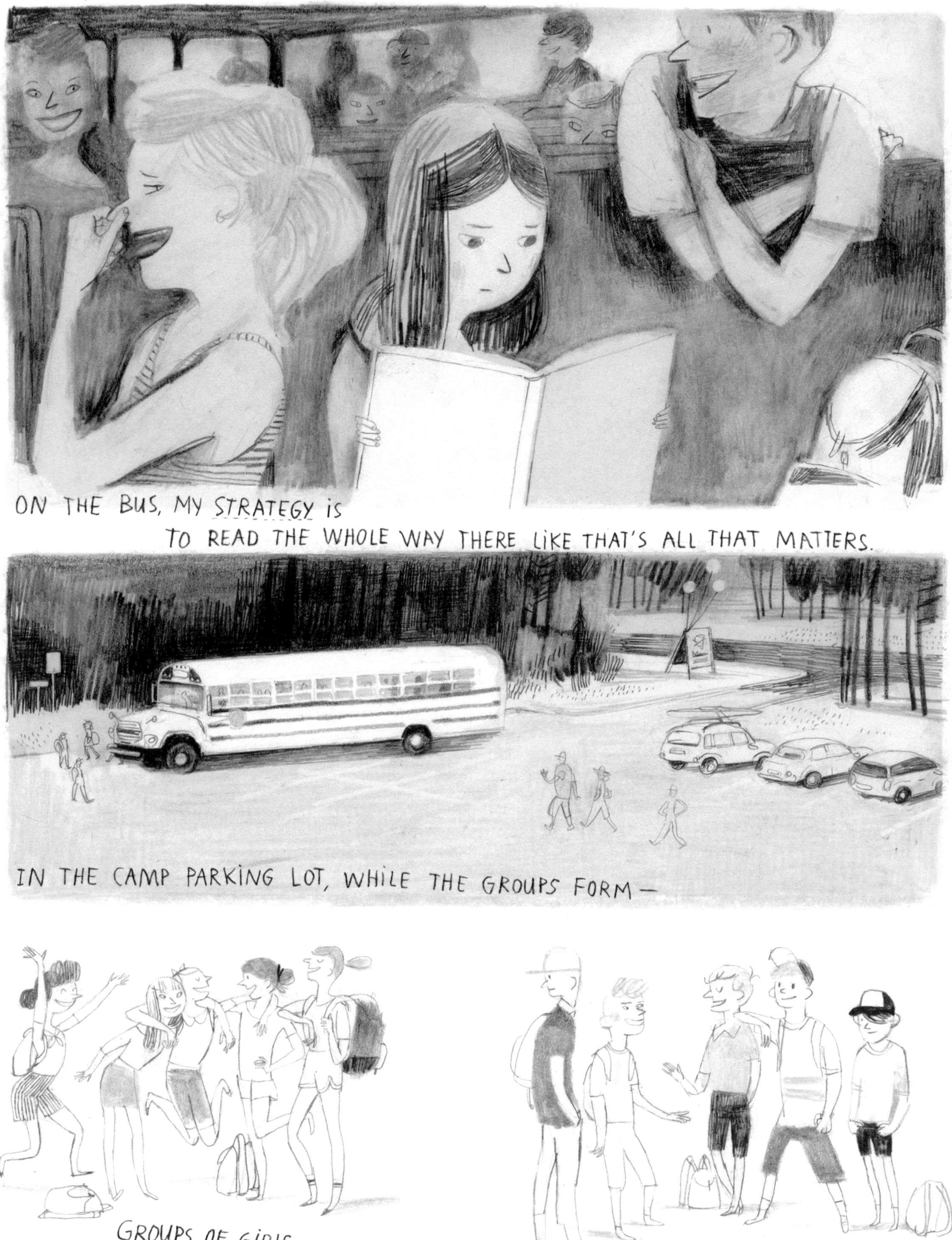
ON THE BUS, MY STRATEGY IS
TO READ THE WHOLE WAY THERE LIKE THAT'S ALL THAT MATTERS.
IN THE CAMP PARKING LOT, WHILE THE GROUPS FORM—
GROUPS OF GIRLS
GUYS

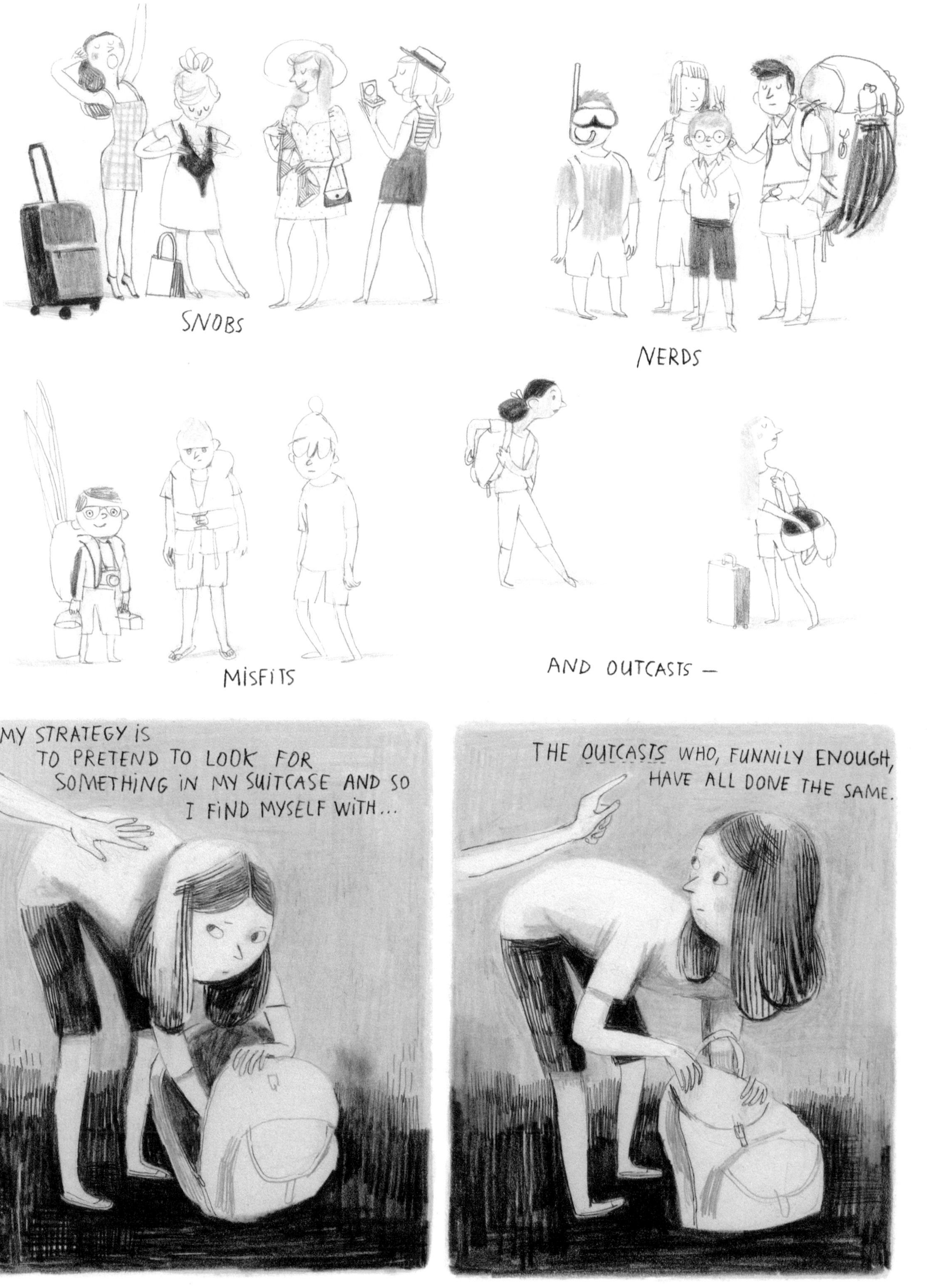
SNOBS
NERDS
MISFITS
AND OUTCASTS —
MY STRATEGY IS TO PRETEND TO LOOK FOR SOMETHING IN MY SUITCASE AND SO I FIND MYSELF WITH...
THE OUTCASTS WHO, FUNNILY ENOUGH, HAVE ALL DONE THE SAME.

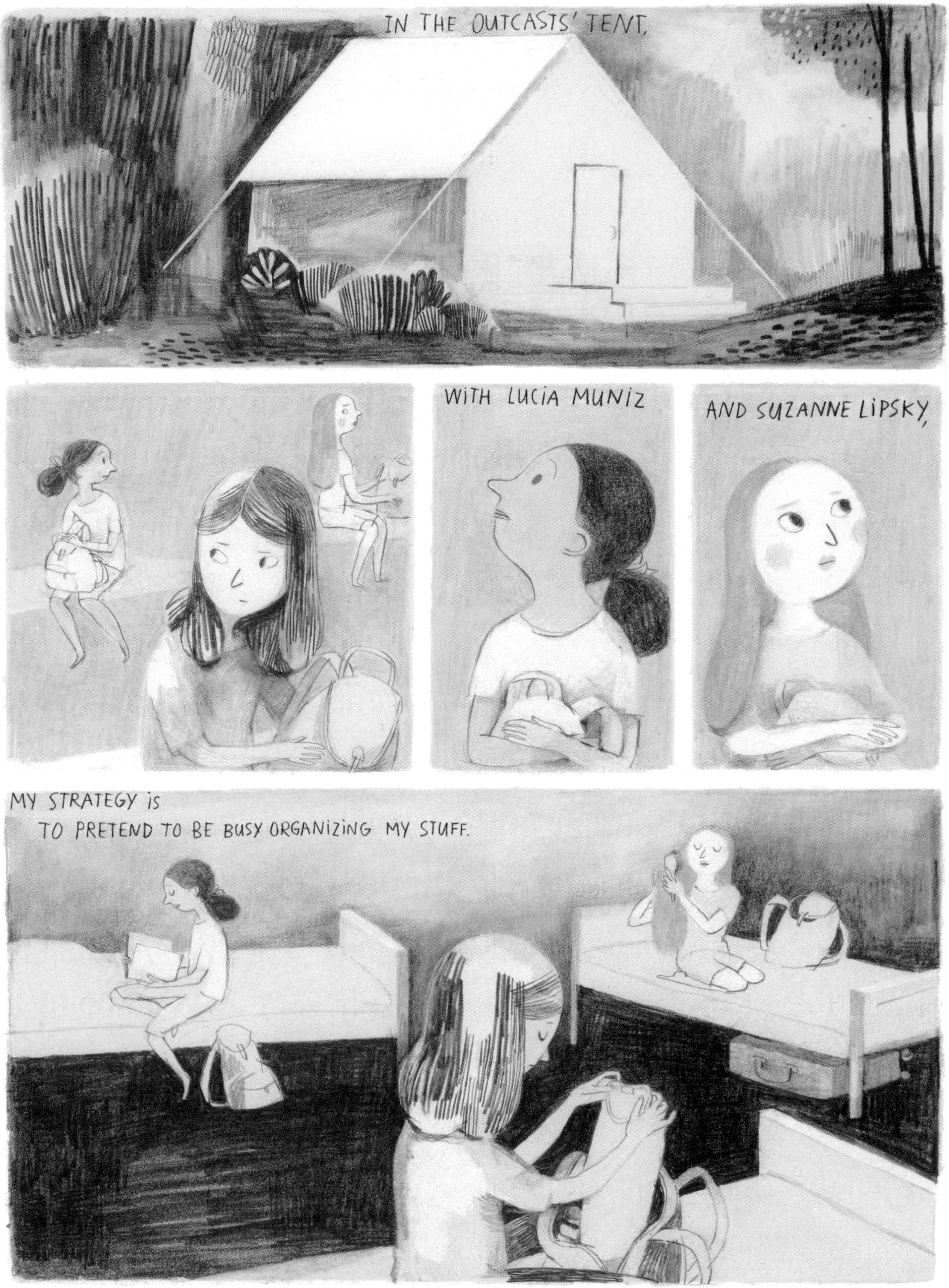
IN THE OUTCASTS' TENT,
WITH LUCIA MUNIZ
AND SUZANNE LIPSKY,
MY STRATEGY IS
TO PRETEND TO BE BUSY ORGANIZING MY STUFF.

AT THE CAMPFIRE, WHEN I ARRIVE AND THE BOYS CHANT,

BOUM! BA-DA-BOUM!
BA-DA-BOUM!

MY STRATEGY IS
TO SMILE SOFTLY

AS I WONDER WHETHER
LAMEBRAIN OR NUMBSKULL
SUITS THEM BEST.

THEN, AS SOON AS THEIR
BACKS ARE TURNED,

RUN,
RUN,
RUN.

THE OUTCASTS' TENT IS THE
FARTHEST FROM THE
MAIN CABIN.
FROM THERE TO HERE
IS LIKE CHANGING
COUNTRIES.

THANK
GOODNESS.

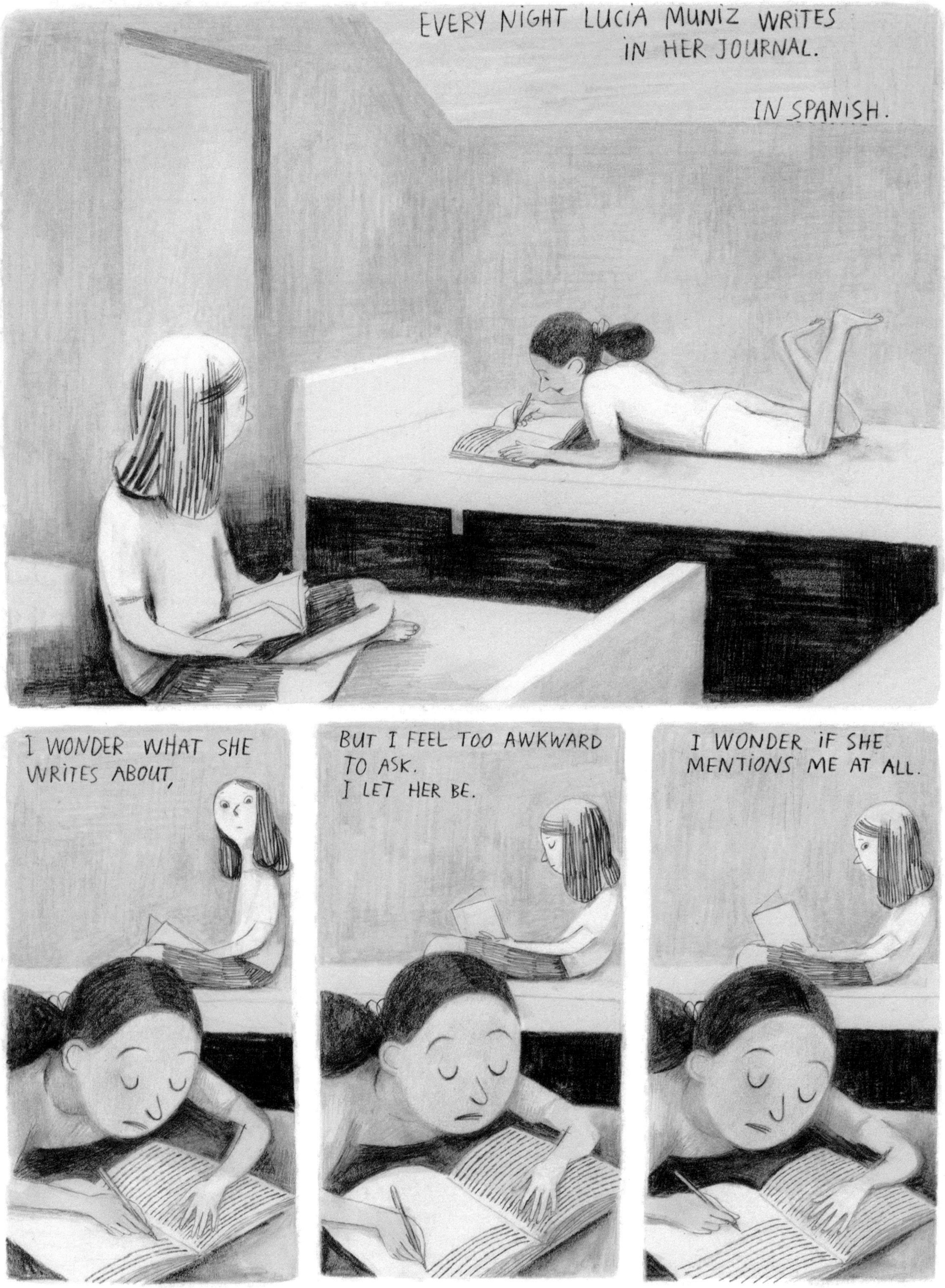
EVERY NIGHT LUCIA MUNIZ WRITES IN HER JOURNAL.
IN SPANISH.
I WONDER WHAT SHE WRITES ABOUT,
BUT I FEEL TOO AWKWARD TO ASK.
I LET HER BE.
I WONDER IF SHE MENTIONS ME AT ALL.

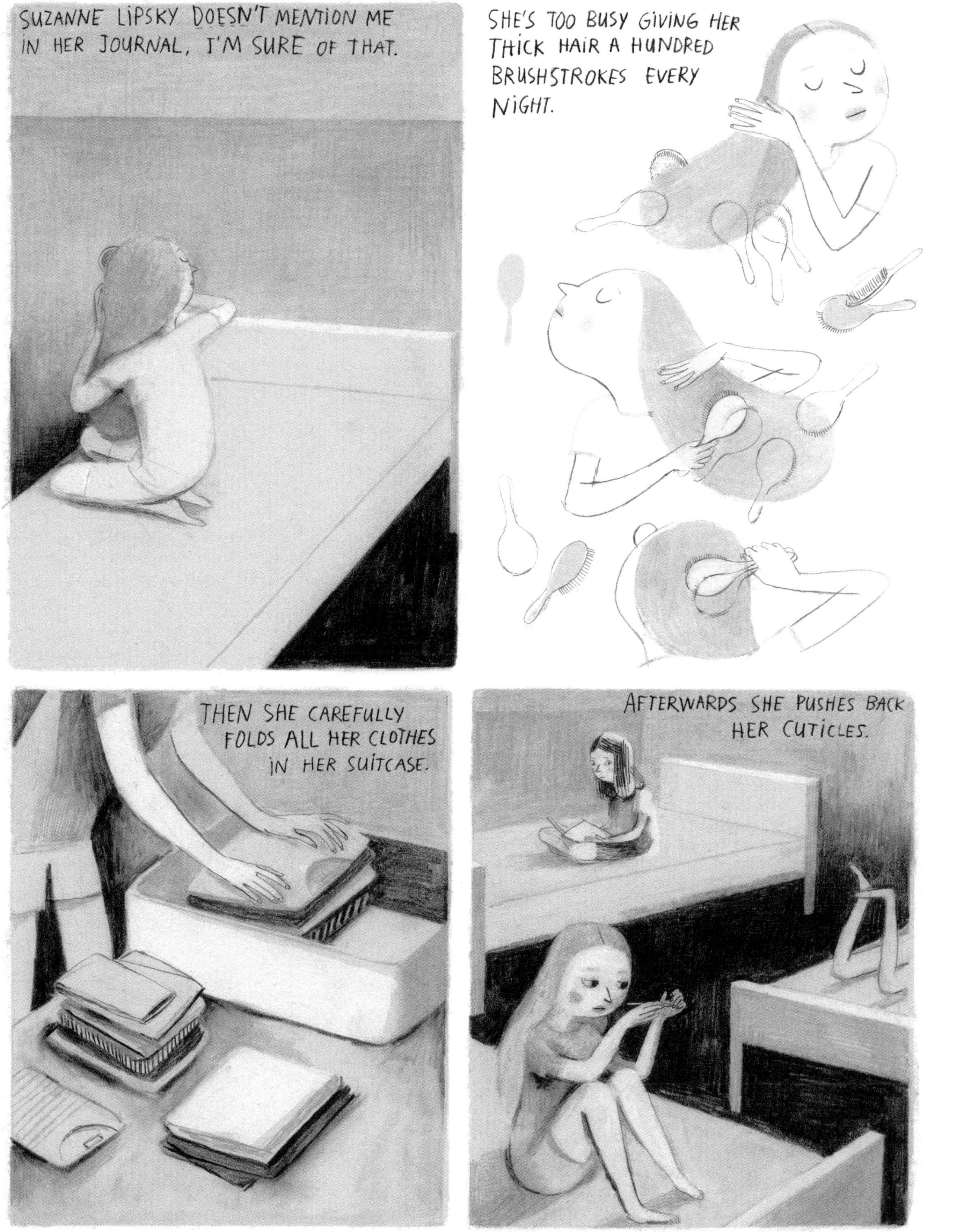
SUZANNE LIPSKY DOESN'T MENTION ME IN HER JOURNAL, I'M SURE OF THAT.
SHE'S TOO BUSY GIVING HER THICK HAIR A HUNDRED BRUSHSTROKES EVERY NIGHT.
THEN SHE CAREFULLY FOLDS ALL HER CLOTHES IN HER SUITCASE.
AFTERWARDS SHE PUSHES BACK HER CUTICLES.

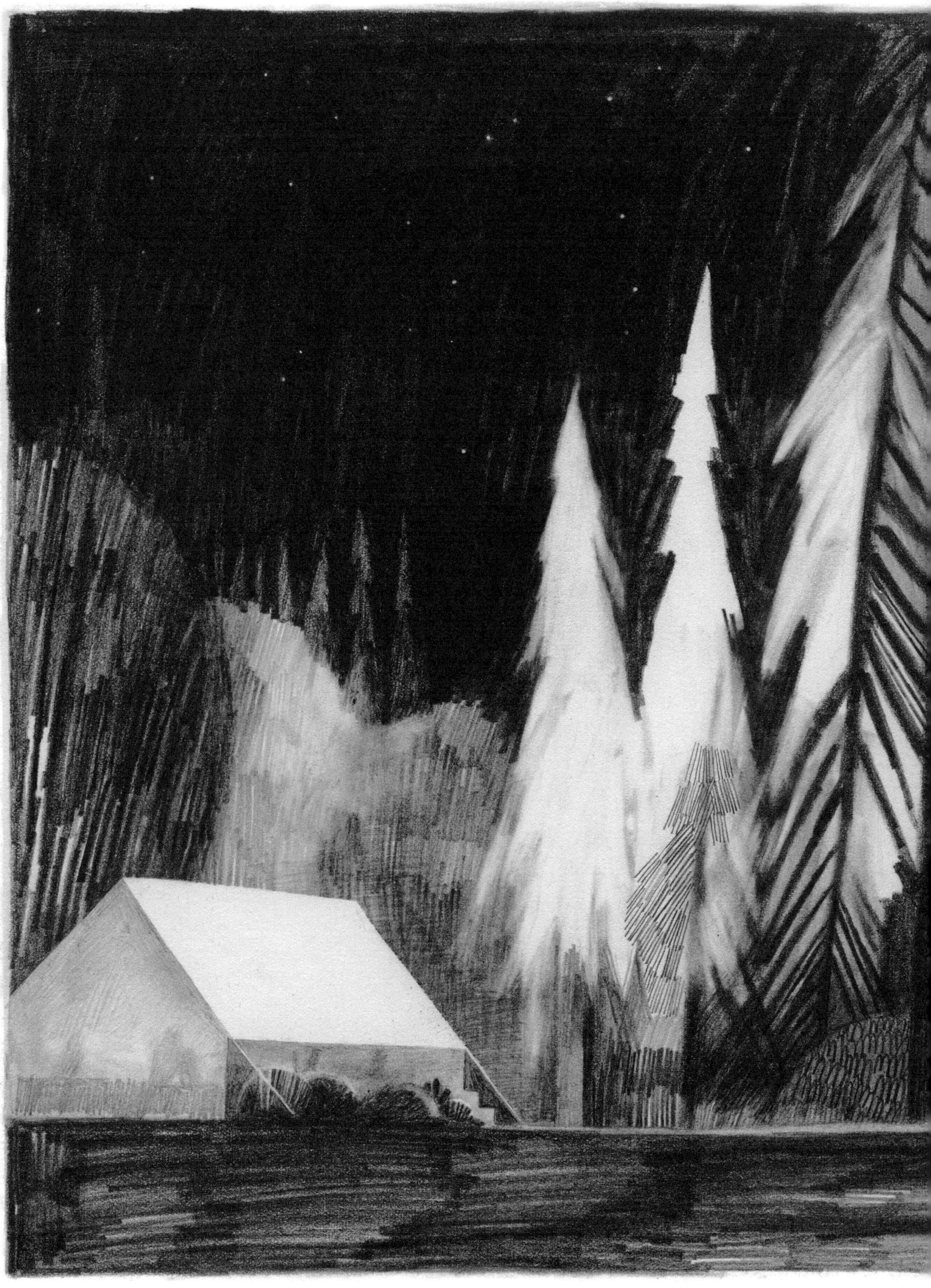

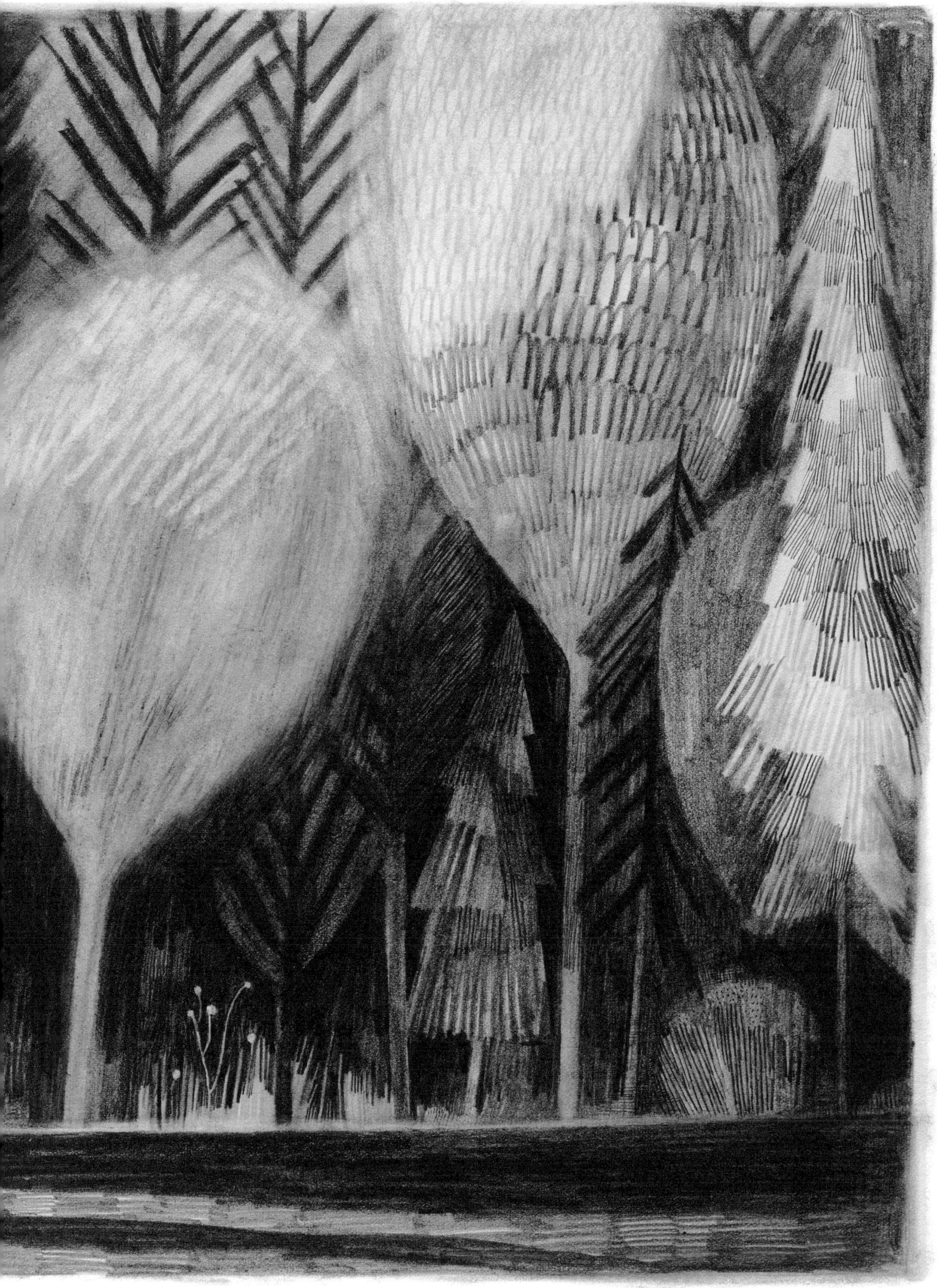

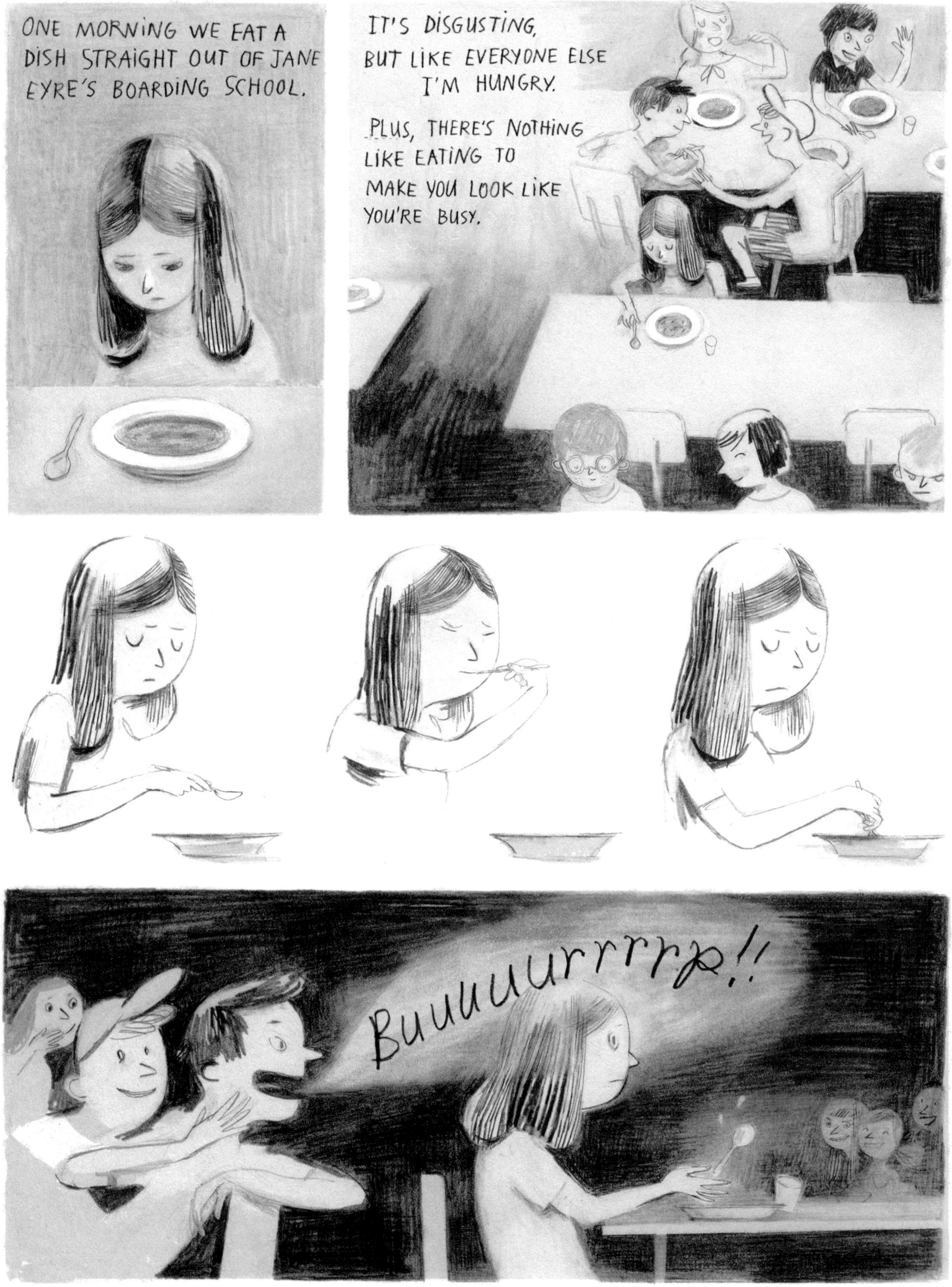
ONE MORNING WE EAT A DISH STRAIGHT OUT OF JANE EYRE'S BOARDING SCHOOL.
IT'S DISGUSTING, BUT LIKE EVERYONE ELSE I'M HUNGRY.
PLUS, THERE'S NOTHING LIKE EATING TO MAKE YOU LOOK LIKE YOU'RE BUSY.
Buuuuurrrrp!!

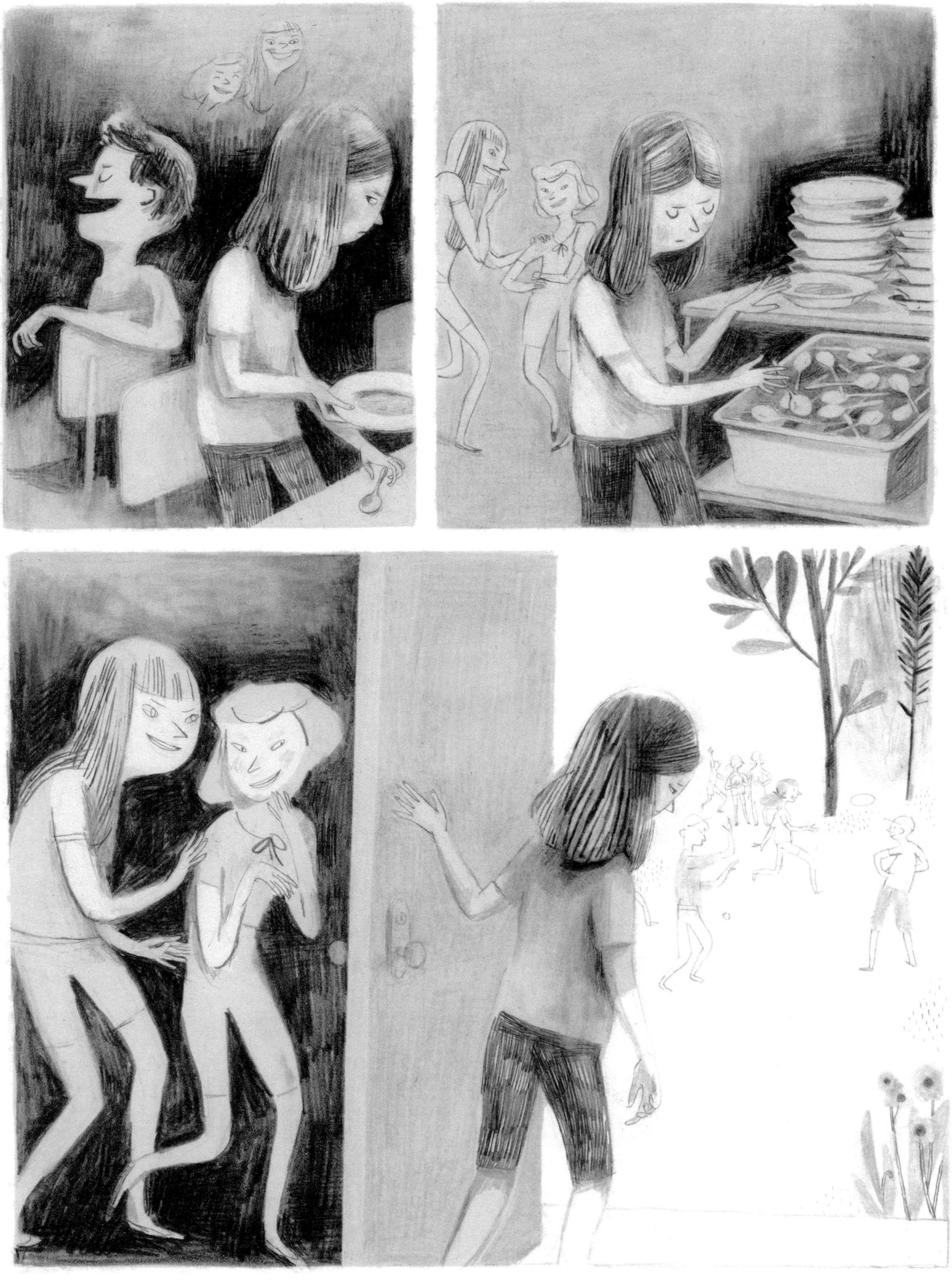

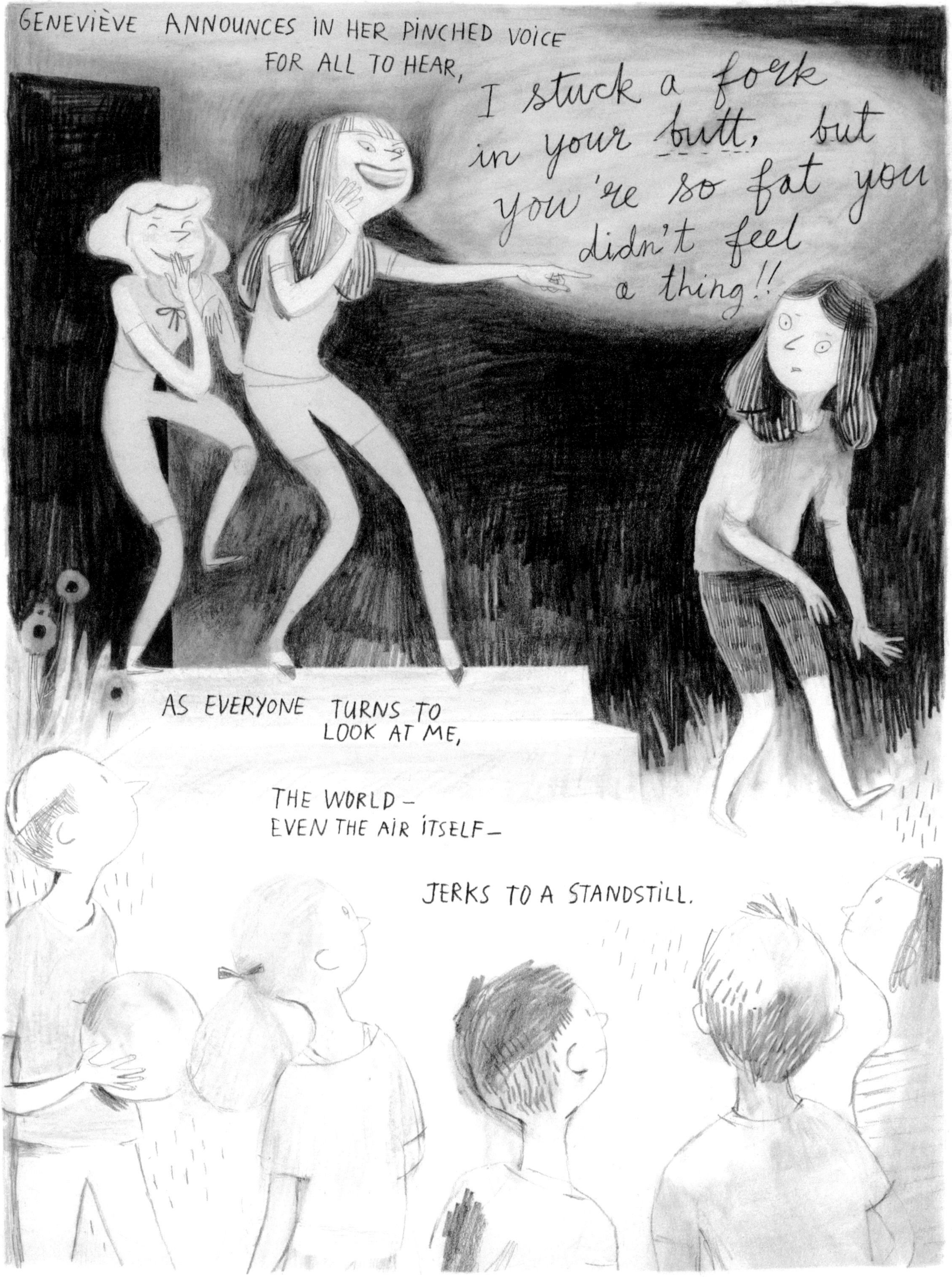
GENEVIÈVE ANNOUNCES IN HER PINCHED VOICE FOR ALL TO HEAR,
I stuck a fork in your butt, but you're so fat you didn't feel a thing!!
AS EVERYONE TURNS TO LOOK AT ME,
THE WORLD – EVEN THE AIR ITSELF –
JERKS TO A STANDSTILL.

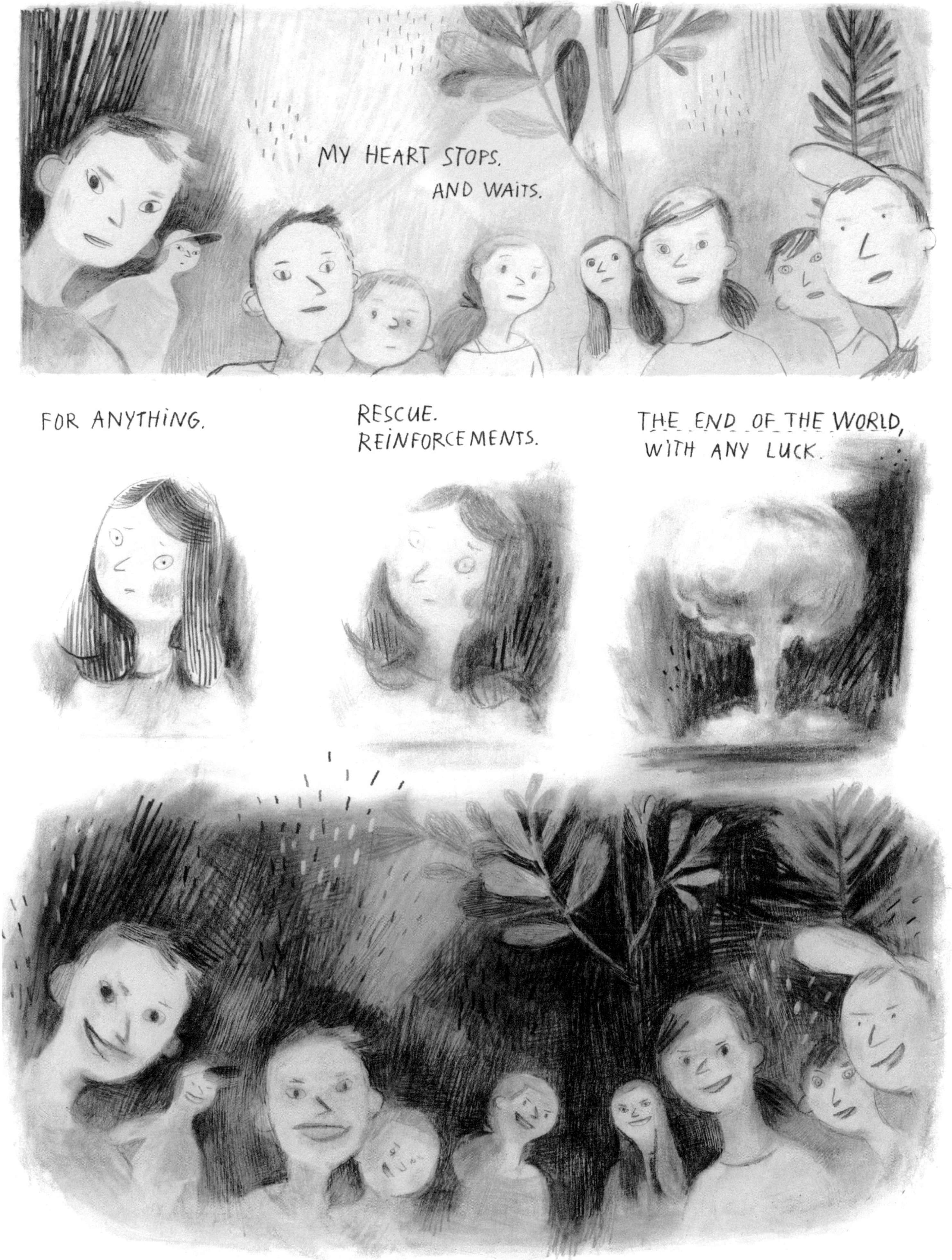
MY HEART STOPS.
AND WAITS.
FOR ANYTHING.
RESCUE.
REINFORCEMENTS.
THE END OF THE WORLD,
WITH ANY LUCK.

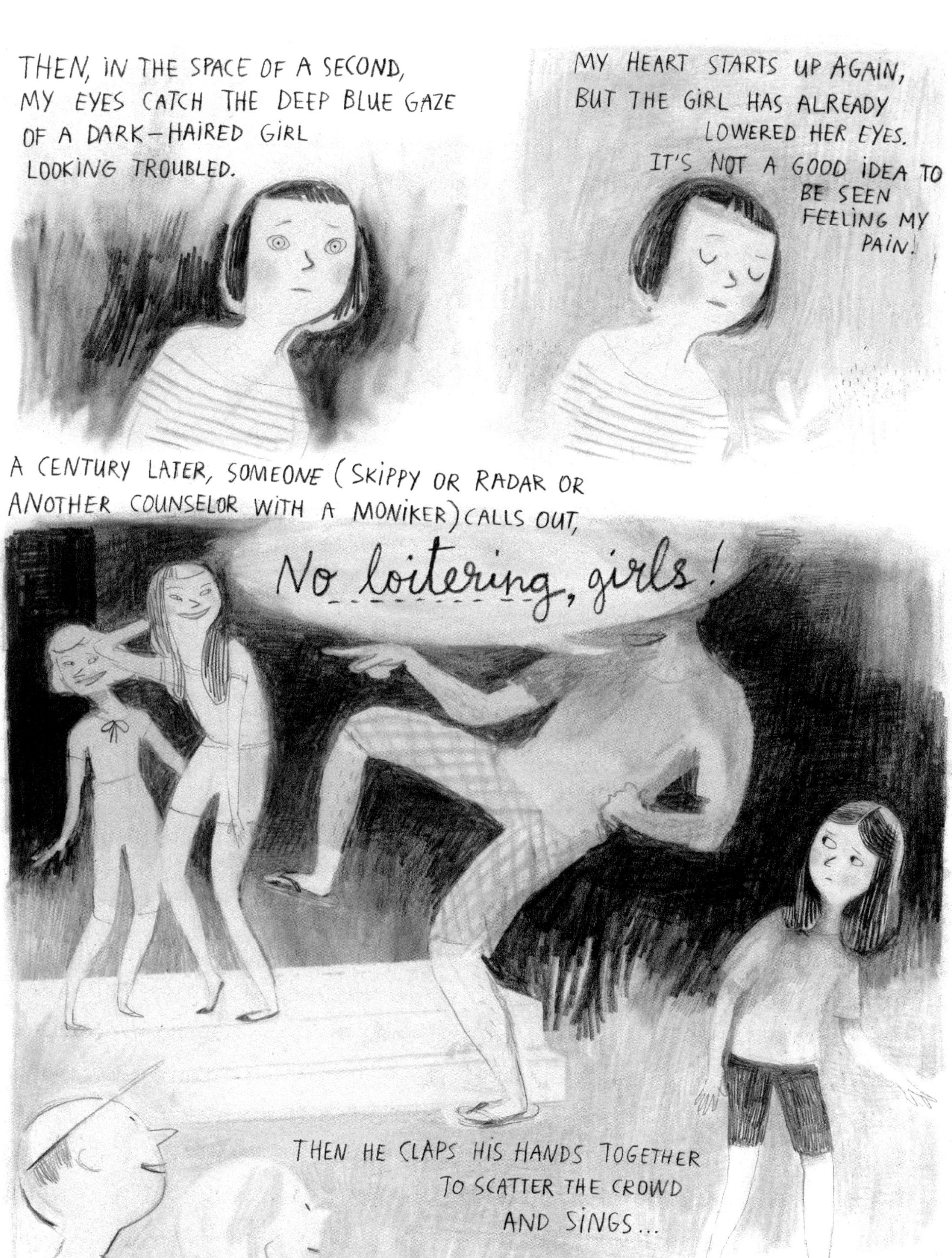
THEN, IN THE SPACE OF A SECOND, MY EYES CATCH THE DEEP BLUE GAZE OF A DARK-HAIRED GIRL LOOKING TROUBLED.
MY HEART STARTS UP AGAIN, BUT THE GIRL HAS ALREADY LOWERED HER EYES.
IT'S NOT A GOOD IDEA TO BE SEEN FEELING MY PAIN!
A CENTURY LATER, SOMEONE (SKIPPY OR RADAR OR ANOTHER COUNSELOR WITH A MONIKER) CALLS OUT,
No loitering, girls!
THEN HE CLAPS HIS HANDS TOGETHER TO SCATTER THE CROWD AND SINGS...

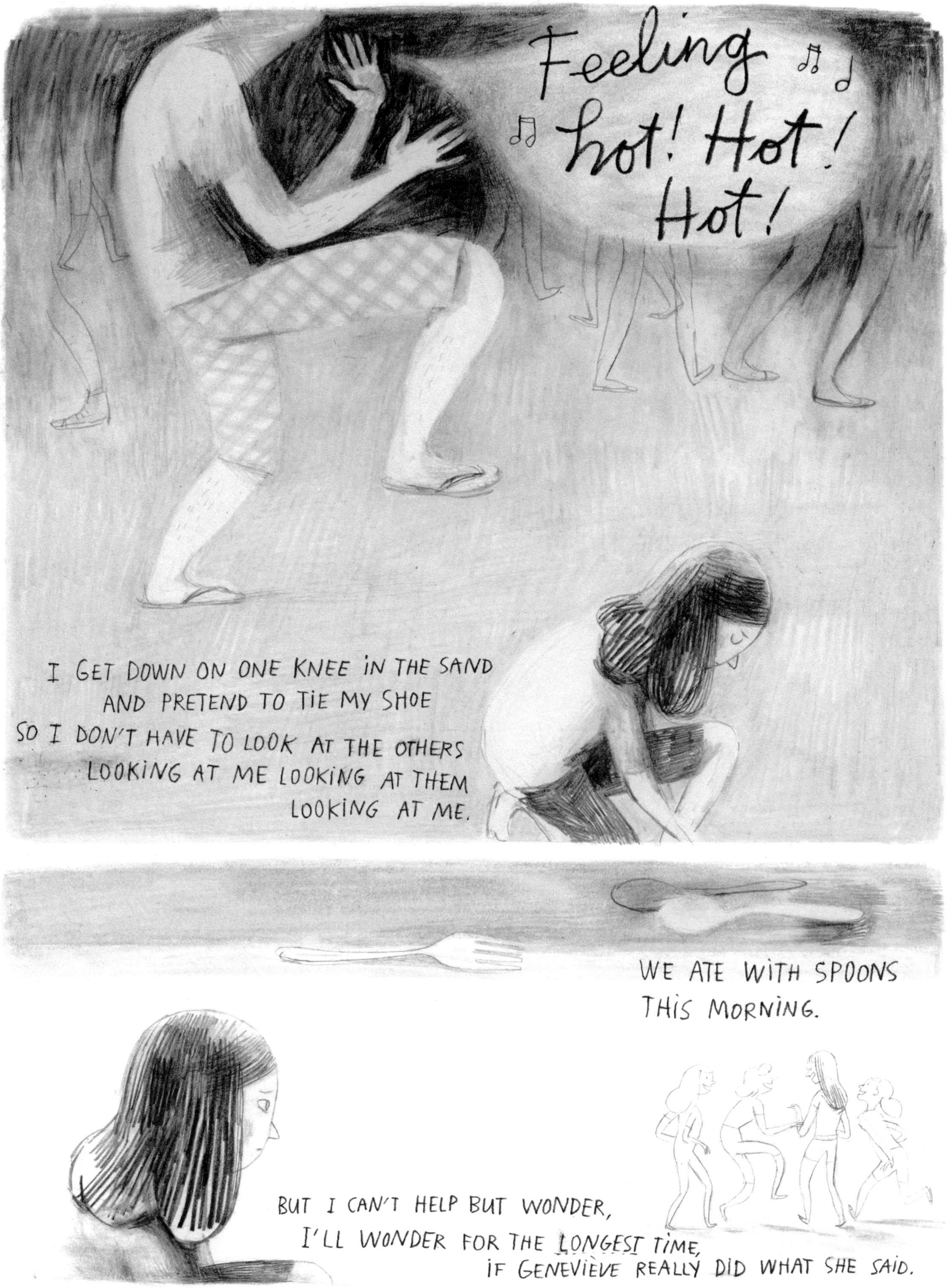
Feeling hot! Hot! Hot!
I GET DOWN ON ONE KNEE IN THE SAND AND PRETEND TO TIE MY SHOE SO I DON'T HAVE TO LOOK AT THE OTHERS LOOKING AT ME LOOKING AT THEM LOOKING AT ME.
WE ATE WITH SPOONS THIS MORNING.
BUT I CAN'T HELP BUT WONDER, I'LL WONDER FOR THE LONGEST TIME, IF GENEVIÈVE REALLY DID WHAT SHE SAID.

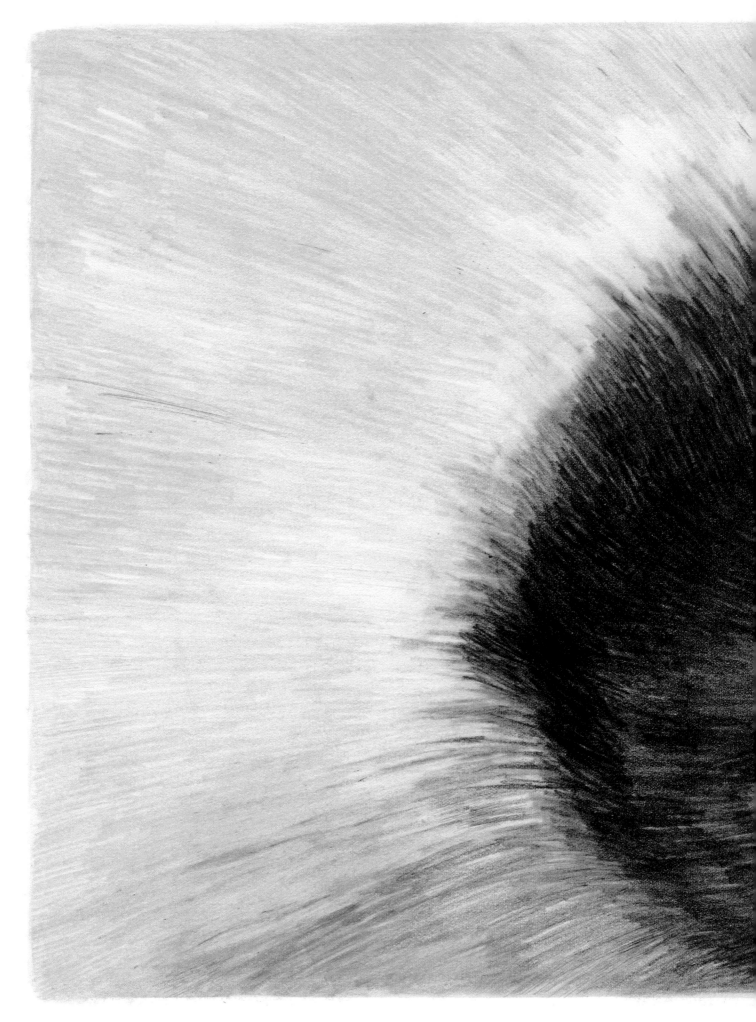

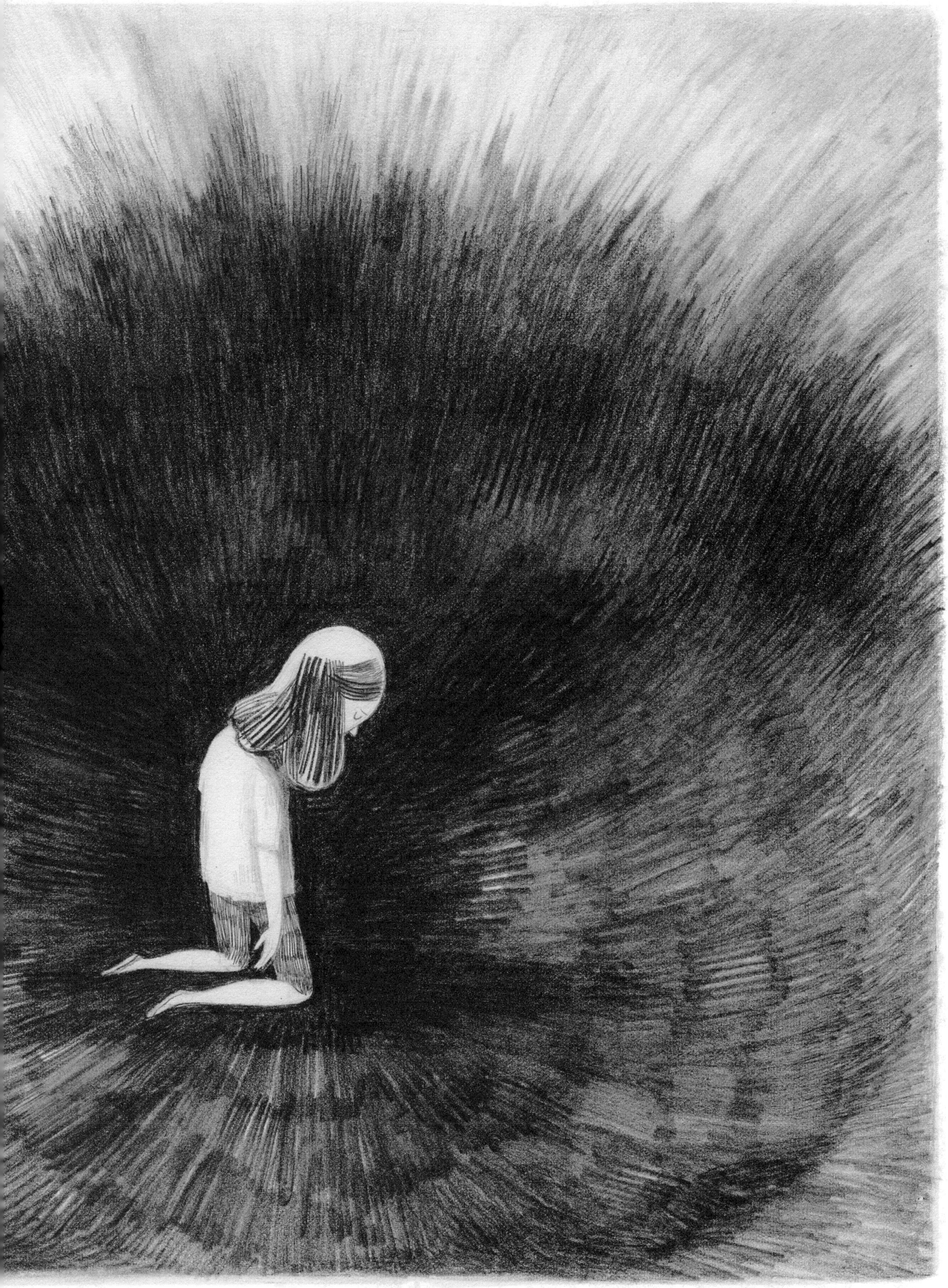

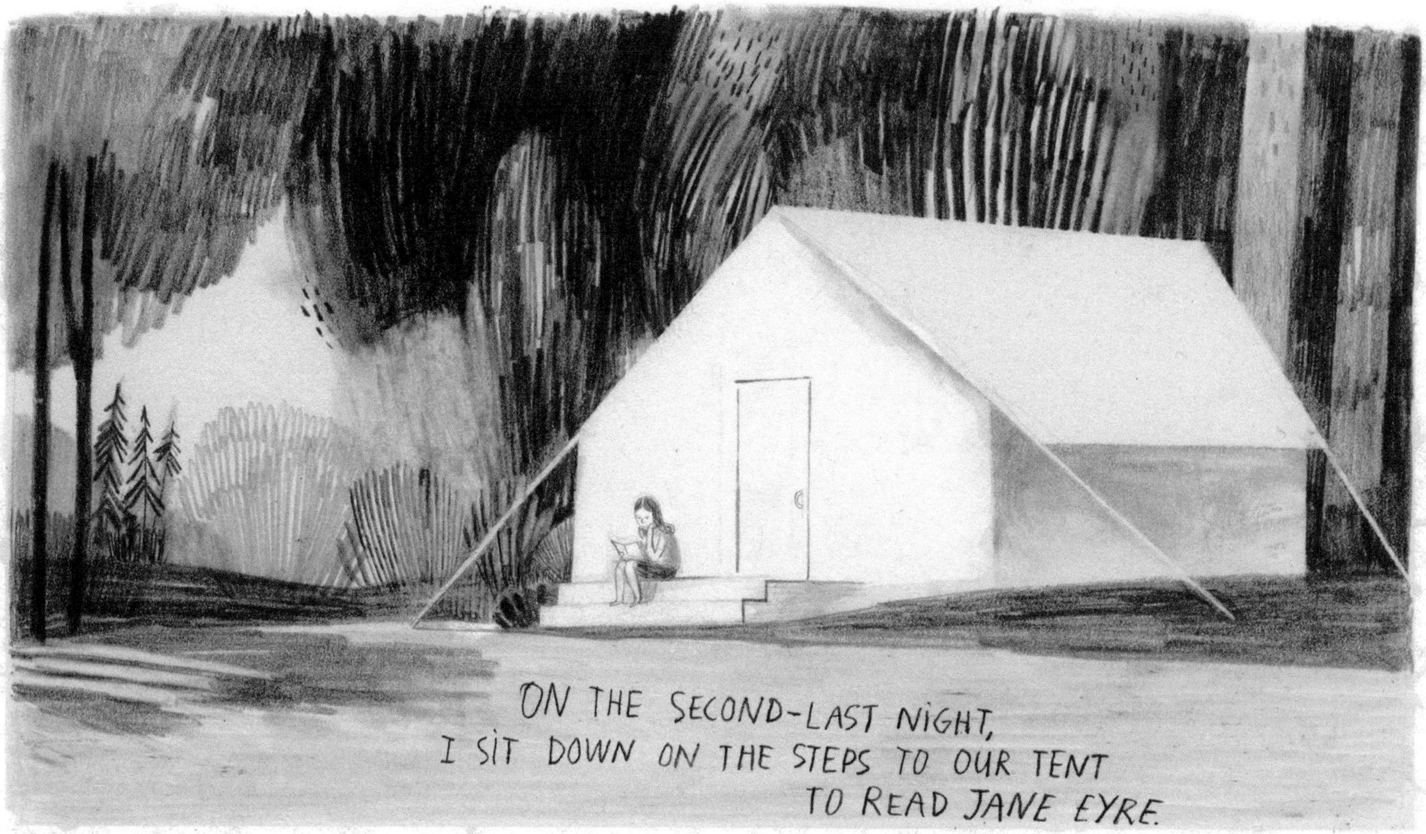
ON THE SECOND-LAST NIGHT, I SIT DOWN ON THE STEPS TO OUR TENT TO READ JANE EYRE.

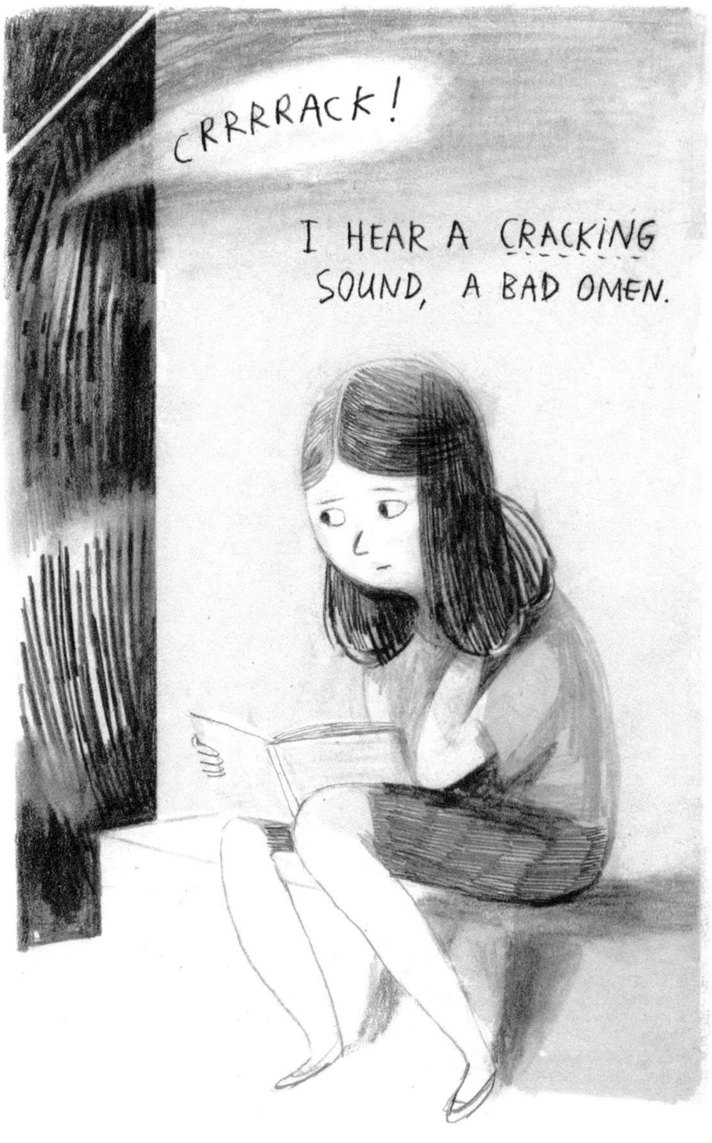
CRRRRACK!
I HEAR A CRACKING SOUND, A BAD OMEN.

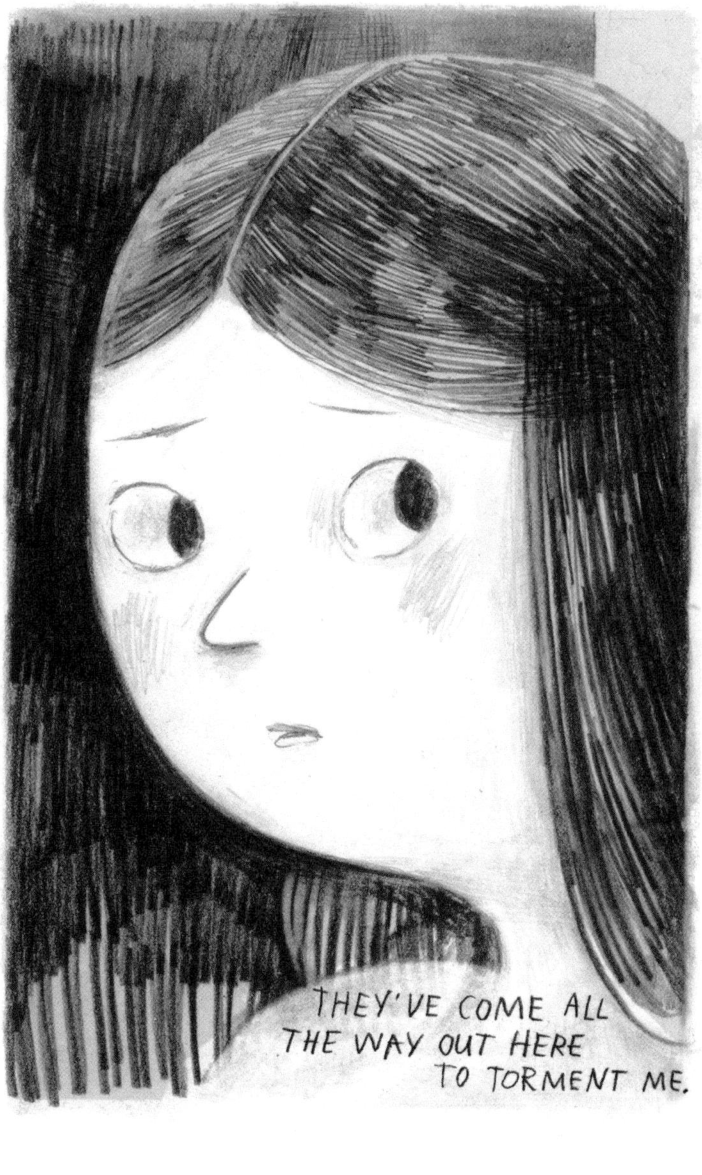
THEY'VE COME ALL THE WAY OUT HERE TO TORMENT ME.

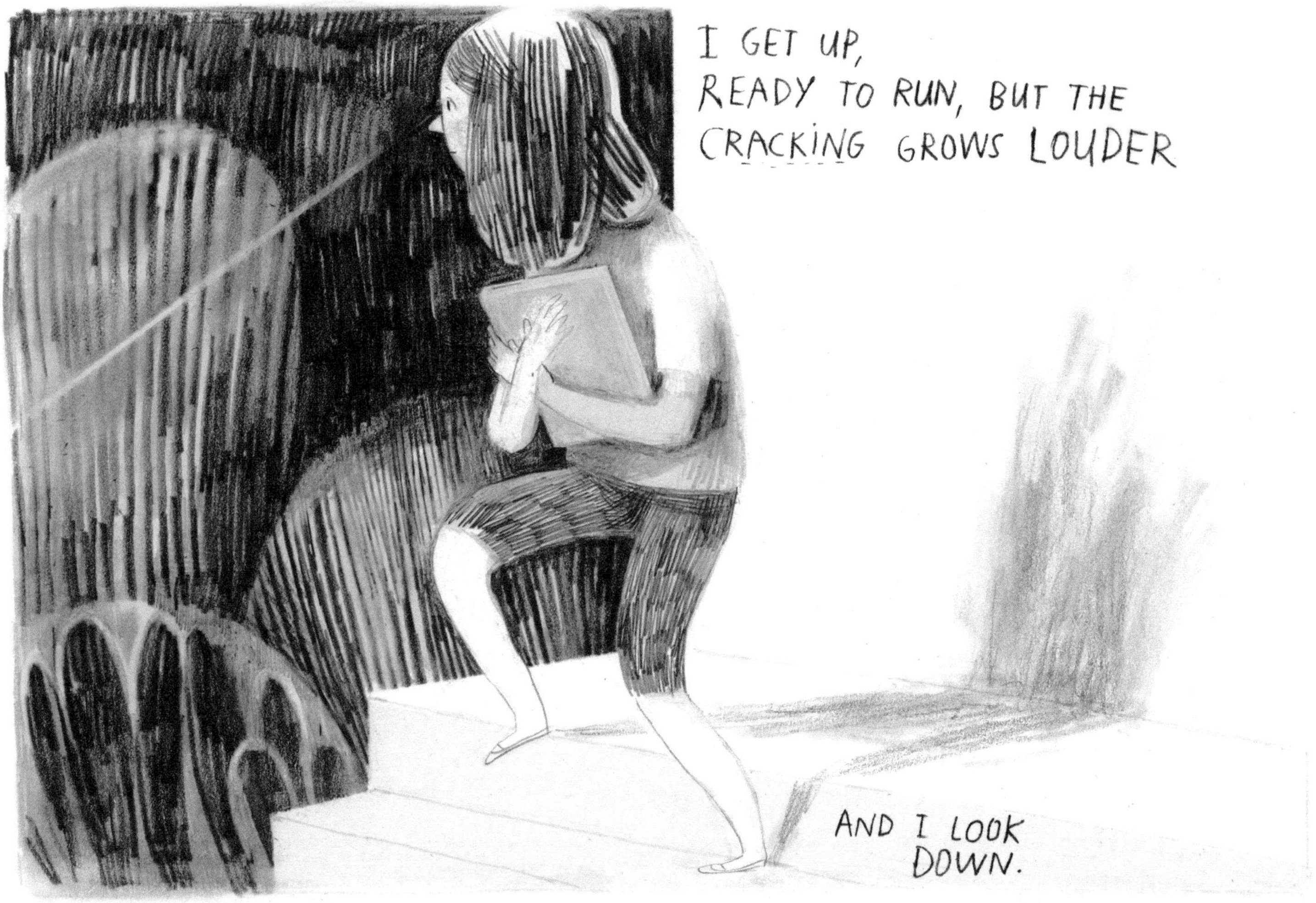
I GET UP,
READY TO RUN, BUT THE
CRACKING GROWS LOUDER
AND I LOOK
DOWN.

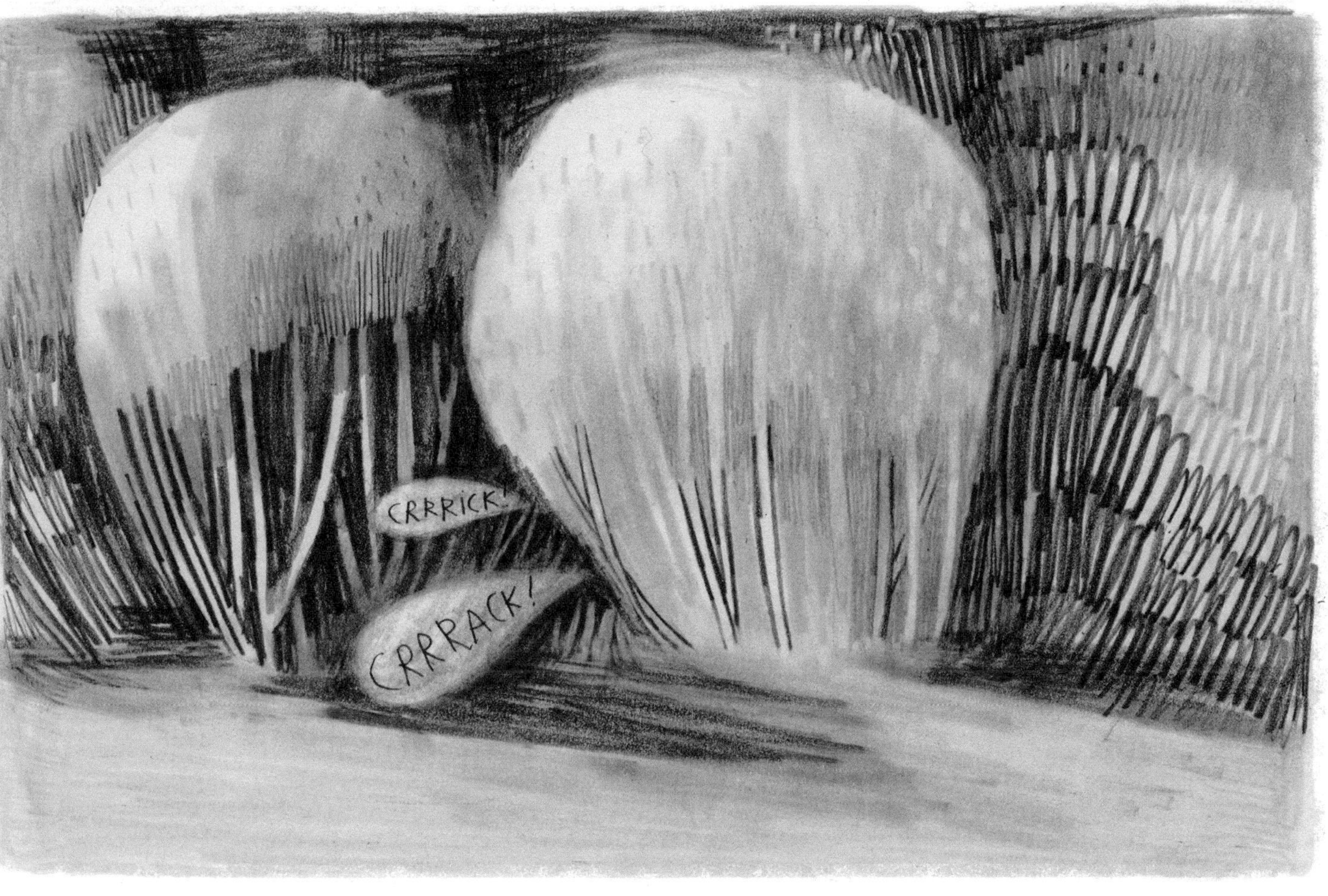
CRRRICK!
CRRRACK!

A FOX.
A REAL LIVE RED FOX,
TINY, WITH A SMALL PATCH OF DARKER FUR
JUST ABOVE ITS LEFT FRONT LEG. LIKE A BEAUTY SPOT.

ITS EYES ARE SO KIND
I JUST ABOUT BURST.

THAT SAME LOOK IN ANOTHER HUMAN'S EYES,
AND MY SOUL WOULD BE THEIRS FOR SURE.

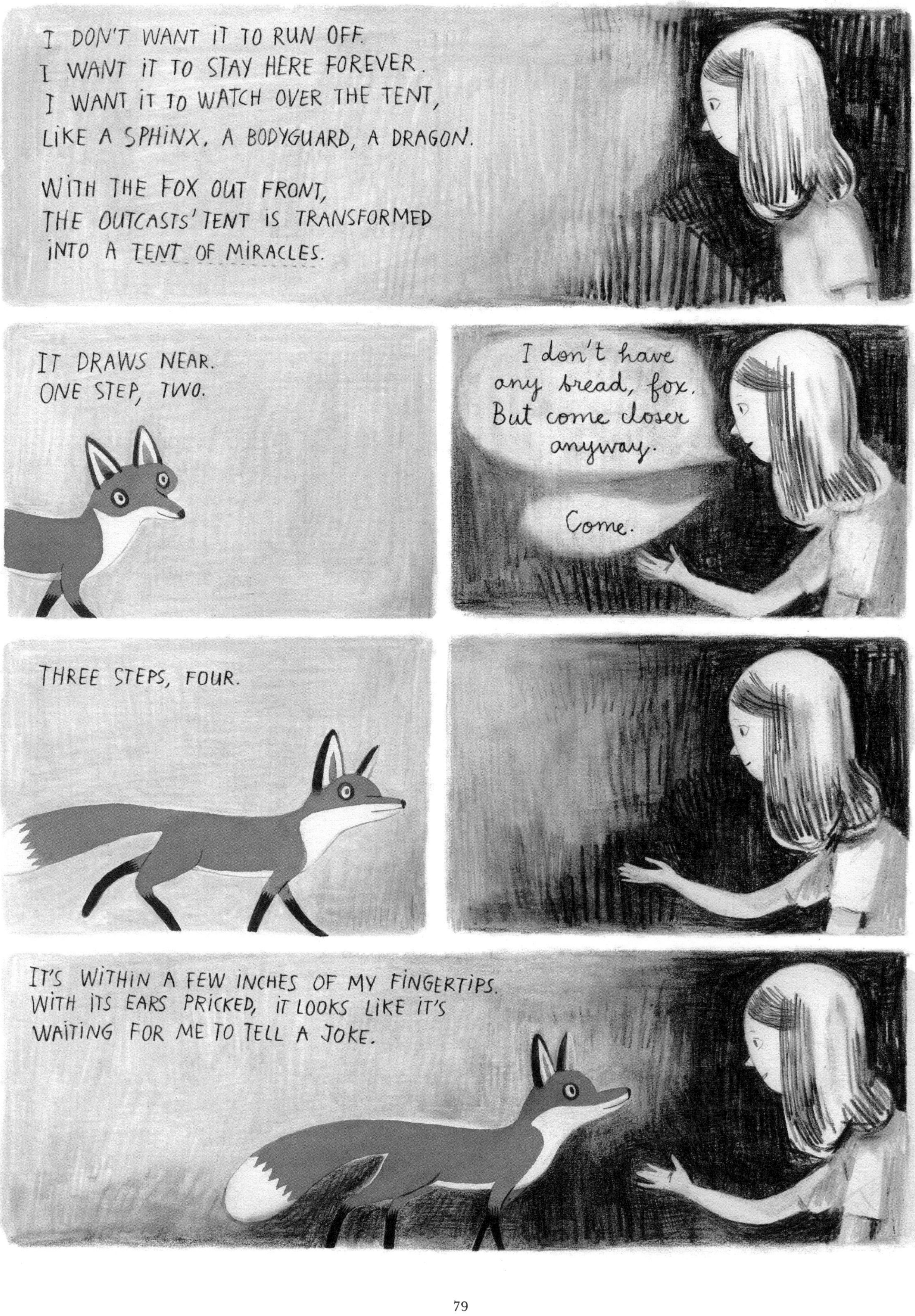
I DON'T WANT IT TO RUN OFF.
I WANT IT TO STAY HERE FOREVER.
I WANT IT TO WATCH OVER THE TENT,
LIKE A SPHINX, A BODYGUARD, A DRAGON.
WITH THE FOX OUT FRONT,
THE OUTCASTS' TENT IS TRANSFORMED
INTO A TENT OF MIRACLES.
IT DRAWS NEAR.
ONE STEP, TWO.
I don't have any bread, fox. But come closer anyway.
Come.
THREE STEPS, FOUR.
IT'S WITHIN A FEW INCHES OF MY FINGERTIPS.
WITH ITS EARS PRICKED, IT LOOKS LIKE IT'S
WAITING FOR ME TO TELL A JOKE.

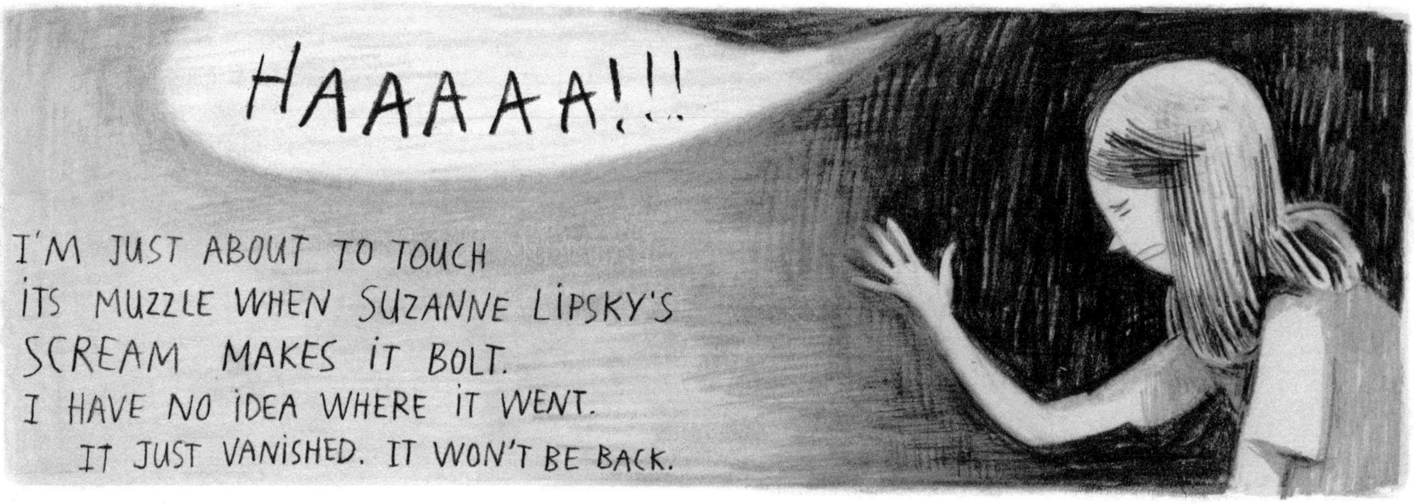
HAAAAA!!!
I'M JUST ABOUT TO TOUCH ITS MUZZLE WHEN SUZANNE LIPSKY'S SCREAM MAKES IT BOLT.
I HAVE NO IDEA WHERE IT WENT.
IT JUST VANISHED. IT WON'T BE BACK.

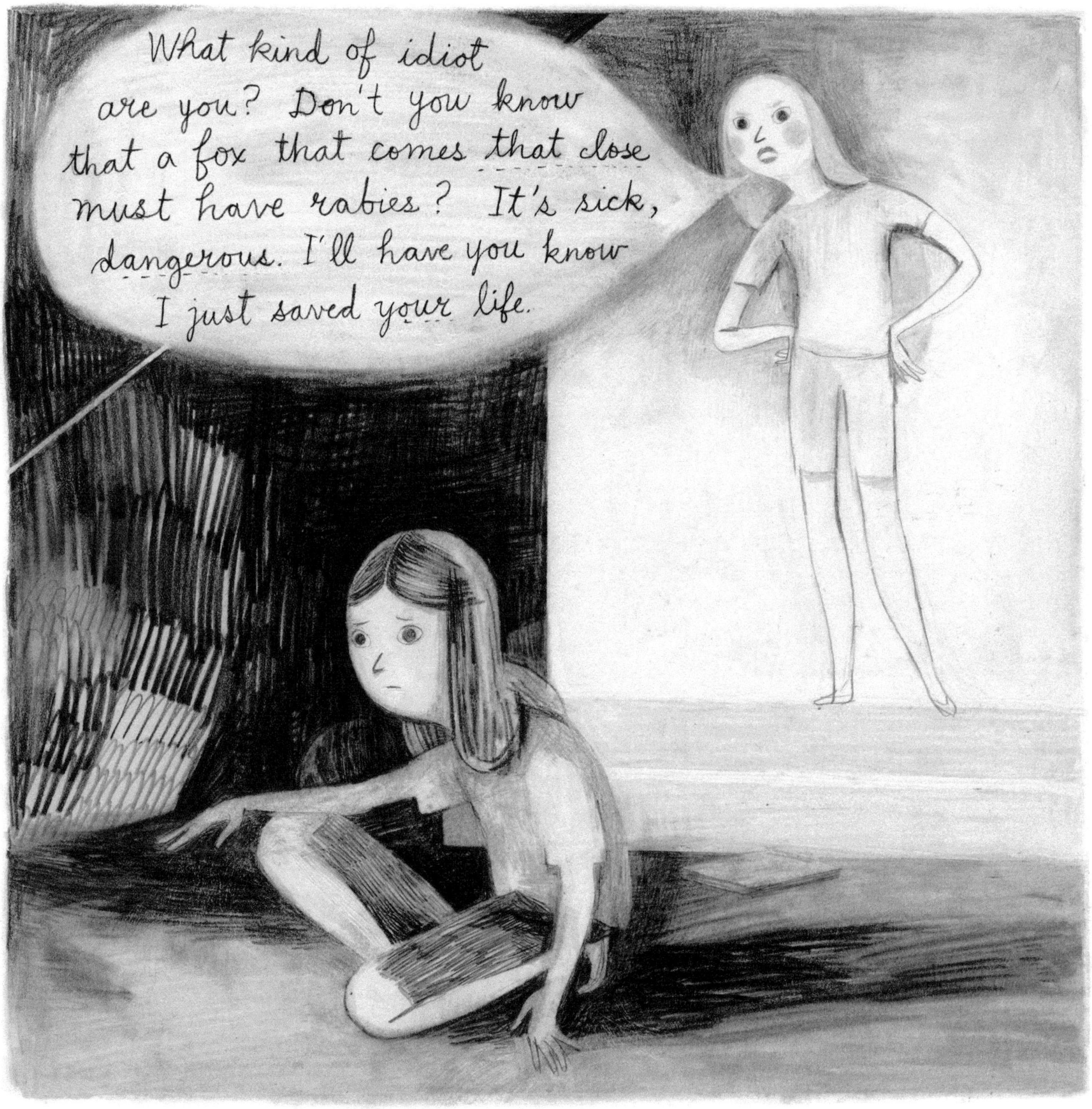
What kind of idiot are you? Don't you know that a fox that comes that close must have rabies? It's sick, dangerous. I'll have you know I just saved your life.

I DIDN'T KNOW
THAT ANY FOX WHO DARES
APPROACH ME —
HÉLÈNE WHO WEIGHTS 396
HÉLÈNE WHO HAS NO FRIENDS
HÉLÈNE A FORK IN HER BUTT
HÉLÈNE WEARING A CRINOLINE
WHEN IT'S LAST SUMMER'S FAD
HÉLÈNE WHO GETS ON EVERYONE'S
NERVES, EVEN SUZANNE LIPSKY'S —
HAS GOT TO BE
RABID,
SICK,
DANGEROUS.

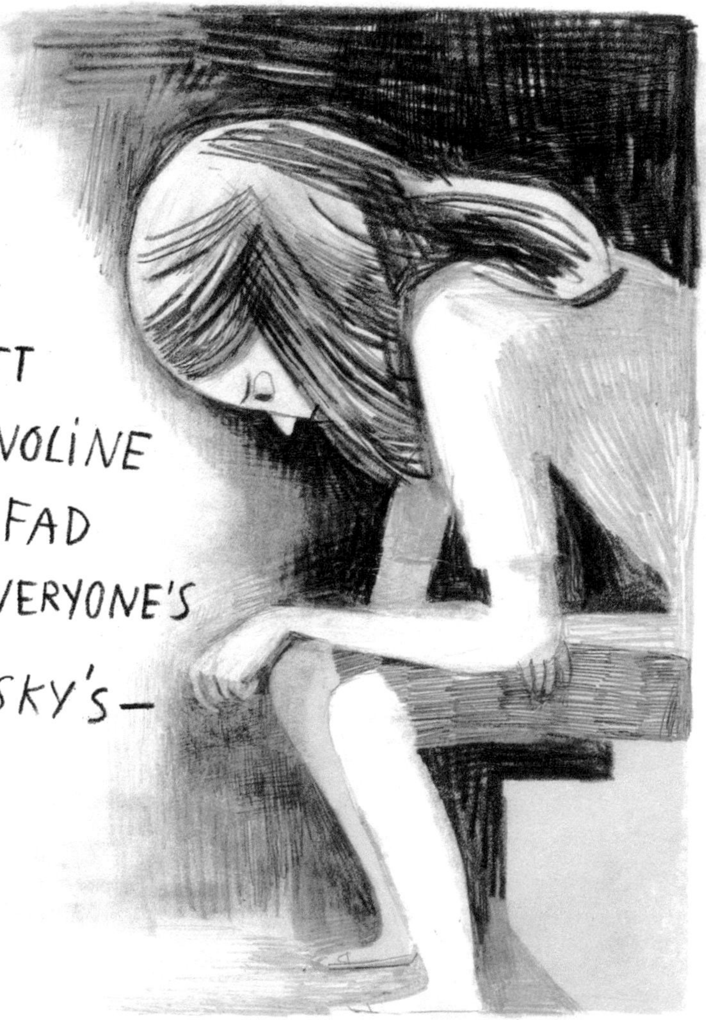

I DIDN'T KNOW.

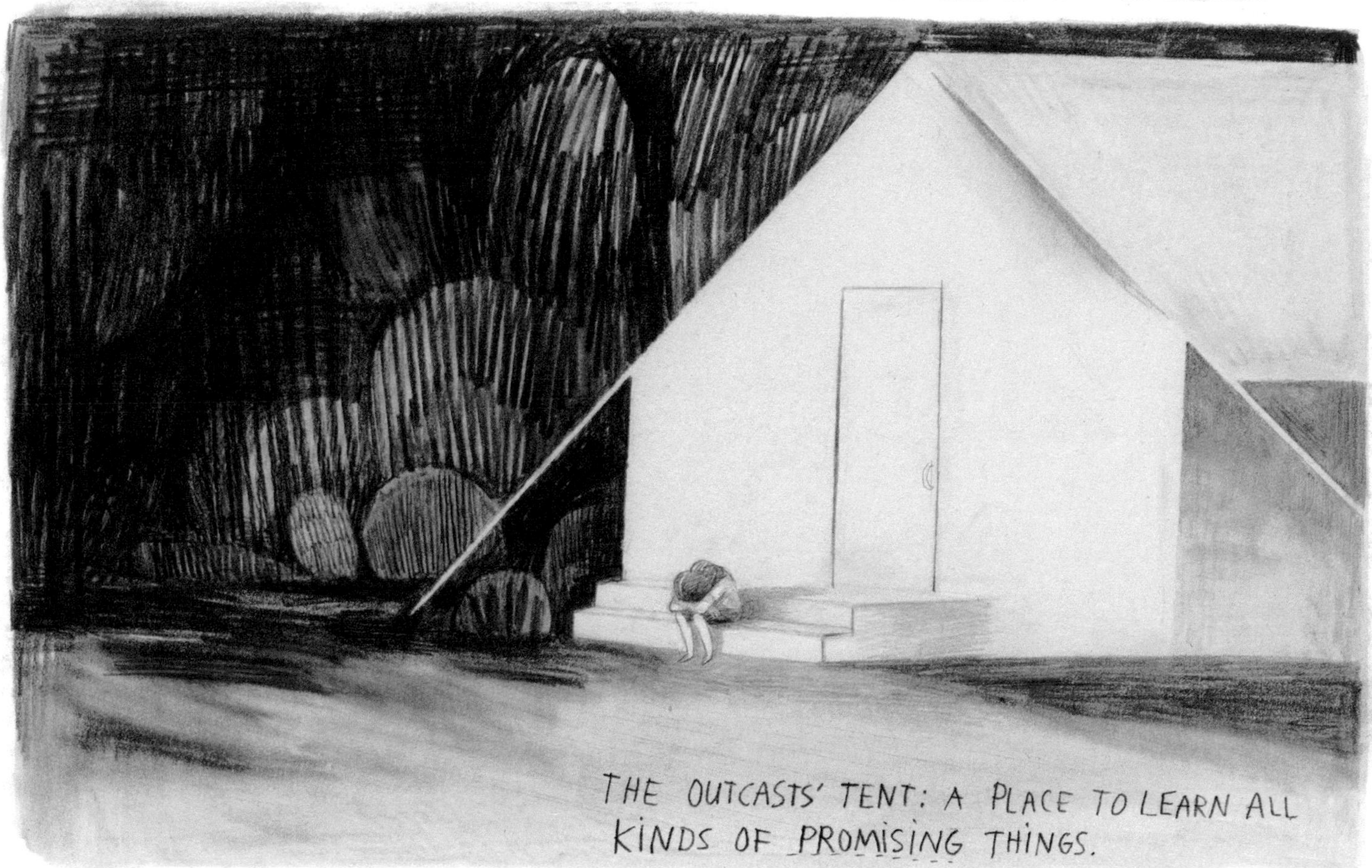
THE OUTCASTS' TENT: A PLACE TO LEARN ALL KINDS OF PROMISING THINGS.

Mr. Rochester loves Jane Eyre
and asks her to marry him.

Strange and serious,
brown dress and all,
he loves her.

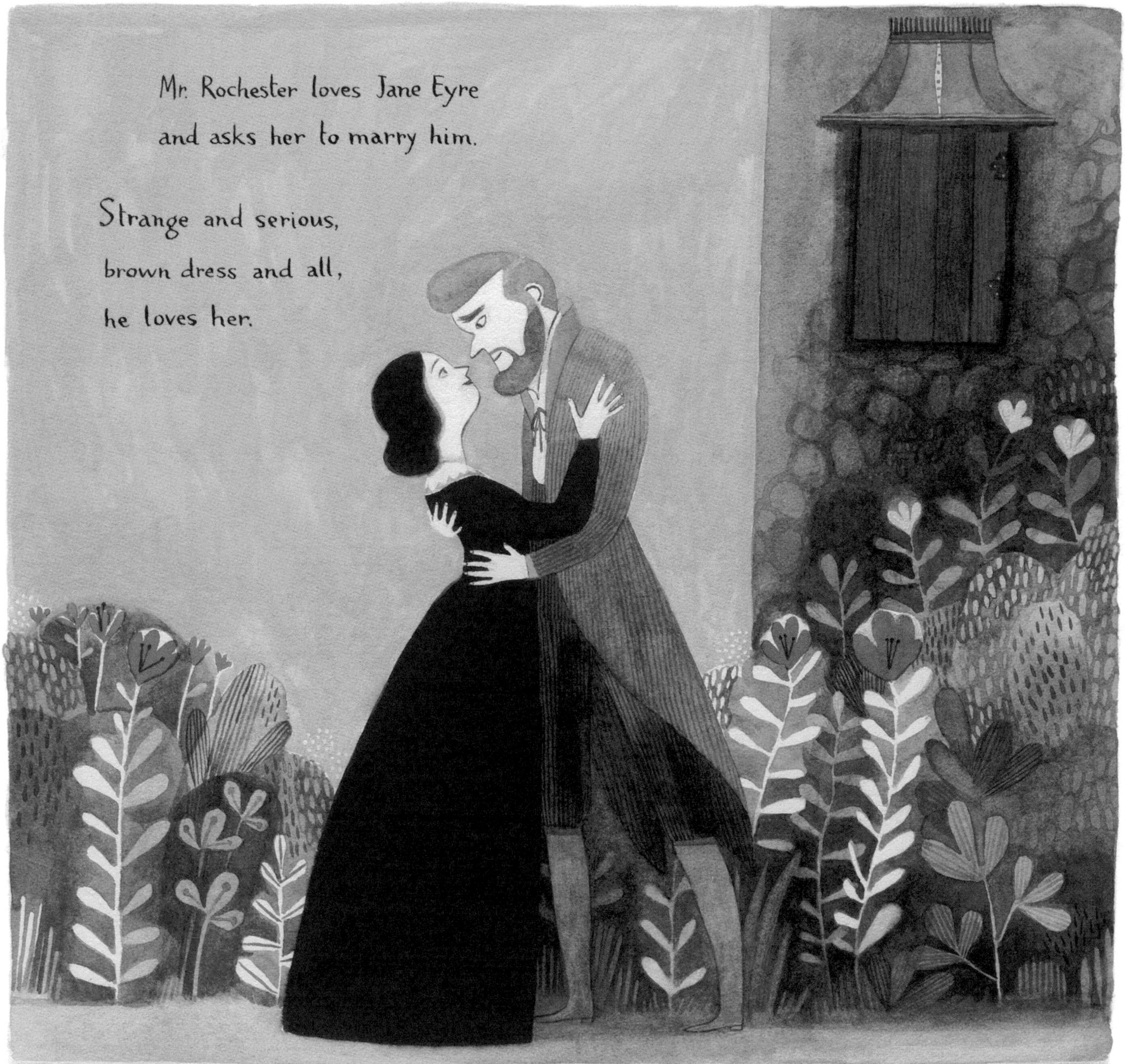

How wonderful, how impossible.

Any boy who'd love a sailboat-patterned, swimsuited sausage
who tames rabid foxes would be wonderful.
And impossible.

Just like in *Jane Eyre*, the story would end badly.

Just like in *Jane Eyre*,
she'd learn the boy already has a wife as crazy as a kite, shut up in the manor tower, and that even if he loves the swimsuited sausage, he can't marry her.

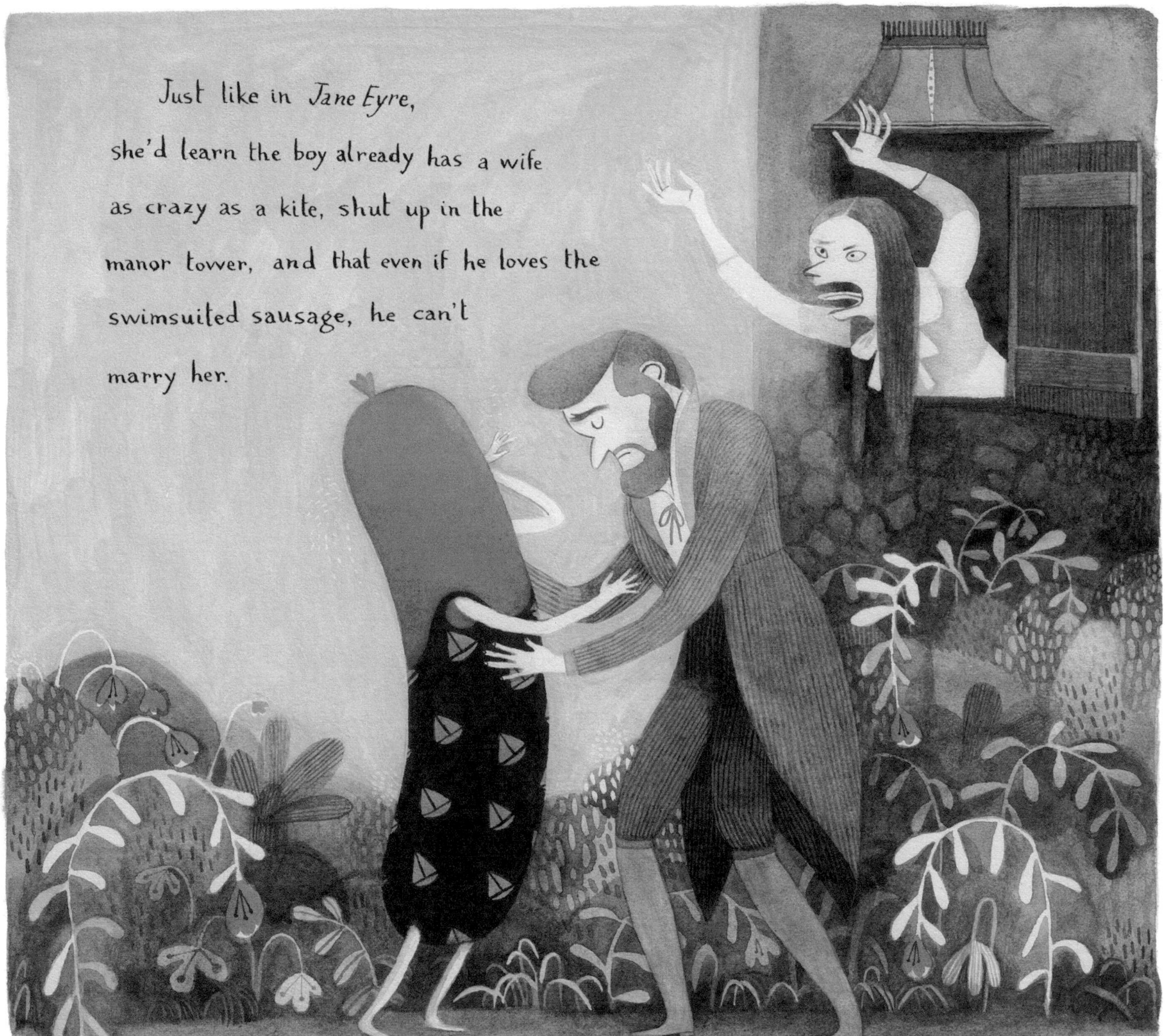

Then the sausage would have to leave the manor in shame and travel to the ends of the earth, her heart in a thousand pieces.

Just like in *Jane Eyre*, the moral of the story would be "never forget that you're nothing but a sad sausage."

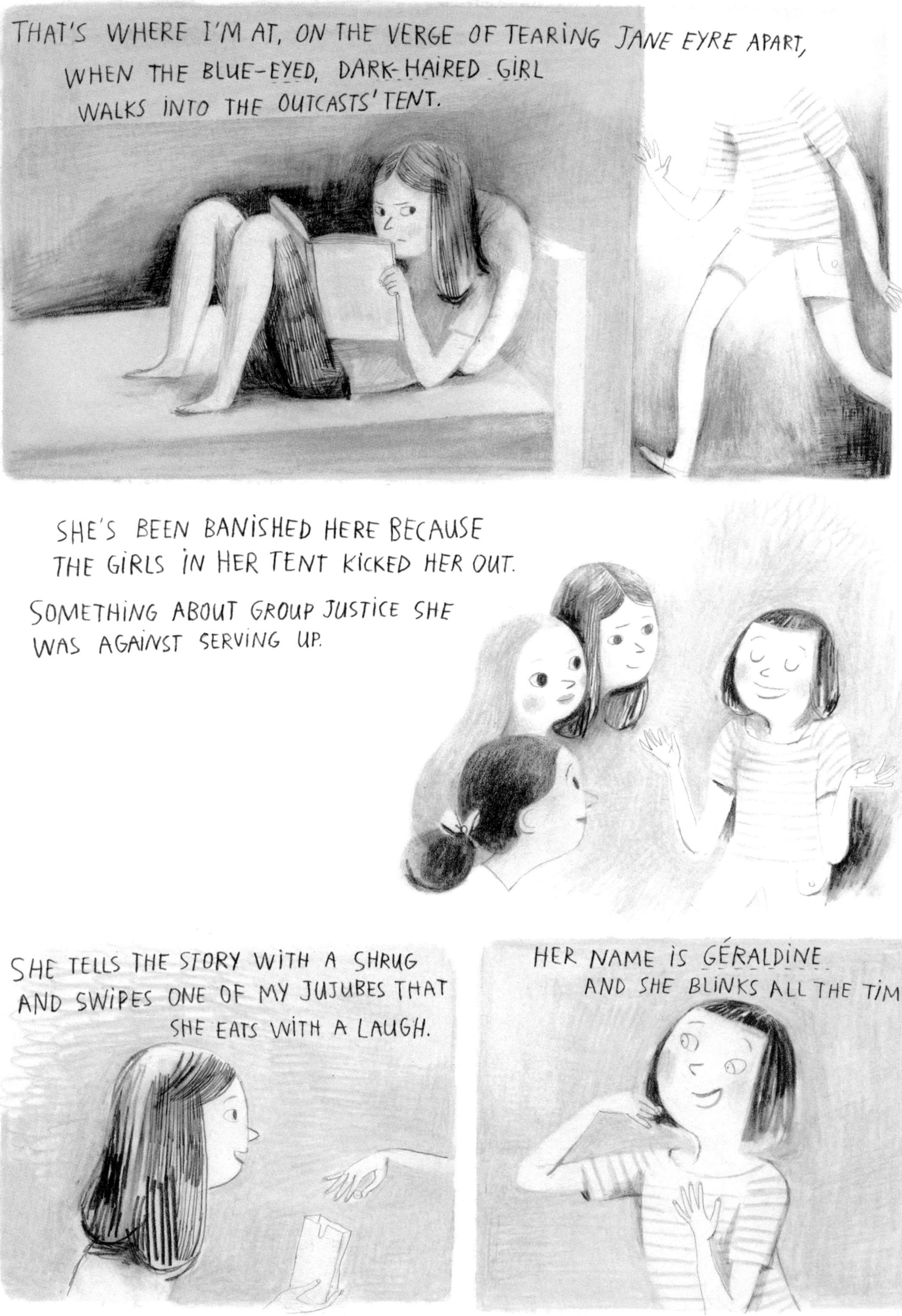
THAT'S WHERE I'M AT, ON THE VERGE OF TEARING JANE EYRE APART, WHEN THE BLUE-EYED, DARK-HAIRED GIRL WALKS INTO THE OUTCASTS' TENT.
SHE'S BEEN BANISHED HERE BECAUSE THE GIRLS IN HER TENT KICKED HER OUT.
SOMETHING ABOUT GROUP JUSTICE SHE WAS AGAINST SERVING UP.
SHE TELLS THE STORY WITH A SHRUG AND SWIPES ONE OF MY JUJUBES THAT SHE EATS WITH A LAUGH.
HER NAME IS GÉRALDINE AND SHE BLINKS ALL THE TIME.

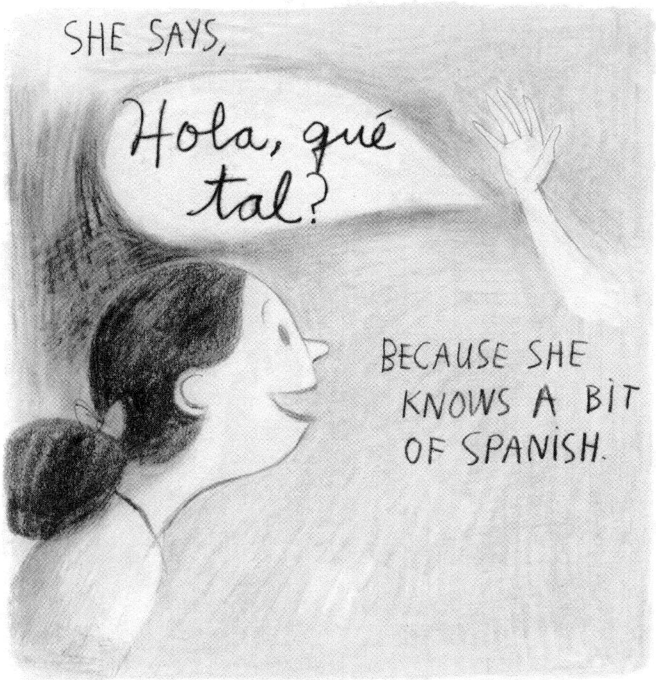
SHE SAYS,
Hola, qué tal?
BECAUSE SHE KNOWS A BIT OF SPANISH.

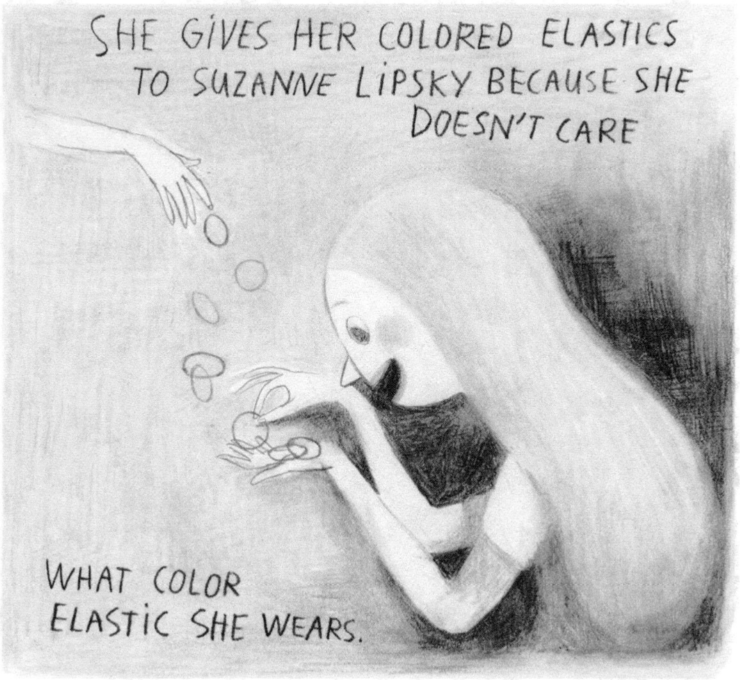
SHE GIVES HER COLORED ELASTICS TO SUZANNE LIPSKY BECAUSE SHE DOESN'T CARE
WHAT COLOR ELASTIC SHE WEARS.

WITH HER, THE OUTCASTS' LAST NAMES ARE DROPPED.

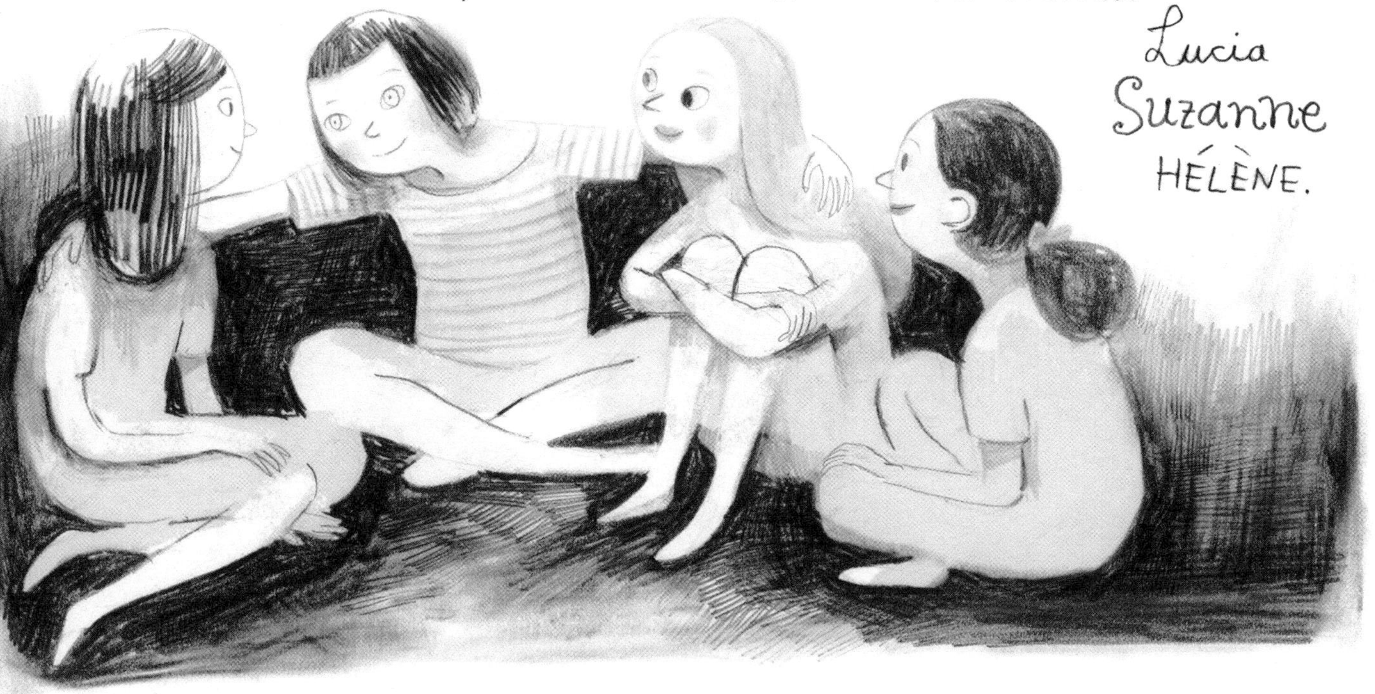
Lucia
Suzanne
HÉLÈNE.

THEN SHE GRABS MY HAND AND PULLS ME OUTSIDE. SHE SAW SOME EARLY STRAWBERRIES IN THE WOODS SHE WANTS TO SHOW ME.

ME, NOT LUCIA OR SUZANNE OR ANYONE FROM HER EX-GANG OF SNOBS.

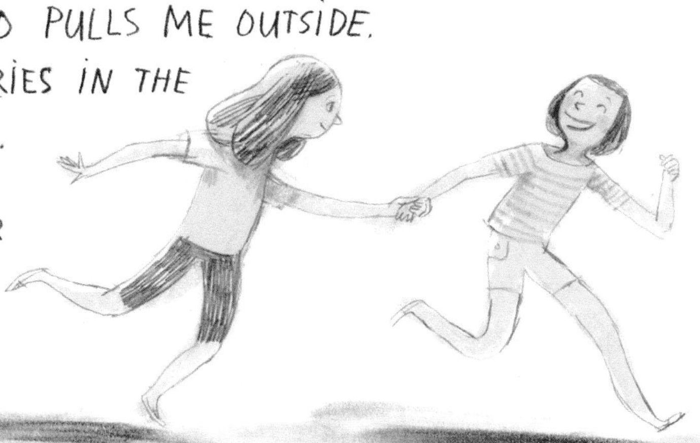

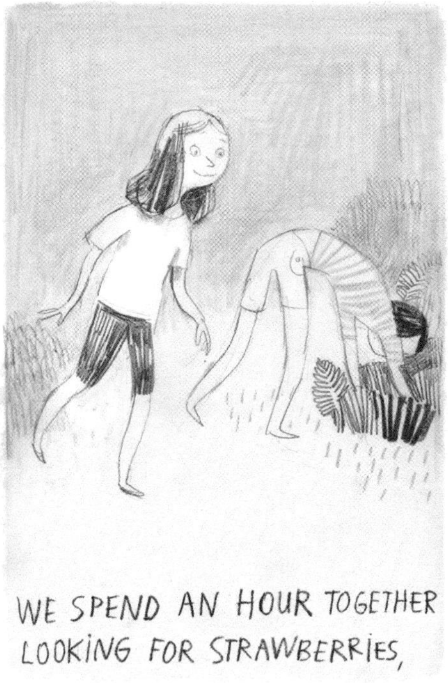
WE SPEND AN HOUR TOGETHER LOOKING FOR STRAWBERRIES,

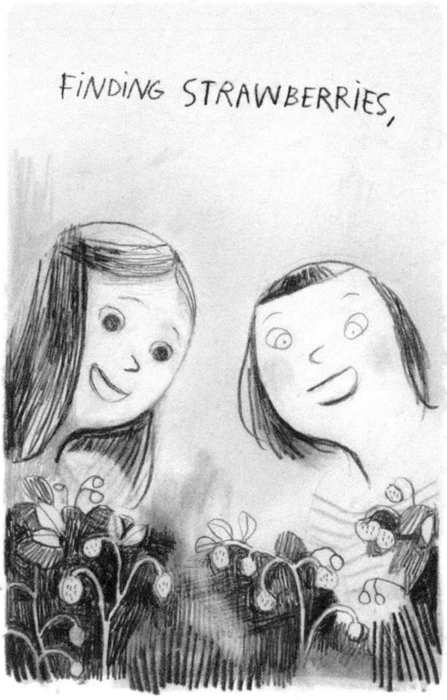
FINDING STRAWBERRIES,

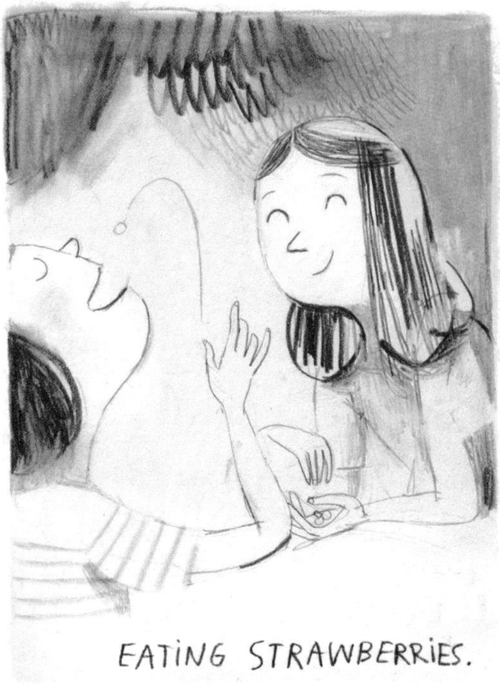
EATING STRAWBERRIES.

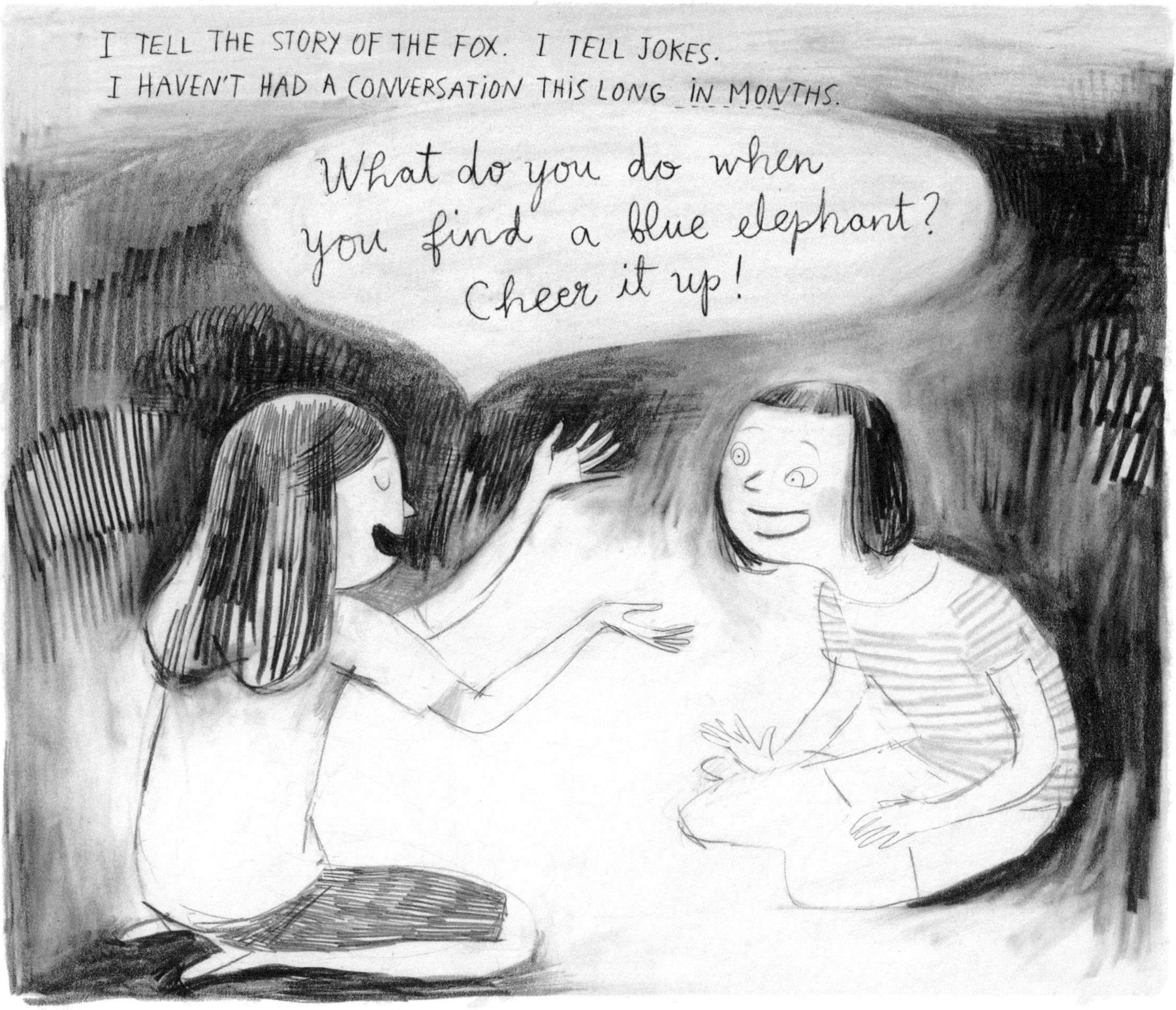
I TELL THE STORY OF THE FOX. I TELL JOKES.
I HAVEN'T HAD A CONVERSATION THIS LONG IN MONTHS.
What do you do when you find a blue elephant? Cheer it up!

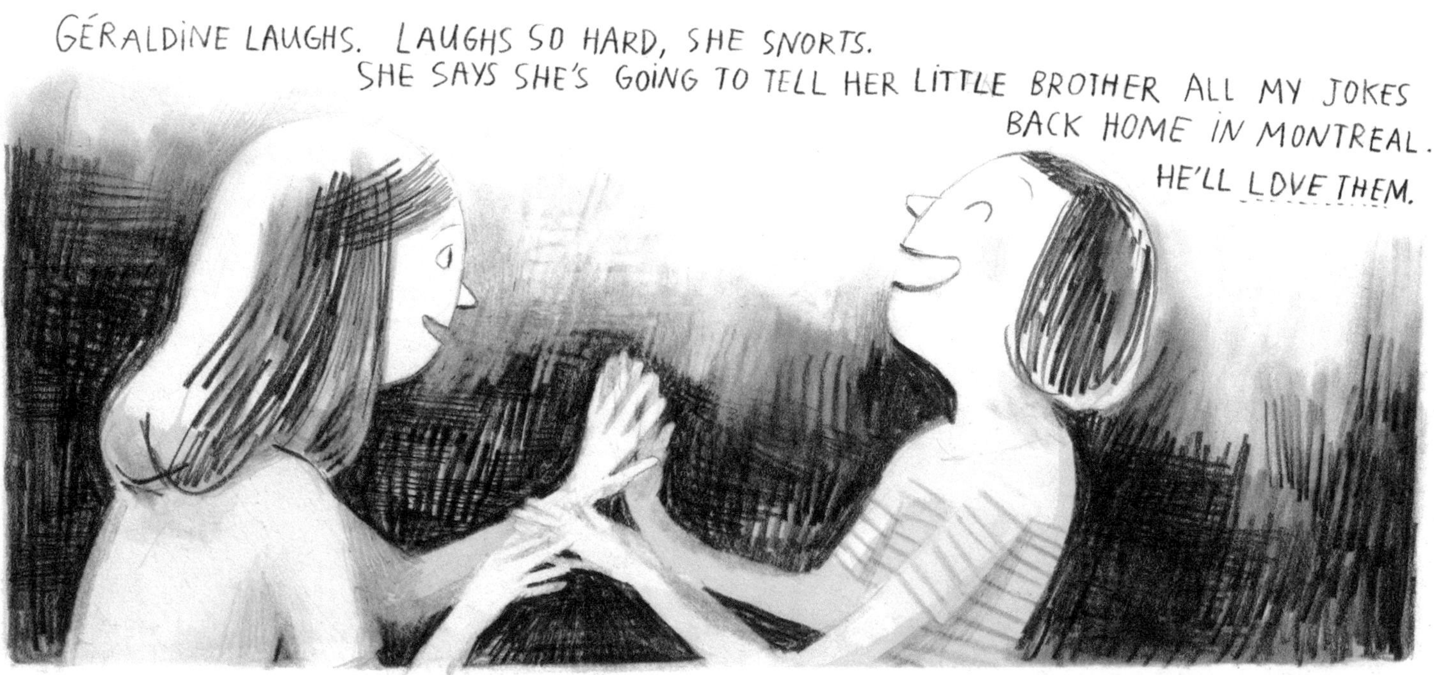
GÉRALDINE LAUGHS. LAUGHS SO HARD, SHE SNORTS.
SHE SAYS SHE'S GOING TO TELL HER LITTLE BROTHER ALL MY JOKES BACK HOME IN MONTREAL.
HE'LL LOVE THEM.

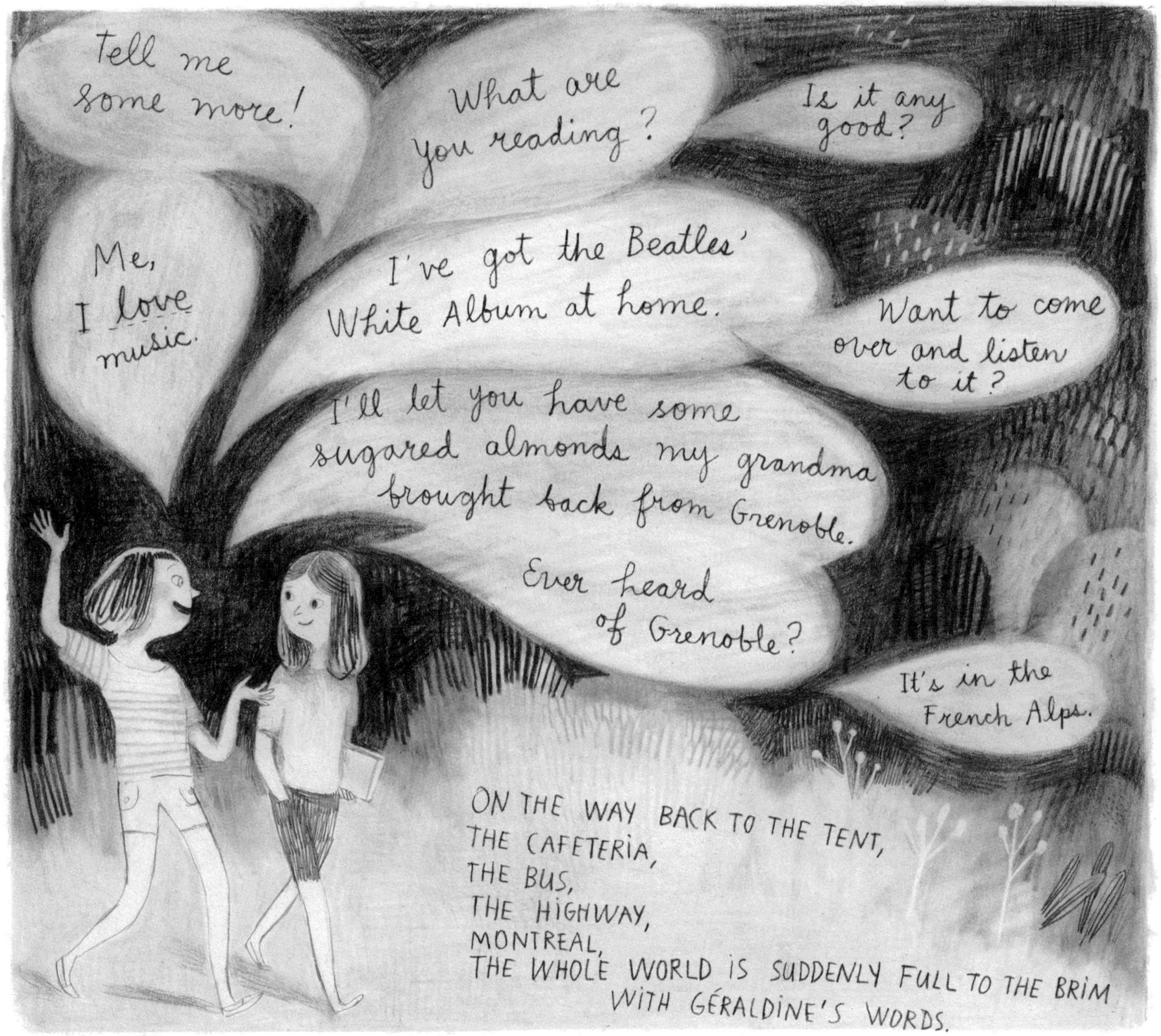
Tell me some more!
What are you reading?
Is it any good?
Me, I love music.
I've got the Beatles' White Album at home.
Want to come over and listen to it?
I'll let you have some sugared almonds my grandma brought back from Grenoble.
Ever heard of Grenoble?
It's in the French Alps.
ON THE WAY BACK TO THE TENT,
THE CAFETERIA,
THE BUS,
THE HIGHWAY,
MONTREAL,
THE WHOLE WORLD IS SUDDENLY FULL TO THE BRIM WITH GÉRALDINE'S WORDS.

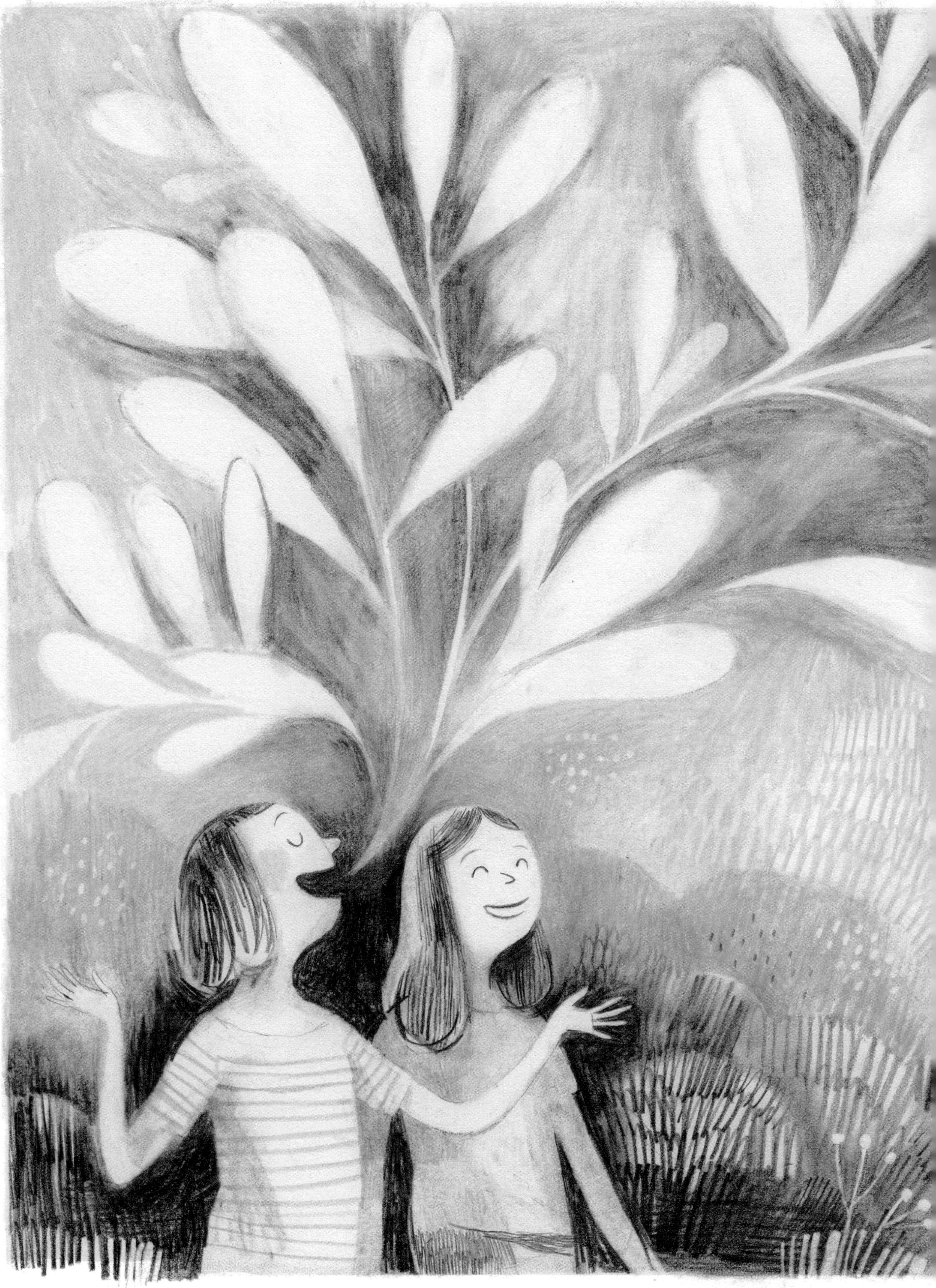

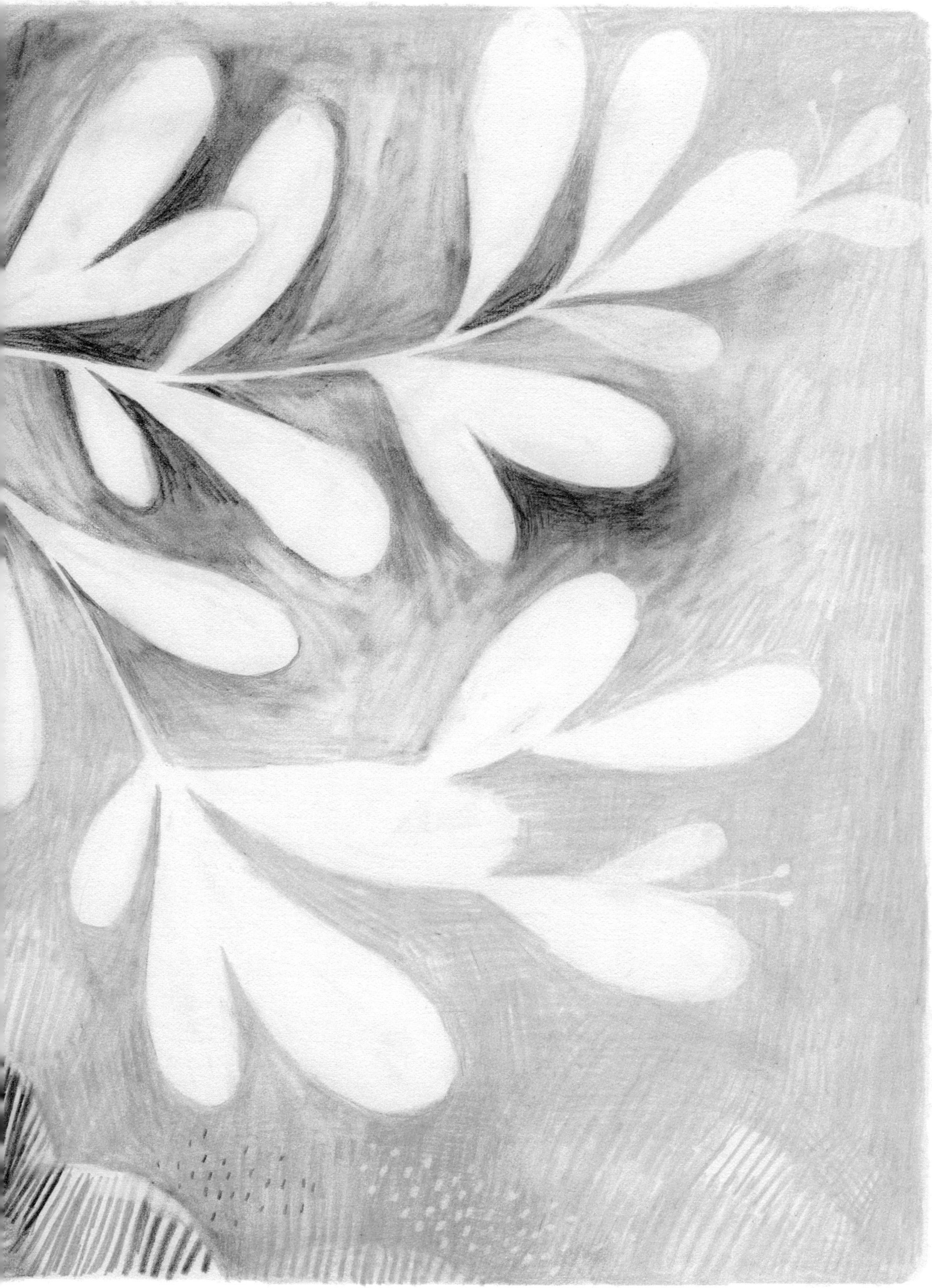

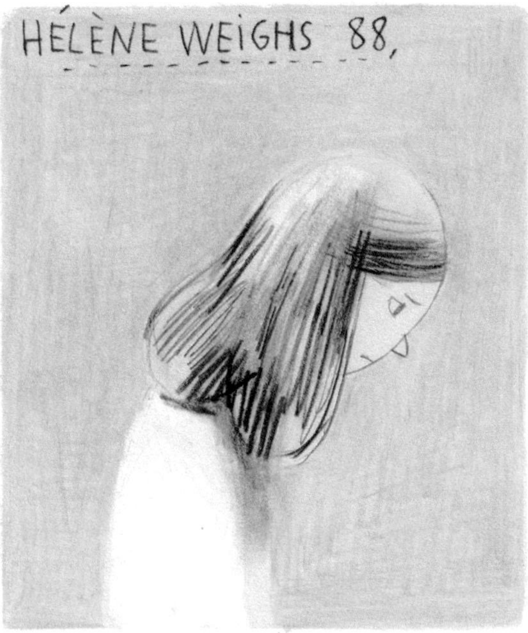
HÉLÈNE WEIGHS 88,

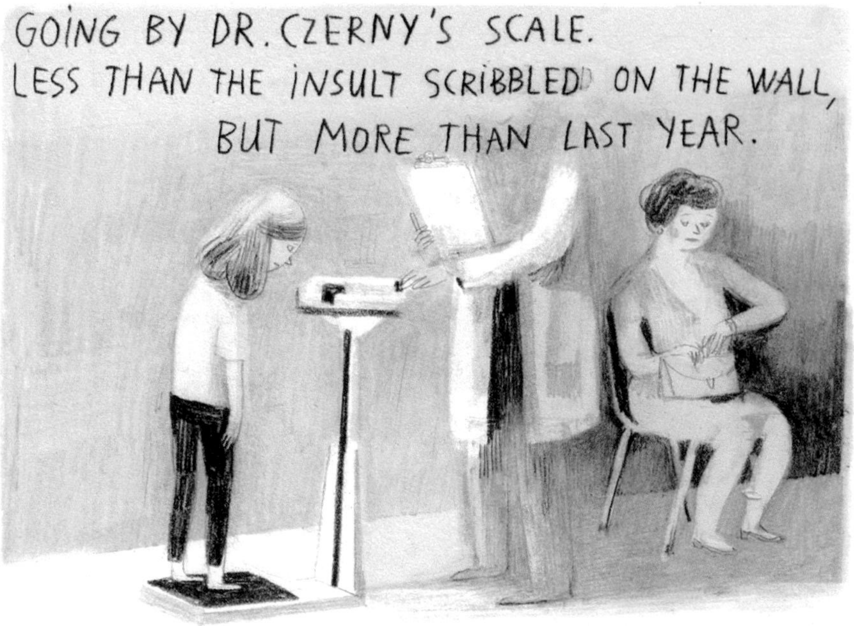
GOING BY DR. CZERNY'S SCALE.
LESS THAN THE INSULT SCRIBBLED ON THE WALL,
BUT MORE THAN LAST YEAR.

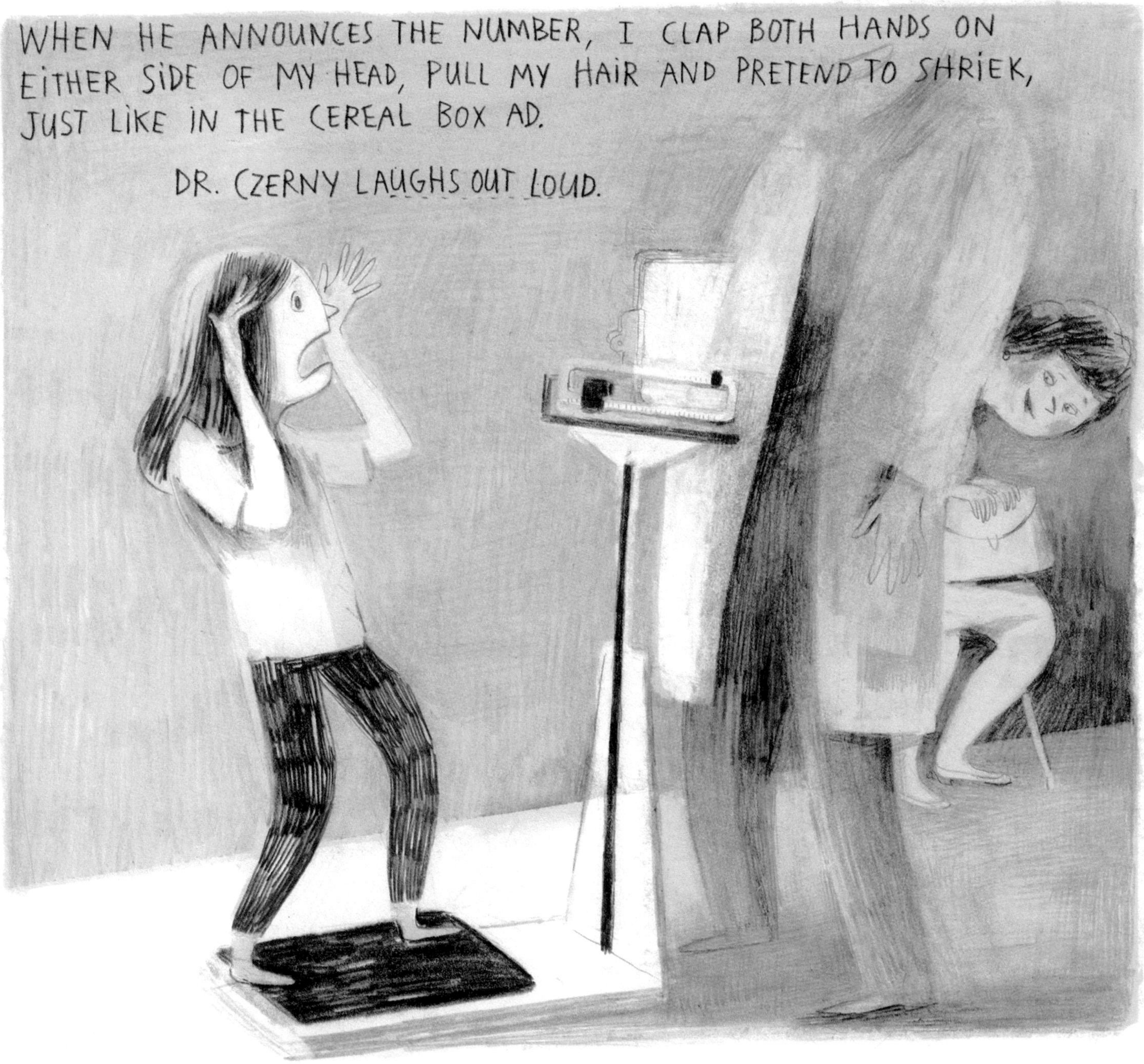
WHEN HE ANNOUNCES THE NUMBER, I CLAP BOTH HANDS ON EITHER SIDE OF MY HEAD, PULL MY HAIR AND PRETEND TO SHRIEK, JUST LIKE IN THE CEREAL BOX AD.
DR. CZERNY LAUGHS OUT LOUD.

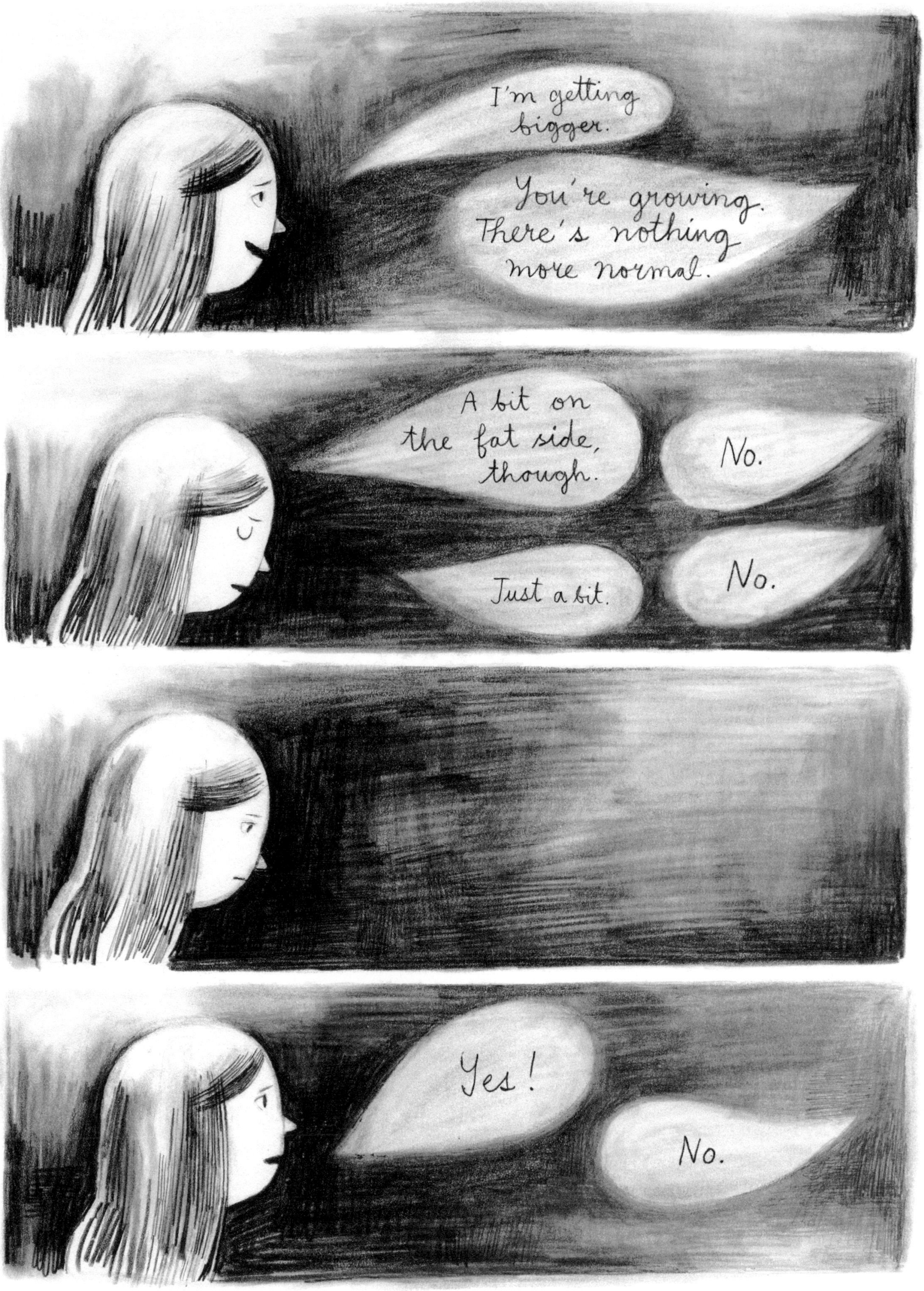
I'm getting bigger.
You're growing. There's nothing more normal.
A bit on the fat side, though.
No.
Just a bit.
No.
Yes!
No.

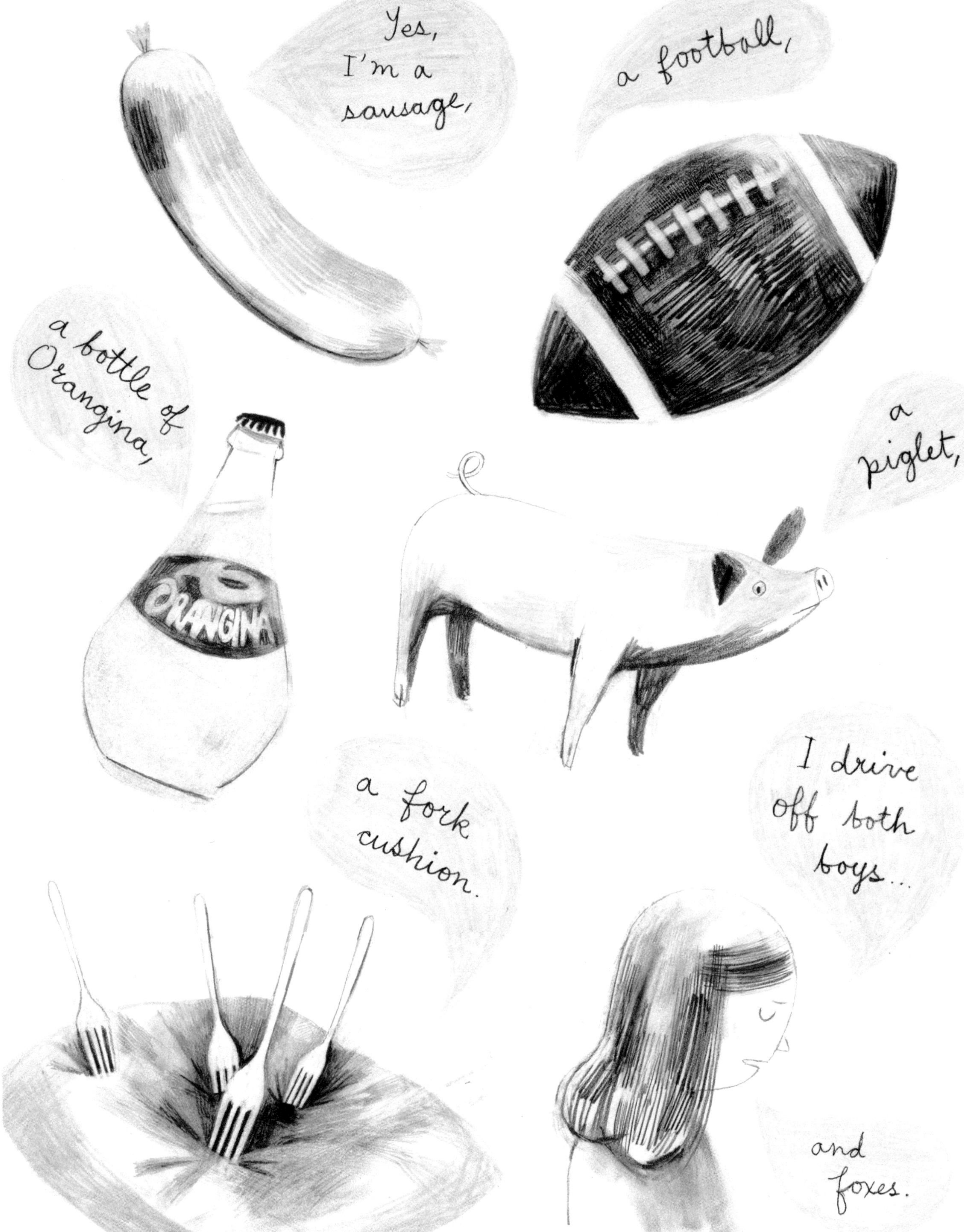
Yes, I'm a sausage,
a football,
a bottle of Orangina,
ORANGINA
a piglet,
a fork cushion.
I drive off both boys...
and foxes.

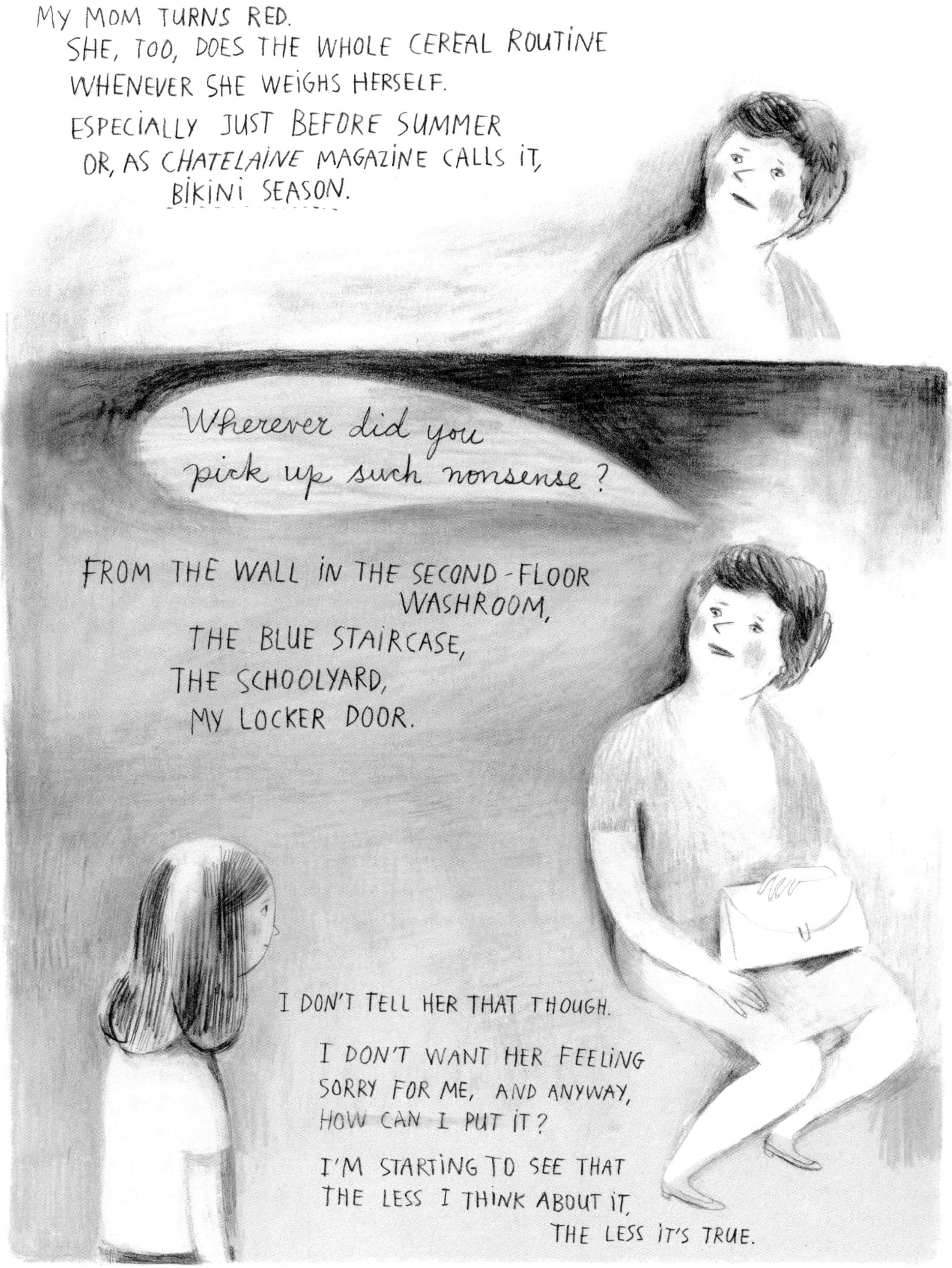
MY MOM TURNS RED.
SHE, TOO, DOES THE WHOLE CEREAL ROUTINE WHENEVER SHE WEIGHS HERSELF.
ESPECIALLY JUST BEFORE SUMMER OR, AS CHATELAINE MAGAZINE CALLS IT, BIKINI SEASON.
Wherever did you pick up such nonsense?
FROM THE WALL IN THE SECOND-FLOOR WASHROOM,
THE BLUE STAIRCASE,
THE SCHOOLYARD,
MY LOCKER DOOR.
I DON'T TELL HER THAT THOUGH.
I DON'T WANT HER FEELING SORRY FOR ME, AND ANYWAY, HOW CAN I PUT IT?
I'M STARTING TO SEE THAT THE LESS I THINK ABOUT IT, THE LESS IT'S TRUE.

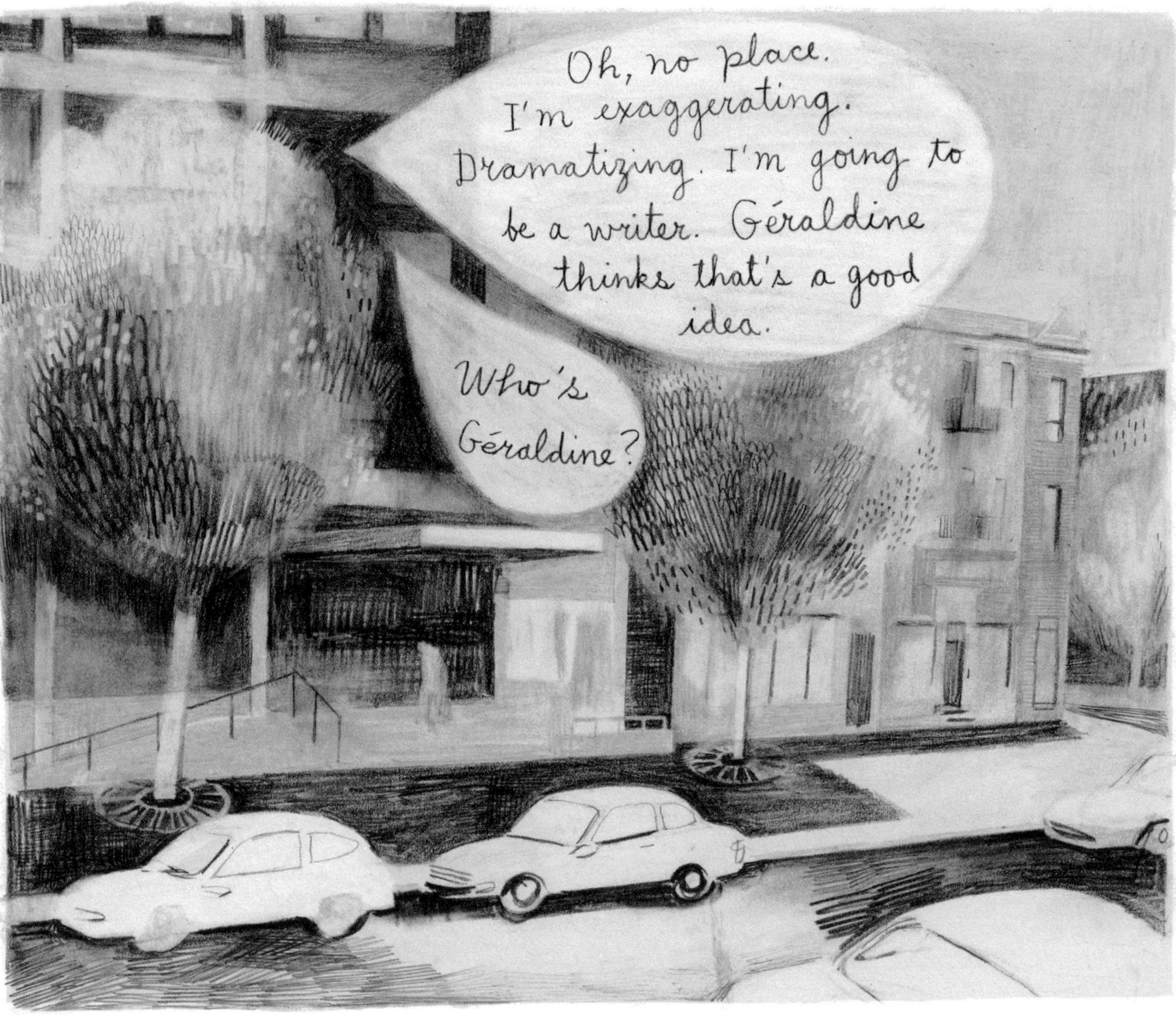
Oh, no place. I'm exaggerating. Dramatizing. I'm going to be a writer. Géraldine thinks that's a good idea.
Who's Géraldine?

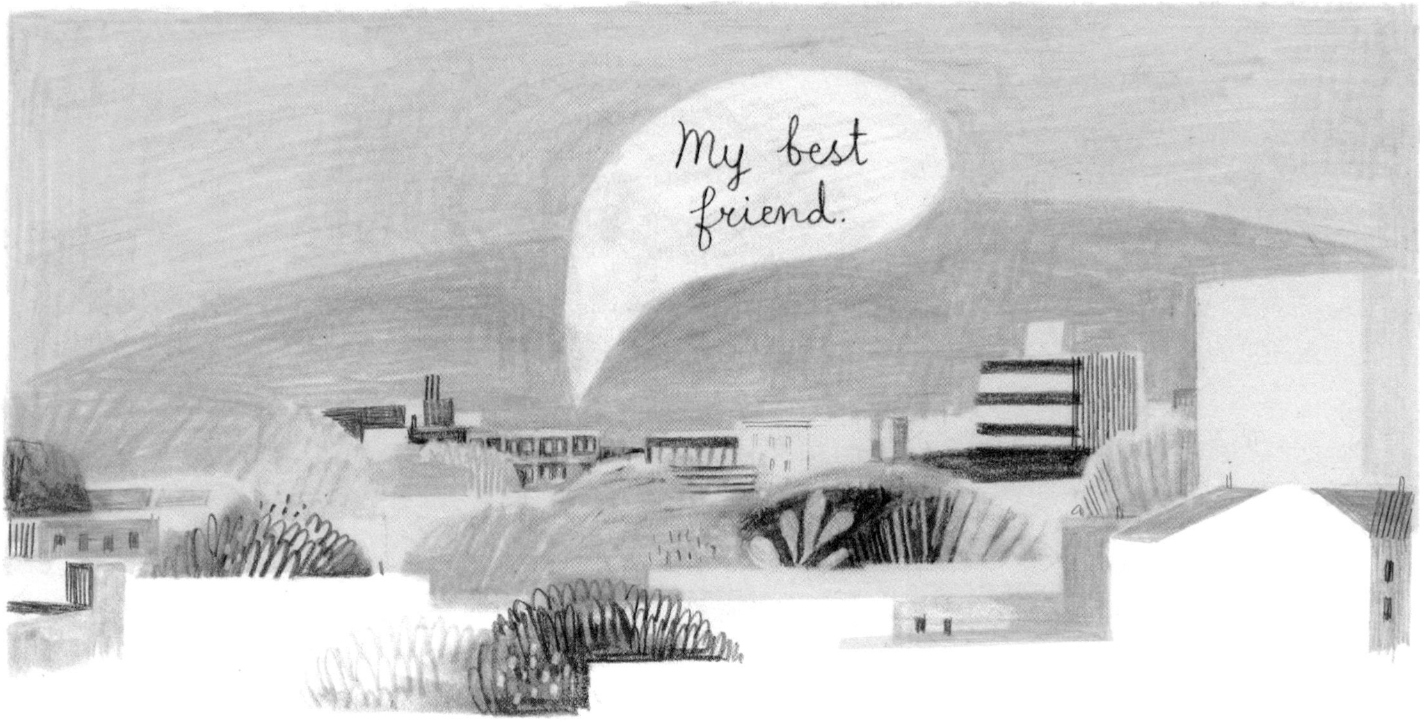
My best friend.

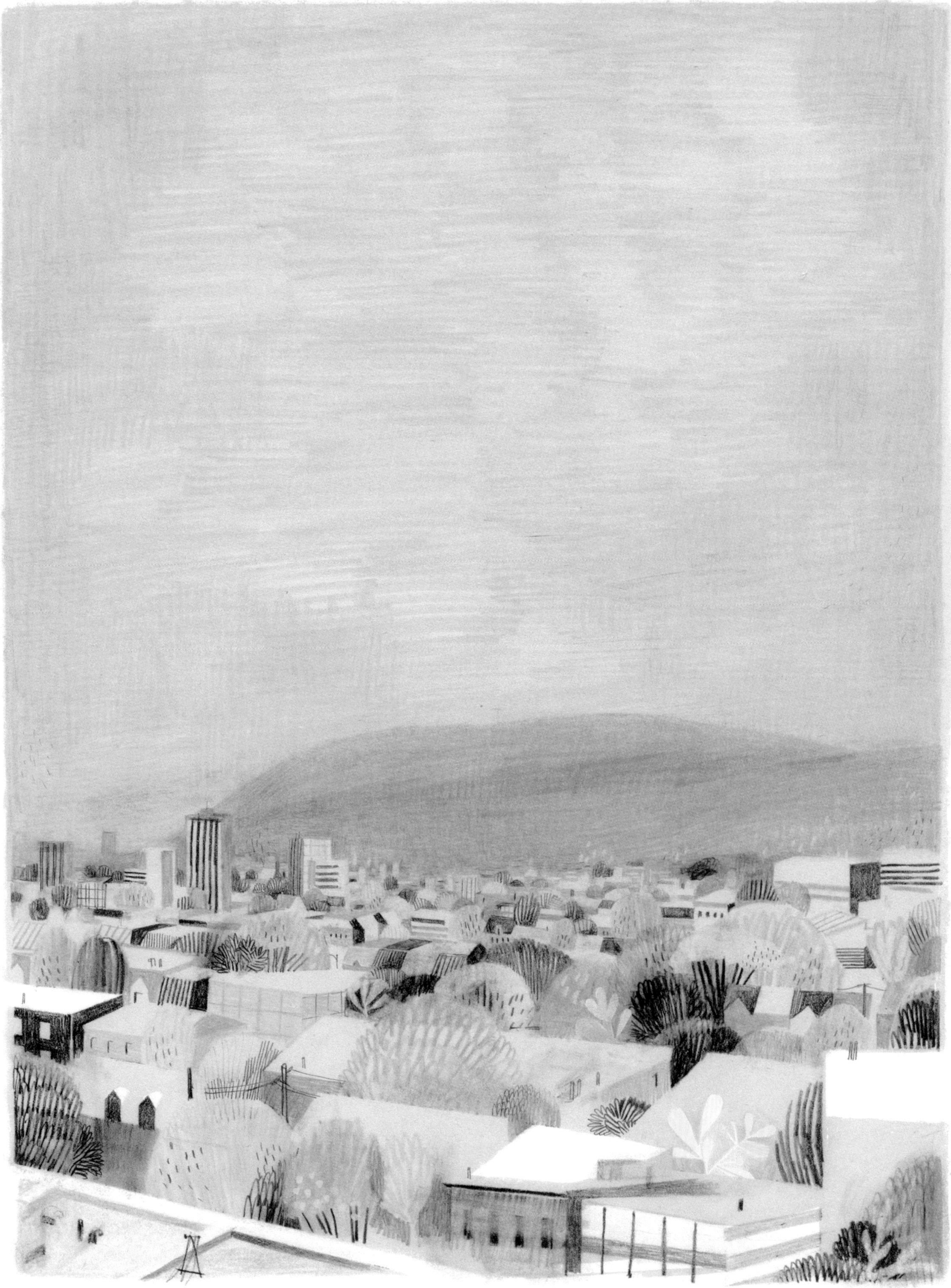

Oh right, I forgot.

Jane Eyre returns to Thornfield one day and discovers the crazy-as-a-kite wife set the manor on fire and did Mr. Rochester some serious harm before dying herself.

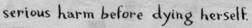

When Jane shows up at the manor, she discovers Mr. Rochester in the dark, surrounded by the ruins of his castle.

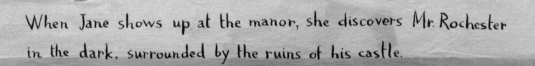

He is maimed, blind, unkempt.

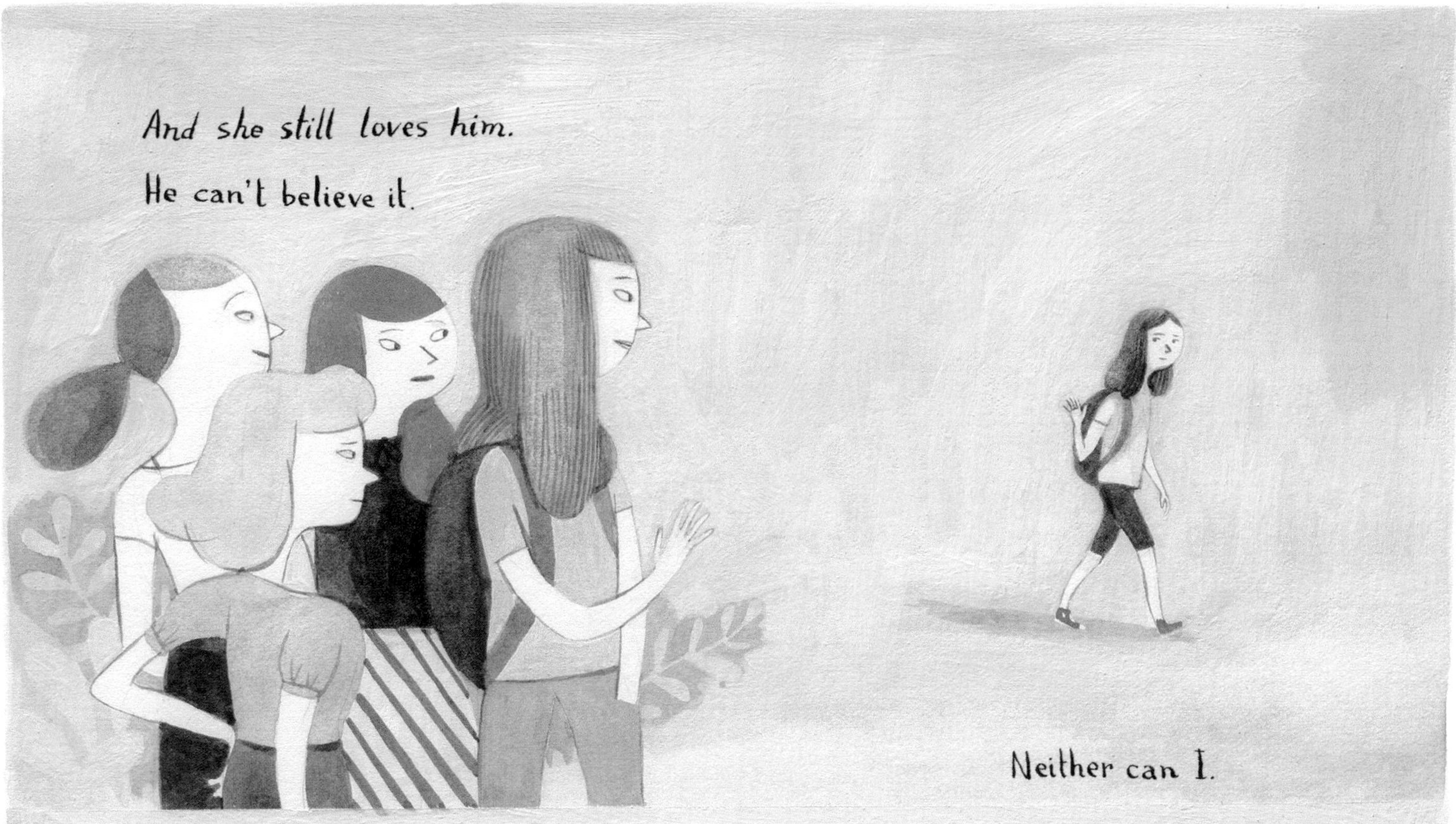
And she still loves him.
He can't believe it.
Neither can I.

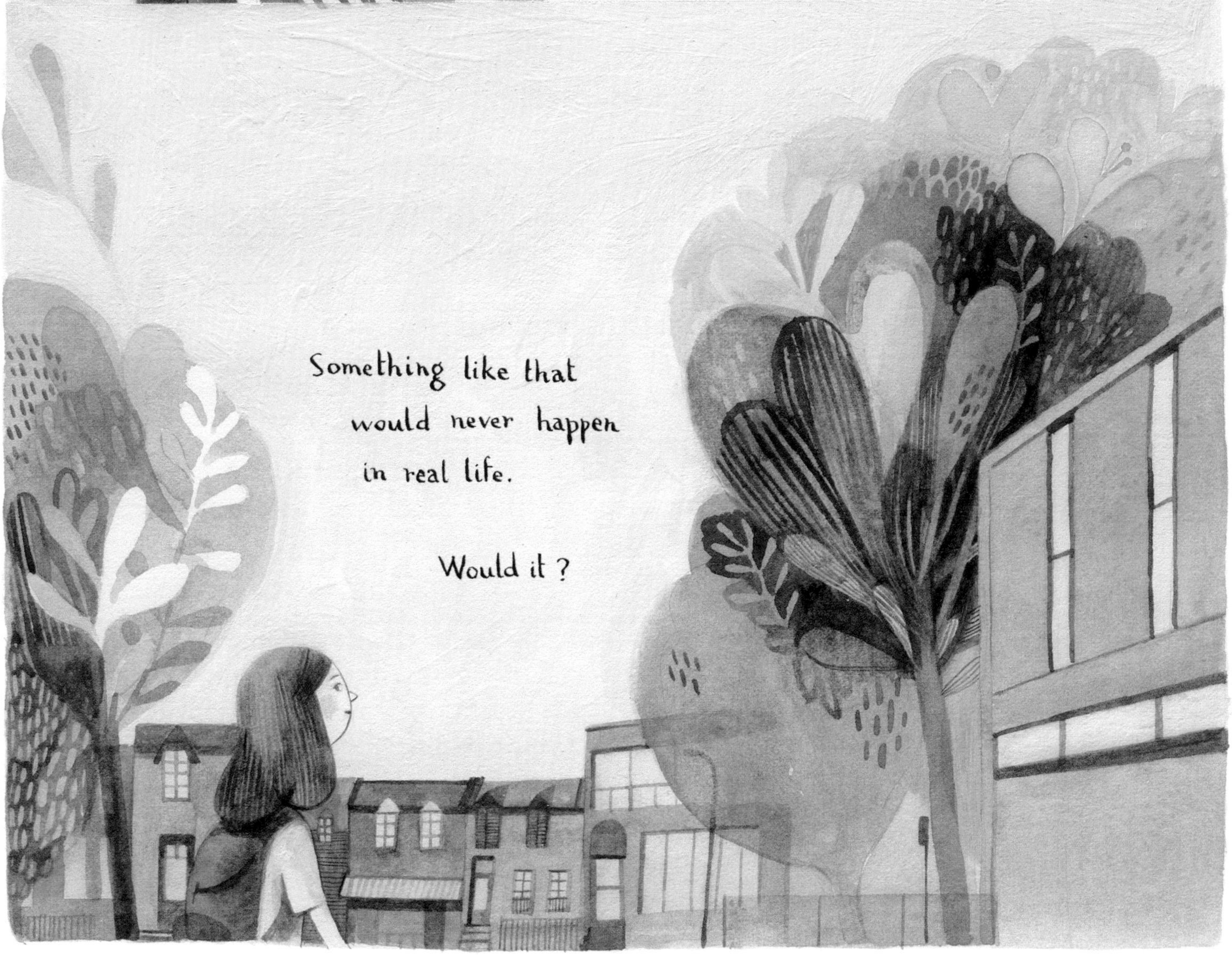
Something like that
would never happen
in real life.
Would it?

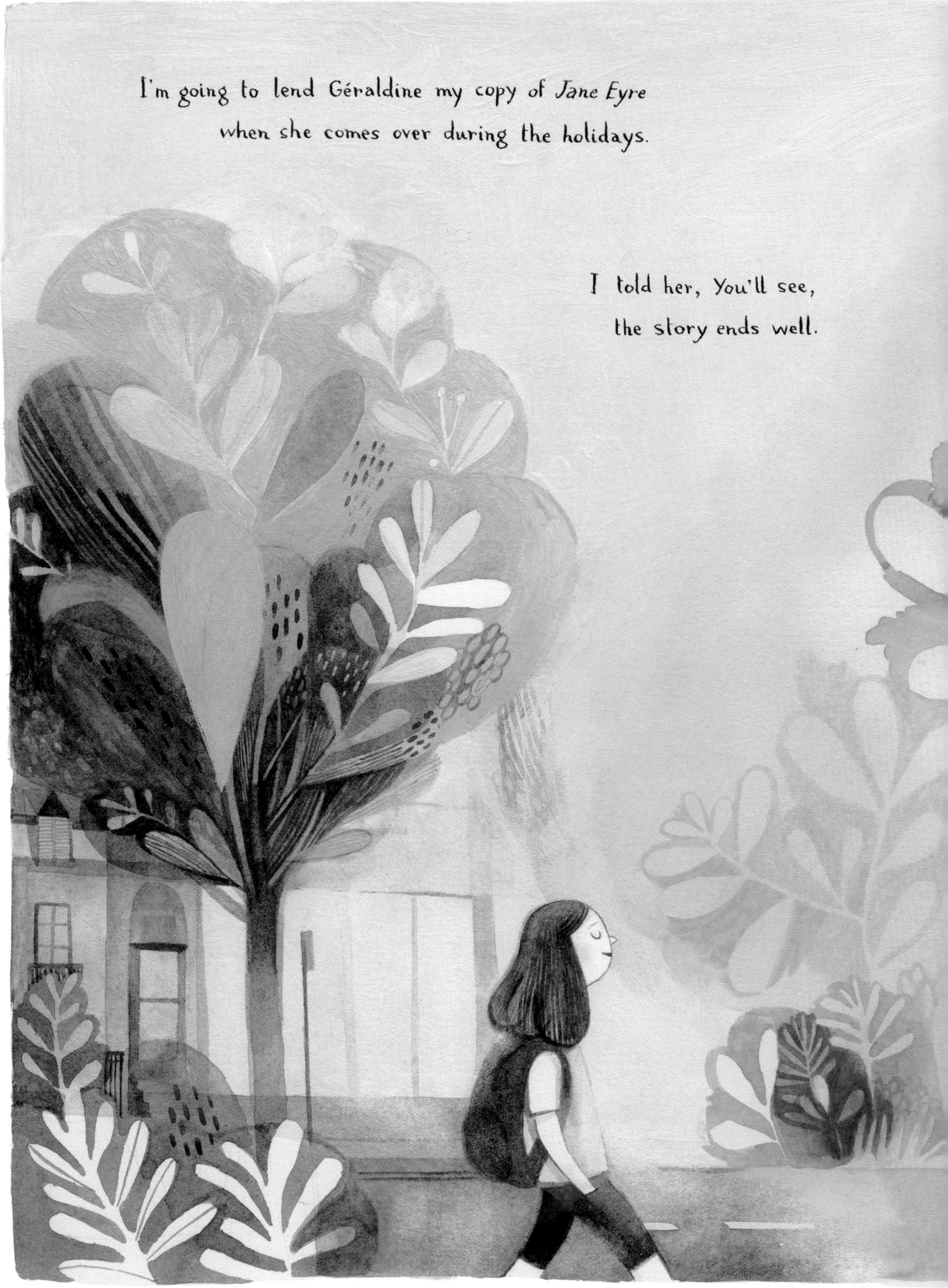
I'm going to lend Géraldine my copy of *Jane Eyre* when she comes over during the holidays.
I told her, You'll see, the story ends well.

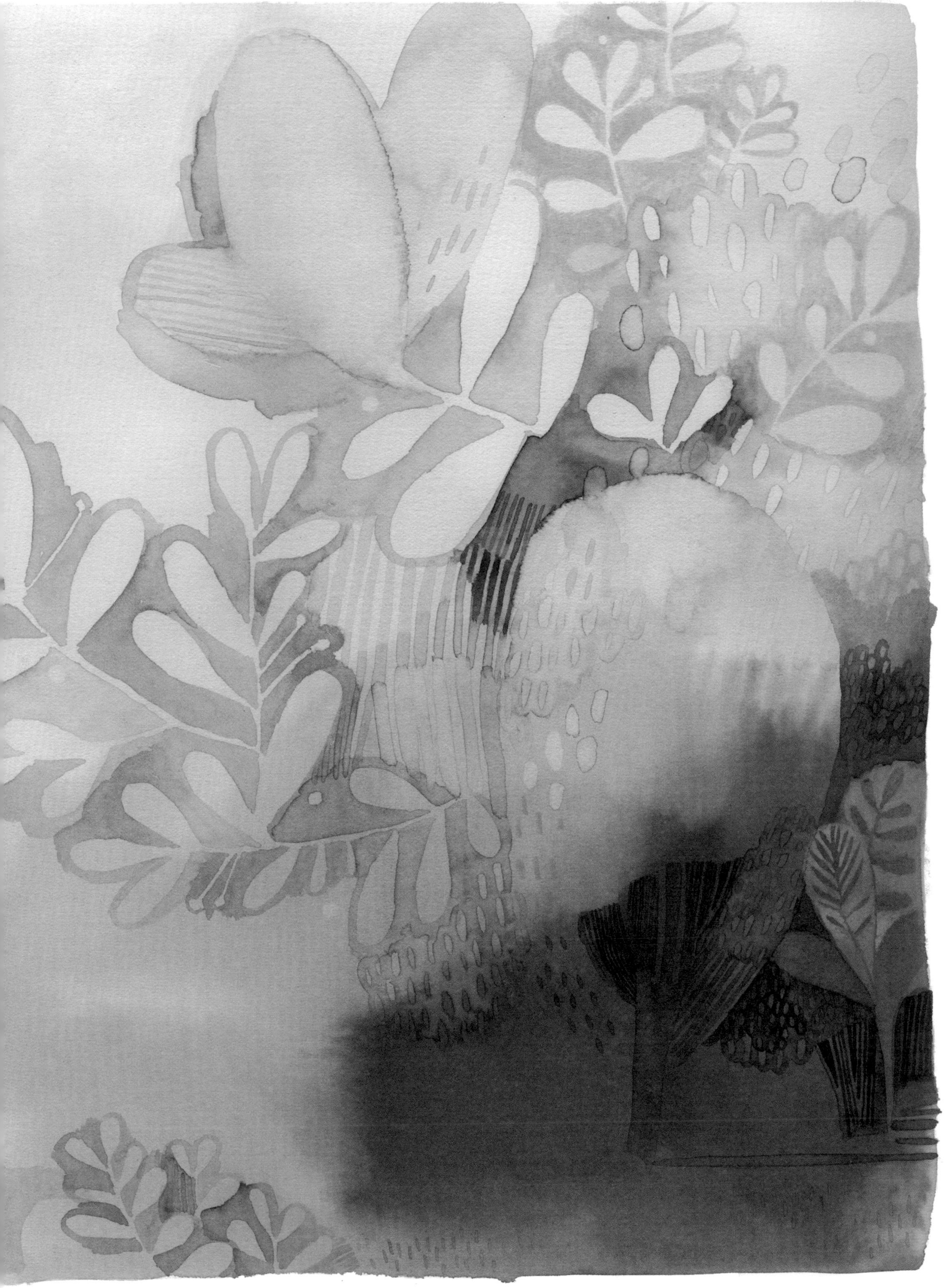

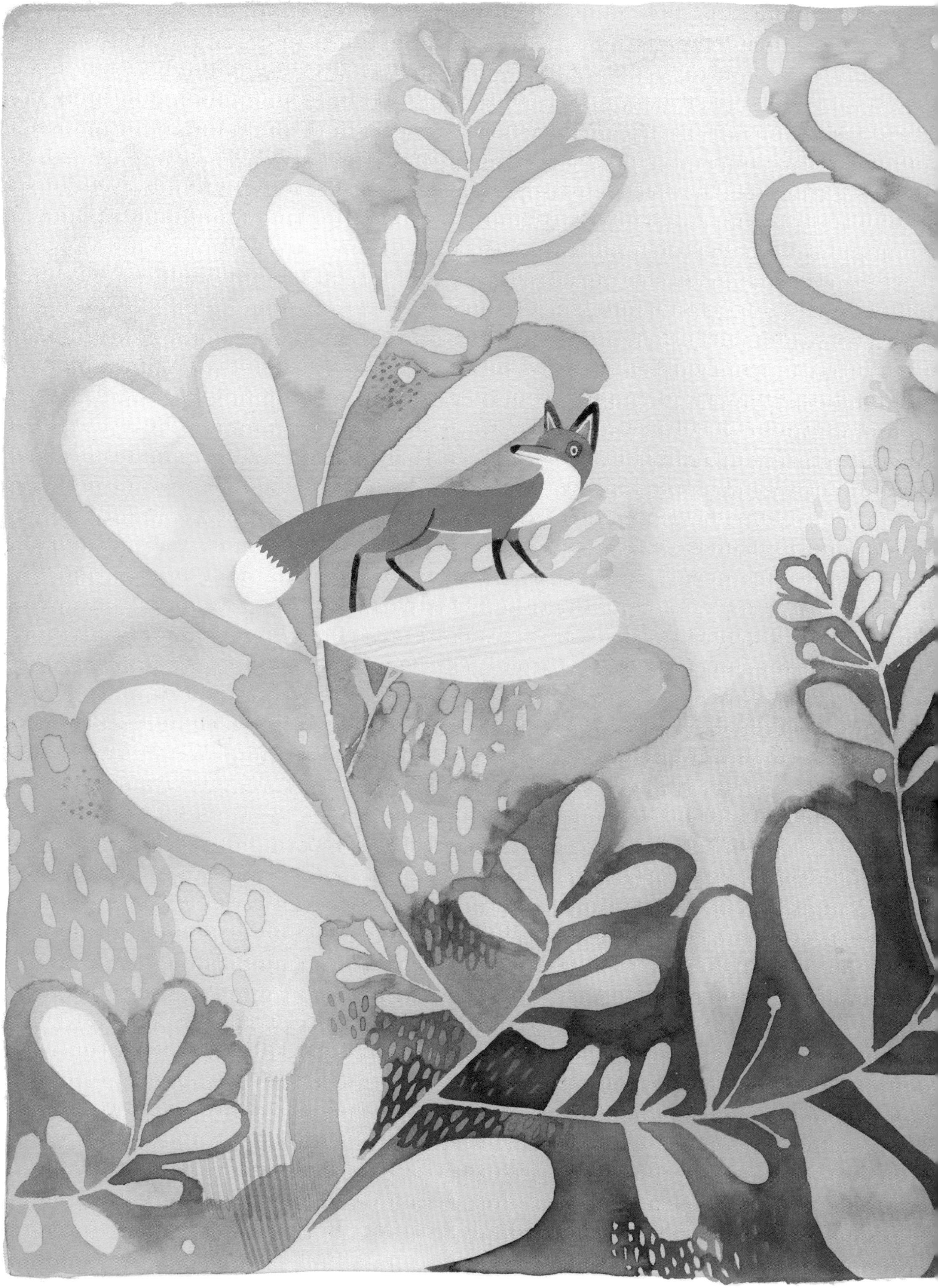

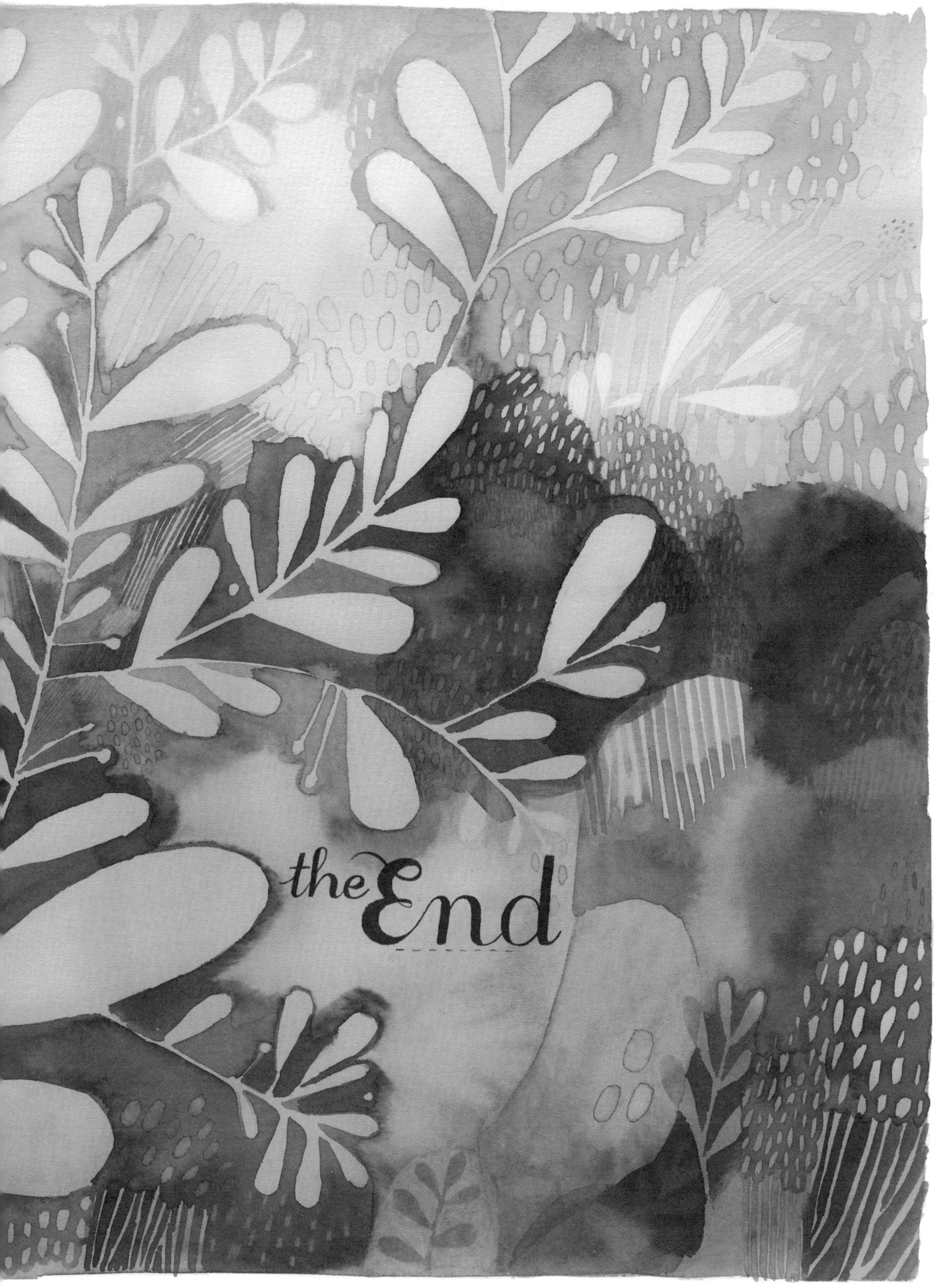
the End

ABOUT THE AUTHORS

FANNY BRITT is a Quebec playwright, author and translator. She has written a dozen plays (among them *Honey Pie*, *Hôtel Pacifique* and *Bienveillance*) and translated more than fifteen others. She has also written and translated several works of children's literature. *Jane, the Fox and Me* is her first graphic novel.

ISABELLE ARSENAULT is a Quebec illustrator who has won an impressive number of awards and has achieved international recognition. Her picture books include *Migrant* by Maxine Trottier, a New York Times Best Illustrated Children's Book and a finalist for the Governor General's Award, and *Once Upon a Northern Night* by Jean E. Pendziwol.

ABOUT THE TRANSLATORS

CHRISTELLE MORELLI, like Géraldine's sugared almonds, comes from Grenoble, France. And like Hélène, SUSAN OURIOU's strategy is reading, too.